CW00429847

ANNIE PEPPER
COMES HOME

by

SANDRA SAVAGE

Copyright © Sandra Savage 2019

This book is sold subject to the condition that it shall not,
by way of trade or otherwise, be lent, resold, hired out,
or otherwise circulated without the publisher's prior consent in any
form of binding or cover other than that in which it is published
and without a similar condition including this condition being
imposed on the subsequent publisher.
The moral right of Sandra Savage has been asserted.

ISBN: 978-0-9931332-9-9

Acknowledgements

To my wonderful cousins Gerald and Neil Dawson,
who have demonstrated, in so many
ways over the years, that
'blood is thicker than water'.

To Roberta

Happy reading.

Sandra Dawson

Also by Sandra Savage

Chapter 1

"Billy......Billy......wake up." Annie's voice whispered into the early morning light filtering into the small bedroom of their son's home. Her husband moaned, softly, as he turned towards the sound of her voice. She'd seemed.....well, a bit frightened of late and he'd noticed a change in her usual contented mood, but the next few words she uttered brought instant awakening to his mind.

Her eyes were wide and dark and wet with pregnant tears. "I want to go home," she whispered, simply, "please, Billy, take me home." Billy pulled his wife closer and wrapped his arm around her shoulders, as tears began to spill down her cheeks.

"Hey, hey," he murmured, "what's all this?" Annie sniffed, she knew that Billy wanted to stay in Belfast with their son, John and his wife Mary, but it was April now and a long time since they'd left Dundee last Christmas and she was homesick.

Billy sighed and squeezed her tighter. "I'll get us a nice cup of tea," he said, "and you can tell me what's troubling you...... alright?" He kissed the top of her head and threw back the covers, his mind searching for words to comfort Annie, but also to convince her that there was nothing back in Dundee for them, but in Belfast was their son, HIS son.

All these years ago, Billy had found work gathering in the flax at Mr Pepper's small farm outside Belfast, where he'd first met Annie and her sister Mary. He knew Annie had fallen in love with him, but in his arrogance, he'd made love to her before leaving to find work in Scotland, without ever finding out that he had fathered a son. The secret was held by Annie alone, until her son found out where she lived from his adoptive parents and they had met......then Billy, his father, had to be told. Having been unaware of his existence until then, the secret wrecked his marriage and when Annie's husband, Euan McPherson, was killed during the war, he was determined to make Annie his again and embrace their son fully.

The kitchen was warm and brightly lit and John had already boiled the kettle and was just finishing his first cup of tea when Billy entered.

"There's plenty of tea in pot," he said smiling, "help yourself." He closed yesterday's newspaper that he'd been reading and handed it to Billy, "I'm on duty at seven so I'd best get moving." He checked his watch, it had just gone six and he looked, quizzically, at his father. "There's no need for you to be up at this time," he said, "couldn't you sleep?"

Billy shrugged his shoulders. "It's your mum who couldn't sleep," he said, "but I'm sure a nice cup of tea will settle her down." John frowned, he loved his mum very much and especially since she and Billy had been living with them, he felt closer to her than ever. Their first family Christmas in 1946 had been wonderful, with his parents at his wedding to Mary and catching up on all the years they'd missed together. And the more he'd got to know his father, the many questions he'd had about the past had now been answered.

"I'll see you this evening then," he said, accepting that nothing much was amiss with his mum, "Mary's cooking a special meal tonight," he added grinning from ear to ear, "we've got something to tell you both, so don't make any plans to go anywhere else to eat."

Billy watched him go, hurrying out of the garden gate to his car, his unbuttoned coat flapping in the breeze as he set off for Belfast General Hospital where he was the Senior Paediatric Doctor. Billy felt a surge of pride as John's car disappeared from view and Annie came into the kitchen.

Her eyes were red rimmed and Billy hurried towards her. "I'm sorry, my dear," he said, "I was just having a bit of a chat with John before he left for his shift and I forgot about the tea." He ushered Annie to sit down at the table. "I'll make us a fresh pot," he said, annoyed at himself for his thoughtlessness, "and you can tell me what's wrong."

Annie's whole body seemed diminished as she gazed at the cup of tea Billy had placed in front of her. "I just want to go home," she said again, "to Dundee."

Billy's lips tightened. He had to get to the bottom of this or his plan that they spend the rest of their lives in Ireland was threatened. He pulled his chair closer to Annie's and took hold of her hand. "But why," he asked, "there's nothing left for us there and everything we love is here?"

Annie turned to face her husband, "Dundee is my home," she said simply "it's where my happy memories are and where Lexie and Nancy are and........." "But Lexie's happy at the Air Base at Montrose and Nancy and her bairns are fine, I've seen to that," Billy interrupted, anxiously, so I think you're just feeling a bit blue, that's all and John says that he's got something to tell us tonight, isn't that exciting?"

His grip tightened on Annie's hand. "Please, Annie," he begged, "put this out of your head. We can go for a nice walk later and maybe buy a new Spring frock for you...you'd like that, wouldn't you?"

Annie extricated her hand from his. "The only place I want to walk to, is the Swannie Ponds in Dundee," she said, a determination creeping into her voice "and if you won't take me home... then I'll go myself!" Billy felt cold with shock, whatever it was that had gotten into his wife, he knew he couldn't reach it and he could only hope that whatever John had to say would bring her to her senses. He hoped it was that Mary was pregnant and Annie would surely want to stay then!

"ALRIGHT, ALRIGHT," Billy said, his calmness deserting him, "if you really want to go back then, of course, I'll take you...but Annie," he took her hand again, "please think about John and Mary and how upset they'll be that you want to leave their home." Annie's eyes levelled with her husband's. "Home," she said quietly, "home is where the heart is Billy and my heart is in Dundee."

Billy remained sitting at the kitchen table for a long time after Annie had gone back to their bedroom. How can her heart be in Dundee, he wondered again and again, trying to find a way to convince her that Belfast was now her home, along with him and their son and perhaps……..a new baby!

"Penny for them," quipped Mary as she joined Billy in the kitchen and, like John, wondered why he was sitting there alone and so early in the morning. Annie was usually the first to appear, busying herself with preparing breakfast for the two of them and washing the dishes from last night's supper.

Two women in one kitchen was never a good idea and although Mary loved Annie and Billy living with them, there were times when she just wanted the place to herself. But John had been adamant that both his mum and dad were to treat the house as their own, so it was with relief that he had decided they should find a much bigger house with enough room for all of them to be together but with separate living space.

Billy looked at John's wife closely. She didn't look pregnant, in fact she seemed slimmer than ever and any hopes he had of a bairn on the way, quickly diminished.

"It's Annie," he said, "she's got it into her head that she wants to go back to Dundee."

Mary's eyes widened in surprise, "GO BACK," she echoed, "TO DUNDEE?"

Billy nodded, "I know," he said, his voice heavy with resignation, "don't ask me why," he added, "she just said that home is where the heart is and that's inDundee."

Mary sat down with a bump. She'd noticed the change in Annie herself, but had thought it was just having to share the house with another woman that was getting Annie down a bit; but that would soon be remedied when John found a bigger house and his mum could have her own kitchen.

"Don't worry," she said kindly, "I'm sure she doesn't mean it" and hoping that John's announcement at dinner that night, would throw a different light on Annie's thoughts. He wanted more than anything for his mum and dad to spend the rest of their lives in Belfast and he could be very persuasive; especially when he found out what his mum was thinking of doing.

Annie sat in the bedroom and took out the letter from her handbag and re-read it. She hadn't shown it to Billy and never would, she only knew she had to go home and soon.

At the sound of Billy's footsteps returning, she stuffed the letter back into her bag and pretended to search through her wardrobe for something to wear.

"Mary's up," Billy said, not wishing to broach the subject of going back to Dundee again, "breakfast will be ready in half an hour..... if you're hungry that is?"

He looked at Annie hopefully, maybe something in her stomach would stop this anxiety taking hold.

"I won't change my mind," Annie said, softly, "but breakfast sounds fine."

Billy knew to quit while he was ahead. He could see there was no point in trying to change his wife's mind, he just had to hope that John's news, whatever that was, would get through to her.

The rest of the day passed in mundane activities, both of them avoiding any more talk about going back to Dundee and Billy counting the hours till John came back from the hospital and made his announcement, hoping that his wife and change her mind about leaving Belfast.

Cloistered in their bedroom, both wanting to avoid John's return home, Annie had picked up her knitting needles and began casting on stitches for another cardigan while Billy read the Belfast Times from end to end, each lost in their own thoughts while the sounds of dinner being prepared emanated from the kitchen.

At six o'clock, "Dinner's ready," Mary called out, brightly, from the dining room, making Annie drop a stitch and Billy to feel his stomach muscles tighten. Annie had re-read her letter in her mind for the umpteenth time and although she loved her son, she couldn't ignore the urgency of its contents.

Mary had set the table with all the best crockery and cutlery and Annie blinked at the flickering candles at its centre. Whatever it was John was going to announce, it must be something special and she prayed it wasn't that Mary was pregnant.

"Sit down here," John said, ushering his mother to the top of the table. "Dad," he continued, "you sit here next to mum." No one spoke as John took his place and began slicing the roast beef while Mary arranged the dishes of steaming potatoes and vegetables, along with a jug full of meaty gravy, around the candles.

A quick glance at his parent's faces brought a slight frown of concern to his own.

His mum and dad weren't usually this quiet, but once he told them his news, he reasoned, he as sure they'd soon cheer up.

The food was probably delicious, but Annie's appetite had deserted her, as she picked at the beef and tried to swallow the small bites she'd forked into her mouth.

"Everything alright mum?" John asked, unable to ignore the unhappiness that was hanging over Annie like a black cloud. "Mary's made your favourite especially....."

"I'm sorry John," Billy interrupted, "maybe a sleep would help, your mum's been a bit tired all day." John was on his feet immediately, swiftly moving to his mum's side and taking her pulse and checking her forehead for signs of a temperature, but found nothing amiss. Annie clenched his hands together and nodded towards Billy, "I am a bit tired," she whispered, pushing back her chair and slowly standing up, "so maybe a sleep will help." Wordlessly, Billy watched as Annie left the room, before turning to his son and Mary.

"What's wrong," John demanded to know and it's nothing to do with tiredness is it?"

Billy took a gulp of the red wine in front of him. "No," he said, "the long and short of it is.........your mother wants to go home......to Dundee."

Confusion was written all over his face, "but why?"

"I don't know," Billy answered, honestly, "she's been a bit...... distant.....for a couple of days now, but I thought it was something and nothing, then this morning she told me that she wants to go back to Dundee.....with or without me!"

Disbelief filled the room. "Maybe you should tell Billy your news," Mary said, quietly, "it may make a difference."

John looked at his wife and nodded. She'd been saying for a

while now, how two women in one kitchen can be difficult and his idea to move to somewhere big enough for all of them had been turned into action. That very day, he'd signed the documents for the purchase of a rambling farmhouse on the outskirts of the city, sure that his mum and dad would love it, but now...

When Billy heard the news, his heart leapt with hope, surely, this would make Annie change her mind. "But that's wonderful," he told John, "it's everything we could have hoped for and more. Let me speak with Annie again," he said, his voice cracking with emotion, "she'll see sense when she hears this." But it wasn't about seeing sense for Annie, it was about love, a love that she couldn't ignore and that Billy was soon to find out about.

"Annie, Annie," Billy called, rushing into the bedroom, "you won't believe what John has just told me!" Annie's eyes met his. "It'll make no difference," she said, handing her husband the letter. Read this."

Billy frowned, "but you haven't heard the news," he rushed... ....as his hope began to ebb like the Spring tide.

"Just read the letter," Annie repeated, handing him the single sheet of paper.

Dearest Mum

The job at Montrose Air Base is no more and I've returned home to Albert Street.
The year began with so much hope, but fate has dealt me blow after bitter blow and I'm now afraid for the future. I wish you were here and I'm sorry for all the hurt I must have given you when I went away, my thoughts were of no one but myself.
But now, well now, I'm older and wiser and I don't know how I'm going to handle the shame that is now upon me. I need some of your wise words, mum, not that I deserve them, but I don't know who else to turn to. Write soon, I miss you very much.

Your loving daughter,
Lexie

Billy read the words twice over, unable to believe that the feisty and brave Lexie had written them.   "Shame!" he exclaimed. "What shame?"

Annie shook her head, "I don't know," she said, trembling, "but it must have something to do with leaving Montrose.......or being told to leave," she added, miserably.

Billy handed the letter back, all excitement about John's proposition forgotten.

Of course Annie had to go back and so did he, he wouldn't have let anything harm either of them and wrapped his arm around Annie's shoulder.

"So, you see, Billy, I must go back to Dundee, Annie said shakily, "Lexie needs me and I can't turn my back on her, no matter what she's done."

"Hush now, sweetheart," he whispered into her hair as he kissed the top of her head, "I'll make the arrangements first thing tomorrow and explain to John and Mary why we must leave."

"NO, NO," gasped Annie, "don't let them know about Lexie, please, not until we know ourselves what's happened!"

"But, we have to tell John and Mary something, you must see that!"

"I know, I know, but please don't let Lexie's shame be told to anyone else, especially not John......."

Billy sighed. "Calm yourself Annie, if you don't want John to know the real reason why we're going back to Dundee, then I'll try to think of something believable to tell him. Now get some rest," he added, "we've a long journey ahead of us."

John was staring at the flames in the fireplace when Billy came into the parlour, but jumped up from his chair when his dad came into the room. He could see by the look on his father's face that something was very wrong.

"Is mum alright?" he asked, anxiously, as Billy took a seat opposite his son.

Billy took a deep breath, the dilemma that Annie had set him deepening within his heart. The woman he loved was asking him to lie to their son, but his conscience rebelled against the deceit.

"Can we talk.....man to man?" he asked.

"I wouldn't want it any other way," he son replied, the worry lines on his forehead increasing.

"You mum has had a letter.......from Lexie..."

"But, Lexie's a grown woman.......with her own life.....so...."

"Please," Billy held up a stopping hand, "let me finish."

"I read her letter a few minutes ago and Lexie's in great distress." John leaned forward in his seat. "Go on!"

"It looks like something has happened at the Montrose Air Base and Lexie's either left or has been dismissed. She didn't say why."

John sat back in his chair. "But can't she just get another job?" he asked reasonably, with her abilities, surely that wouldn't be too difficult."

"I agree," Billy said, "but there's more to it than that." She talks about 'fate dealing her blow after bitter blow' and how she's 'fearful for her future' and begging her mother for help."

John absorbed the news with disbelief. "This doesn't sound like the Lexie I know," he said, pondering the situation, "but surely she's not thinking of doing anything.........stupid?"

Billy's lips tightened. "You never knew Lexie's father, Alexander Melville," he began, "but he committed suicide and Annie's fear is........."

It was John's turn to stop Billy from telling him anything further: It was true he hadn't known Lexie's father, in fact he'd assumed that Lexie was Euan McPherson's daughter, but as a doctor, he did know that suicide was a possibility when the trials of life became overwhelming, especially when they had to be faced alone.

"Let me speak to mum," he said, standing up again, "let her know I understand!"

"NO, NO," Billy almost shouted, "she didn't want me to tell you any of this, so please, never let her know what we've spoken about, nor tell Mary what's happened. Let this just be between ourselves and I'll write and tell you more when things become clearer." Billy's hands were gripping his son's shoulders tightly, "I'd like nothing more than to spend the rest of my days living here with you and Mary," Billy emphasised, "and so would your mum, but it looks like fate has dealt us all a bitter blow and until we can sort things out, remaining in Belfast can't happen."

"Then, the quicker you both get back to Dundee, the better," John said, decisively "and you can depend on me to keep this between us. Just remember," he added "the farmhouse will be here whenever you can return to Belfast, you can count on that." He shook his father's hand, "say goodbye to mum for me," he said, unable to trust his feelings at her going "and tell her how much I love her."

John hurried from the room before tears of disappointment fell from his eyes. All his plans for the future, sharing his world with his mum and dad, making up for all the years they'd missed were rapidly fading. Lexie's letter had now changed all of that.

Early next morning, Billy managed to book their places on a cargo ship crossing the Irish Sea to Glasgow that afternoon and when John found Billy's note on the kitchen table telling him about their imminent departure, he made sure he'd be on double duty at the Hospital and told a bemused Mary to find something to occupy her time outside the house, for the rest of the day.

Thankfully, their packing only took an hour or so and by noon they were on their way. It would be late by the time they arrived in Glasgow and the next day before they'd be able to get a train to Dundee, so it was with exhaustion and relief that they finally embarked at Dundee West Station.

The familiarity of the place, immediately, took Annie back to the first time she'd made that journey so many years ago now. Mary had been alive then and married to Billy and life in Dundee, for Annie, had only just begun. So much water had flowed under the bridge since then and now, here she was, back where fate and Lexie's letter had brought her, with fear and anxiety gripping her as to what she'd find on turning the key in the lock of her home in Albert Street.

—·—oOo—·—

Chapter 2

Lexie had been waiting anxiously to hear the sound of the 'Postie' bringing her a letter from her mum, so when she heard footsteps on the stairs, she hurried to the door and flung it open.

A look of disbelief washed over her, when she saw her mother standing there, before tears flooded both of their eyes, as she threw herself into Annie's arms.

"Mum," she gasped, "you've come home....... you've come home!"

Billy edged past mother and daughter. "I'll just put these in the bedroom," he said, more to himself, as no one else was listening. Annie had been right to come home, he could see that now, Lexie was in poor shape and not a patch on the lively lass who'd won an Empire Medal for bravery during the war, when she was a WAAF.

"Of course I've come home, Lexie," Annie murmured, her heart aching at the sight of her once lovely daughter, "how could I not, when you needed me?"

Arm in arm, Annie and Lexie went into the kitchen. "Let's have a nice cup of tea," Annie said, with her usual warmth, "the kettle won't take long to boil." Annie fell into her motherly role of setting out the tea things, but looked in vain for any signs of biscuits in the biscuit barrel or cakes in the cake tin. No wonder Lexie looked worn out, she reasoned, she hadn't been eating properly, probably for weeks. A wave of guilt washed over her, that she hadn't been around to look after her sooner, but she would start baking the very next day and try to make it up to Lexie for putting her own needs first.

Billy came into the kitchen, but was immediately despatched

by Annie, as a matter of urgency, to buy some food to put in the empty larder. His cup of tea would have to wait.

Lexie sipped her hot tea as Annie took in the full extent of her appearance.

Mother and daughter would have to speak about what was wrong....and soon.

"Once Billy comes back with the groceries," Annie said, briskly, "we'll have something to eat and then it's into bed for you." Lexie nodded, the relief of having her mother back home allowing her body to ease and with it, a deep tiredness replacing the tension. She hadn't slept well for weeks now, but tonight would be different, tonight she wouldn't be alone.

The meal of meat pies and beans was eaten on automatic pilot for all of them, the weariness of the journey catching up on Annie and Billy as they watched Lexie barely manage to eat the beans and just a little of her pie, before kissing them both goodnight and retiring to her bedroom.

Closing the door quietly behind her, Lexie opened the drawer of her bedside table and took out a little velvet pouch. She tipped the contents into her palm, the light catching a glint of the gold wedding ring Robbie had placed on her finger the day they'd married on board his ship in 1943. Lexie had been on her way to Halifax in Canada to marry Captain Rainbow McGhee of the Royal Canadian Air Force, but fate had returned her to her first love, Robbie Robertson, now the Captain of Lexie's transport ship, and Bo McGhee was left heart-broken.

A tear threatened to fall as Lexie relived the news that Robbie had been killed at sea only a month after their wedding and Lexie had returned to Scotland alone where, thanks to the kindness of Wing Commander Johnny Johnstone, she had been posted back to Lossiemouth to see out the rest of the war.

Alongside the wedding ring was the carved ebony Promise Ring that Bo had given back to her at Christmas when the now, Wing Commander McGhee, had come back into her life at the Montrose Air Base, where Lexie worked as a civilian. But Bo hadn't been alone, he'd brought with him his young son, Louie, the result of his disastrous marriage to Angela Lafeyette from

Quebec and it was plain that Bo wanted to rekindle the love he once had for Lexie, before Robbie Robertson had 'changed her mind.' Meeting Bo again had reminded Lexie of the passion she used to feel in the man's arms and when he'd kissed her as they said goodbye late that Christmas Day, she had willingly responded as all the emotions she had locked away since Robbie's death had surged through her.

The next day, Bo and Louie were gone, back to Canada, with the promise he would write.

She slipped the ring onto the third finger of her left hand and gazed at it. It had been three months since Bo had gone, but no letter had arrived, but by the time February had dawned, Lexie knew for sure, she was pregnant with Bo's child and alone with her shame. Wing Commander Kettlewell was stunned with her resignation and her silence about the reason why, but had to accept her decision that she was leaving and returning home to Dundee.

Sniffing back the tears, she put the rings back into the pouch. How she had sneered at Nancy when she became pregnant out of wedlock and Billy Donnelly had been forced to marry her. A fallen woman, Lexie had called her, a slut, a harlot, a whore even, her 17 year old mind unable to grasp the depth that desire for the love of a man could reach.......but now.... now she knew! At least Nancy and Billy had married, but for her, there would be no happy ending. Bo had had his revenge for being jilted and she'd been a fool to believe otherwise. Sleep evaded her for another night, as she lay curled up in her bed with the covers pulled over her head.

Annie also slept badly. Lexie was thin and gaunt and had obviously been neglecting herself, but the questions and answers would have to wait till Lexie was ready to talk to her and until then, both she and Billy would just have to wait.

The porridge was bubbling gently in the pot and the aroma of pancakes cooking on the griddle filled the air as Lexie came into the kitchen. Annie glanced at her daughter's red-rimmed eyes and winced. "Porridge?" she asked, hovering with pot and Spirtle to dish out a plateful. Lexie shook her head and swallowed hard to keep from retching.

Annie sighed, "there's pancakes, how about a pancake with jam?" Before Lexie could answer, her stomach heaved and she just managed to reach the kitchen sink before last night's beans and pie were vomited up.

Annie felt a cold wave of fear sweep over her. "Surely not... ......?"

She helped Lexie back to the table and filled a glass of water from the well.

"You're pregnant........aren't you!" she said, quietly, handing her daughter the cold water. It was more of a statement than a question. Lexie looked at her mother for understanding and acceptance, before whispering... "yes."

The years melted away with that one word and Annie was once more in the Poor House in Belfast giving birth to her own son. All alone and with the bairn's father already married to her sister, she had had to bear the shame of the pregnancy and the guilt of letting her son be taken for adoption by the Nuns. It would be many years before her son, John and his father, Billy Dawson would know of the other's existence and now, fate had come the full circle and here was her daughter living the nightmare again.

Billy came into the kitchen at that moment and knew immediately that something had been said. He looked at Annie, quizzically, unsure whether to stay or go, but she indicated he should stay. "Back to bed with you, Lexie," she said, gently, as she helped her daughter to her feet, "you need rest more than anything... breakfast can wait."

Billy took Lexie's arm and guided her through the kitchen door. "We're here now," he whispered to her, "everything will be alright," as he closed the door behind her and turned to face Annie.

"I think you're going to need something on your stomach," she said, "the worst fate that could have befallen Lexie, has happened."

Billy pulled out a chair and sat down, his eyes narrowing, "Out with it then," he said, "she's not got some disease has she...

... something the doctors can't fix?"

Annie shook her head, "No, it's nothing like that," she said. "Years ago," Annie began, "when Nancy was pregnant with wee Billy out of wedlock and you and Euan had to get Billy Donnelly to marry her........"

"Yes," Billy nodded, "but what's that......"

"Well," Annie continued, "At that time, Lexie hadn't held back with her disgust of Nancy's situation. A fallen woman, she'd called her, among many other bad names and her main concern was that Nancy's shame should not be put onto her through being her cousin." Billy stayed silent while Annie went on with her story. "So, I told her about ME, and my shame."

Billy's head dropped as he felt again the guilt he'd had himself, on finding out about Annie's secret that had almost destroyed her and how she'd lived with the shame of bearing a 'bastard' child......and then finding out that he was the father.

"Who's the father?" Billy asked, looking at Annie for assurance that she'd forgiven him for the past. "Whoever he is, I'll find him and he'll marry her, if it's the last thing I do!"

"I don't know who the father is," Annie said, sitting down heavily on her chair. "If she had someone in her life after Robbie, then she never told me about him."

Billy took in the information: Surely, Lexie wasn't like those women who, since the war, had lost all modesty and sense of morals and were to be found in the Dundee dancehalls, flirting with any man who took their fancy....married or otherwise.

"It has to have something to do with the Montrose Air Base," Billy realised, "that's why she had to give up her job as well". Billy stood up, decisively, "well, I'll soon find out who he is," he said, "breakfast can wait, I think a drive up to Montrose to find out what happened is what's needed."

"WAIT," Annie almost shouted, "don't spread this news around," she said, "remember how ashamed she feels about all this, do you really think she'd want her friends at Montrose, especially the Wing Commander, to know what's happened."

Billy's lips tightened. Annie was right, there was no point in rushing off on a tangent without speaking further to Lexie.

"Alright, alright," he said, calming down. "Let's give it a few days, see what else comes to light."

Annie nodded, "we're here now, so let's try to behave normally till Lexie's able to tell us more about what's happened."

Billy didn't argue further, but he'd decided he'd be going to Montrose to see the Wing Commander as soon as he could without arousing Annie or Lexie's suspicions.

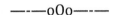

—-—oOo—-—

Chapter 3

Nancy was hard at work at her Looms at Baxters when, to her surprise, she saw her father speaking to the Overseer, John Brannan, at the far end of the weaving flat.

All manner of questions ran through her mind as she watched their interaction and tried to lip-read what was being said. Her main concern was 'why was her father not in Belfast?' But, more to the point, why was he speaking to John Brannan?

Surely, he didn't know about their secret liaisons that had begun at Hogmany, when John had been her first-foot at midnight. He had still been with her in the early hours of New Year's Day when the police had come knocking at her door, to tell her that her estranged husband, Billy Donnelly had been found frozen to death, at the locked gates of Bell Street Jail.

There had been no tears from Nancy when she'd heard of Billy's death. She'd told him their marriage was over for good at Christmas, his obsession with the prostitute Gladys Kelly had seen to that, but it had hit her bairns harder, especially her eldest son, wee Billy, now sixteen. Her first-born, Mary Anne, seemed to cope with the loss of her dad better and King Kevin was too young to understand what had happened, but she knew wee Billy was hurting.

He'd always hoped that they would get back together and hadn't taken too kindly to John Brannan being in the house when the police had come to the door, hence their need for secrecy as they had grown closer over the following weeks. The last thing Nancy needed was for her son to lose respect for her again, especially after her affair with the mill worker, Jim Murphy, had come to light, when Billy Donnelly had been in the

Black watch in France fighting the Nazis.

Nancy had been so lost in her own thoughts that she'd failed to notice that three of the spools of jute had broken and her looms had seized. In a panic, she signalled to John for a Tenter to fix the problem and, after a quick goodbye to her father, he'd come hurrying over to her, signalling for the Tenter to follow.

"Your dad's back," he mouthed over the racket, taking her elbow and edging her past the Tenter who began his repair work, without giving either of them a second glance. He nodded towards the black rubber doors at the end of the weaving flat, but they were being watched by Di Auchterlonie, who had already sniffed out a juicy bit of gossip about Nancy; if she thought that no one had noticed their 'goings-on' Nancy was wrong, very wrong!

Away from the deafening noise of the looms, John squeezed Nancy's shoulders.

"Your dad and Annie are back from Belfast and I think it's for good, so any hopes you had of us moving into the house in Albert Street, are gone.

Nancy frowned, "but I thought they loved life in Ireland," she said, "there's nothing here for them in Dundee, especially not for dad now that he's found his precious son!" Nancy's lips tightened with the words; she'd always been the most important person in his life, till he'd found out her Auntie Annie had borne him a bastard son years ago in Ireland, pushing Nancy into second-place.

"Whatever the reason, he's not saying," John told her, "but I think you need to drop by soon, and find out." Nancy nodded. "I'll go at the weekend," she said, her mind racing with questions, the house in Albert Street was lovely and she could just see herself and John living there and saying goodbye to the cramped hovel in the Cowgate.......but now it looked like all that could change.... but why?

Lexie still seemed bereft at breakfast the following day, but Annie said nothing further about the pregnancy, just offered dry toast and weak tea to her daughter. Lexie seemed determined to keep the identity of the bairn's father secret, but Billy had made it clear to Annie, that he was going to find out who the father was and march the perpetrator of Lexie's distress down the aisle, at the end of a shotgun, if he must.

"Where's Billy?" Lexie asked into the silent kitchen, as she nibbled on the toast.

Annie glanced over her shoulder at her daughter, her hands in the sink of soapy water, tackling the porridge pot and spirtle. "Work," she replied, "now that we're home, Baxters lost no time in asking him to come back."

Lexie nodded in acknowledgement. Billy had been the Mill Manager for many years and the mill had flourished under his watch, but orders for jute were beginning to dry up since the war ended and his expertise and contacts were welcomed back by the owners.

"I was thinking we might visit Nancy soon," Annie said, absently, "see how she's doing. Would you like that?"

"NO!" Lexie exclaimed, suddenly finding her voice again. "The last person I want to see is Nancy," she quivered "and I don't want her to know I'm here either."

Annie slowly dried her hands, she'd been stunned to find out that Lexie had been living back home for weeks, but had told NO ONE, especially not Nancy, the one person who would have understood more than anyone about Lexie's situation.

"Maybe just go for a walk then, get some colour back in your cheeks," Annie suggested, quickly dropping the subject of Nancy, "it looks like the sun's coming out."

"Maybe later," Lexie replied, "sorry mum," she added, before heading back to her bedroom: The last thing she wanted was for Nancy to find out she was pregnant and not married, knowing how she'd behaved to her cousin, when the boot had been on the other foot. The names she had labelled her with, could now be attached to Lexie and her face paled further with shame now she too was a 'slut' a 'harlot' and a 'whore.'

Billy had left the house early, telling Annie he was going into Baxters to 'sort things out,' but had driven instead to Montrose Air Base hoping to see Wing Commander Kettlewell, but he was disappointed. The Wing Commander had been seconded to an air Base in England for three months to manage the changes the end of the war had brought. Men still had to be demobbed and others enlisted, while the War Office was rapidly putting in place plans for the new Air Force. Squadron Leader James Morris, who was temporarily 'holding the fort' for the Wing Commander, welcomed Billy to the Base instead, but wasn't of much help.

"I never really knew your daughter," he said, "I've only been here myself since February, and from what you say, Lexie wasn't it?" he queried, "had gone by then."

Billy frowned in frustration. "She was living with a family in Montrose," he suddenly remembered, "Adams, I think it was, yes, Winnie Adams was their daughter, also working at the Base...... I don't suppose you know if she's still around?"

James Morris smiled. "I can do better than that," he said, winking, before picking up the telephone on his desk. "Sheila," he said, "can you send through Winnie Adams."

"She's here?" Billy gasped, as the sound of knocking swung his attention towards the door.

"Enter," James called and a small, dark-haired woman, wearing a grey skirt and cardigan over a white blouse, came in.

"This gentleman," he said, pointing to Billy, unaware that they had already met, is asking about Lexie Melville and thinks you know her." A startled Winnie nodded, "hello, Mr Dawson," she said.

Billy stood up and extended his hand. "Winnie ," he said, warmly, "Lexie spoke about you often." Winnie's eyes widened, it had been two months since Lexie had disappeared without as much as a goodbye. Winnie had come home from the Base to find that her best friend had packed up and gone, leaving some money with the words 'thank you,' scrawled on the envelope.

"Is she alright?" Winnie asked, fearing bad news. She'd first met Mr Dawson and Lexie's mum many moons ago, when she'd first enlisted and Lexie became her best friend, welcoming her into their home when they had been on a week-end pass from the WAAF.

James Morris interrupted the conversation. "I think you two need to talk in private," he said, "I've a million things to do on the Base so, please, use my office and I'll send in someone with tea and biscuits."

He shook Billy's hand, firmly, "I hope you find what you're looking for," he said, quietly, "I'm a father myself and just glad that my daughter wasn't old enough to get involved in this war......or its aftermath."

Billy pulled up another chair, "please," he said, turning his attention to Winnie, "sit down."

Winnie obliged. "Is Lexie alright," she asked again?"

"Lexie's fine," he told Winnie, "but her mum Annie and me are a bit worried about why she left her job at the Base and came back to Dundee."

Winnie smiled with relief before answering; she knew Lexie would never have gone back to Dundee unless something was seriously wrong, but she'd heard nothing from her since her rapid departure and her letters to her friend had gone unanswered. "I wish I knew," Winnie said, "One day she was here and the next...."

Winnie shrugged her shoulders and Billy winced, his mind searching for a clue, any clue that would point the finger at whoever had done this' thing' to Lexie.

"Did she spend Christmas with you and your family?" he asked, leaning forward so as not to miss a word of Winnie's answer. It was he who had insisted that they spend Christmas with their son in Ireland, but now he was beginning to feel guilty at how swiftly he'd dismissed any problems Annie thought Lexie might have had with their departure.

Winnie's eyes sparkled with the memory. "It was the best Christmas ever," she said, "the war was over and we had a huge party for all the bairns at the Base," she grinned, "even Santa Clause turned up!"

"Anyone else?" Billy asked, his patience beginning to waver, but keeping his fingers crossed that some name would suddenly be in the frame and Billy could force him to face up to his actions!

But Winnie just shook her head. "Only Santa Clause," she said again......"sorry."

An uncomfortable silence began to spread between them as Billy realised that Winnie was none the wiser than he was, about what and who had brought on the grim emptiness that had enveloped Lexie.

"May I go now, please" Winnie asked? Billy looked at the woman standing before him; it wasn't her fault that she couldn't help, nor James Morris's. His only hope was that the Wing Commander may know something more, but it would be months before he'd be returning to Montrose.

"Yes, yes," he replied, dejection sitting heavily on his shoulders, knowing there was nothing more to be said "and thanks for speaking to me."

"Will you tell her that I'm still here if she wants to talk.....or anything?" Winnie asked, now certain that Lexie was deeply unhappy but, as usual, kept her sorrows to herself, especially when Robbie Robertson had been killed at sea a month after their marriage, when Winnie had feared for Lexie's sanity.

———oOo———

Chapter 4

Nancy couldn't wait to pay a visit to Annie and her dad's home in Albert Street and find out why they were back from Ireland. She'd been told by her father that the probability was, they wouldn't be returning to Dundee and that she was 'a big girl' now and could look after herself.

Nancy's lips tightened at the memory of the hurt she'd felt as her dad had plainly chosen his bastard Irish son over her, but a smile crept over her face as she also remembered him telling her that, 'all that would be left would be his empty house'.

Play your cards right, he'd said and who knows.......!

"Penny for them?" John Brannan whispered in Nancy's ear making her jump.

"Nothing for you to worry about," she replied, lightly kissing his lips, "I was just going to pay a visit to my Auntie Annie and my dear father after work tomorrow," she said, "find out a bit more about the reason for their return."

"Good idea," John said, noting the glint of battle in her eyes, but knowing when to keep quiet. "Do you want me to pick up King Kevin from the nursery?"

"No," Nancy replied slowly, knowing how much Annie loved the bairn, it would give her a good excuse for calling uninvited and help break any ice that may have formed since they'd been apart; John shrugged, he knew from experience that what Nancy wanted, Nancy got.

Billy Dawson thanked the Squadron Leader for his help, but had to admit he was no further forward in finding out who the father of Lexie's bairn might be. It didn't help that he couldn't say the real reason for being at the Base, but he knew Lexie would never have forgiven him if he had.

"Sorry we couldn't be of more help," James Morris said, "but if I hear anything about your daughter and why she left us, I'll be sure to let you know."

"Thanks," Billy said, "perhaps you could let the Wing Commander know of my visit?"

James pursed his lips. "Not possible, officially," he told Billy, "but if he gets in touch for any reason, then maybe.....but don't count on it."

By the time Billy got back to Dundee, he'd decided that it was up to Annie to find out more about Lexie's pregnancy and until he had something concrete to go on, he'd just have to hold fire on any 'shotgun wedding'; what a mess.

The next day was spent at Baxters and he made a mental note to get in touch with Nancy, let her know they were back and their stay would be indefinite, but when he climbed the stairs leading to home, he saw a Tansad parked on the landing. Quietly, he opened the door and could hear female voices coming from the kitchen.

He breathed a sigh of relief. Nancy and her toddler son were here and, hopefully, the voices he heard were of Lexie telling Nancy all about what had happened, after all, Nancy was once in the same position, when she got pregnant with wee Billy, all those years ago. But when he opened the kitchen door, he was disappointed, there indeed was Nancy and King Kevin, but the other female voice he'd heard was that of Mary Anne, who'd insisted on joining her mum to visit her Auntie Annie.

"Granddad," she squealed, jumping up to greet him. At 17 years of age, Mary Anne was an independent young woman in her own right and held down a Weaver's job at Baxters, alongside her mum. She'd inherited Nancy's dark hair and eyes but her personality was all her own.

"Where's Annie?" Billy asked, extricating himself from his granddaughter's arms and focussing his attention on Nancy. "She's just gone to get her cardigan, she'll be back in a minute," his daughter told him, "and it's nice to see you too dad," she added pointedly, lifting Kevin onto her knee.

He was about to ask where Lexie was, but thought better of it. "I'm sorry, Sweetheart," he said, tickling Kevin under the chin, "it's been a bit hectic getting back into things....I was going to visit you at the weekend, but now you're here....where's Annie?" he asked again, getting more distracted by her and Lexie's absence.

Nancy frowned, "I told you, gone to get her cardigan, but if you'd like to say hello to your grandson, I'll go and look for her," she said, offering Kevin to him! This wasn't how Nancy had planned the visit to go and her dad's distracted manner had added to her annoyance.

"NO, NO," he cried, loudly enough for his wife to hear and let her know he was home..... "I'll find her myself," he added hastily, leaving the kitchen and Nancy and Mary Anne speechless.

Billy found Annie in Lexie's bedroom, the curtains drawn and his step-daughter was barely visible under the bed covers. "Nancy and Mary Anne are here to see you," he hissed, confusion plain on his face. "Sssshhhhh!" Annie hushed him, "Lexie doesn't want to see them, especially Nancy. She ran into her room when she heard the knock at the door and when she knew it was Nancy, refused to come out."

Billy looked heavenward, exasperated with it all. His patience, at Lexie's behaviour and the ruination of his plans for their future in Ireland with their son, was being stretched to its limit. "Please, Billy," Annie whispered, "tell them I'm not feeling well but I'll come and visit them ..... soon....," but by the time he returned to the kitchen, Nancy, Mary Anne and King Kevin were gone.

Billy sat down, heavily and lit a cigarette, letting the smoke calm his soul as he waited for Annie to come back into the kitchen. Whatever it was that had happened at Montrose, Lexie was going to have to tell all, sooner rather than later and to Hell with the consequences.

But Annie returned alone, her heart heavy and her mind confused. "I don't know what to do," she murmured, silently willing Billy to come up with a solution. "Lexie seems to be getting further and further away from us," she added anxiously "and I can't seem to get through to her......."

Billy could see Annie's distress and saw no betterment would come from getting angry with Lexie's silence; the lass needed help not angry words, but none of them seemed to be able to unlock the door to her silent prison.

Billy's train of thought began winding through the past, searching for inspiration. "Isabella!" he suddenly exclaimed, "Isabella Anderson, of course." Annie's eyes brightened at the sound of her name. Annie had been unhappily married to Alex Melville, Lexie's father and Isabella's brother and it was she who had saved her from despair when she found out that her brother had been beating her.

"Are you still in touch with her?" Billy asked, getting the bit between his teeth.

Annie hurried towards the sideboard and fished out a shoebox. "We lost touch when she and John went to live in Edinburgh," she said, riffling through the contents, "but when the war ended, she wrote to tell me that they had moved to Forfar. John is now the Captain at the Salvation Army Hall there." Her face flushed with hope and waving the letter aloft, she re-opened the envelope. Not only was there an address, but also a telephone number.

"I'll telephone her right away," Annie gushed, "I'm sure she'll help us."

But Billy stopped her, "this is too delicate to speak about over the telephone," he said, wisely, "but I don't think we should lose any more time before driving to Forfar to see Isabella and John face to face." Billy took Annie's hands in his. "First thing tomorrow," he said, "we'll go to Forfar and, God willing, with Isabella's help, we'll find a way through this and bring Lexie out of this dark place she's in."

The next morning, Billy left the house at his usual time for going to work at Baxters, but instead, was waiting for Annie to join him, the engine of his motorcar already warming up for the journey. Annie left a note on the kitchen table, about having to do lots of shopping, along with a plate of pancakes for Lexie's breakfast when she got up. Satisfied that she wouldn't guess the real reason for her mother's absence so early, Annie quietly prayed that Isabella would, once again, come to her rescue, as she hurried down the stairs to the motorcar, parked in Albert Street.

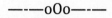

Chapter 5

Nancy was confused and angry at her dad's behaviour and was none the wiser as to why they'd come back to Dundee: and what was all the secrecy, she wondered, with Annie hurrying from the kitchen to fetch her 'cardigan' as soon as they'd come in the door, then never returning?

"Is Granddad alright?" Mary Anne asked, forcing Nancy to turn her attention to her daughter as she pushed Kevin in his Tansad down Albert Street towards the Cowgate. Nancy raised an eyebrow, "why do you ask?" she wanted to know, wondering if Mary Anne had gleaned any insight into her granddad's odd behaviour.

"Well," she said, thoughtfully, "he's usually so happy to see me and Kevin, and I know we haven't seen him for a wee while, but all he seemed to want, was for us to .....go away!"

"You know as much as I do," Nancy replied, briskly, as she bumped the pushchair up the stairs to her home, "but I intend to find out this weekend."

The smell of cooking wafted over them as they came into the kitchen. John Brannan was at the stove stirring a pot of mince and onions, knowing that Nancy had gone straight from work to Albert Street to quiz Annie and her dad on the reasons for their unexpected return to Dundee and especially about their future intentions for the house in Albert Street.

"Mince and tatties do you?" he asked, brightly, trying to gauge Nancy's mood.

"Where's wee Billy?" Nancy asked, immediately, knowing that if her son found John had access to their home when she wasn't in, there would be Hell to pay. The death of his dad at

Christmas, especially of how he was found frozen to death, had left him both grieving and guilty.

"It's alright," John assured her, "he went past my window a good half hour or so with two of his pals, so I doubt he'll be back any time soon." Never the less, Nancy was annoyed that John had taken the risk. "You know how he feels about you," she hissed, as Mary Anne went through to the back room to change out of her mill clothes.

John realised he'd made an assumption that their sleeping together meant that he was accepted as Nancy's 'man' and that entitled him to come and go to her house as he pleased, but her reaction had put paid to that and riled his masculine pride. "Well it's time he grew up," he retaliated, tossing the wooden spoon into the sink "and find out that life's goes on, whether he likes it or not."

Nancy bristled, why was it always the same; once a man bedded you he thought he owned you and it seemed like John Brannan was shaping up to be just like all the rest. "Well," she countered, her hands firmly placed on her hips, "if you're not happy with the way it is, then you know what you can do!"

They glared at one another, each one willing the other to concede but neither of them did. "I know what I can do," John murmured, picking up his jacket from the back of a chair, "enjoy your mince and tatties," he added, his voice heavy with sarcasm as he strode out of Nancy's house.

The sound of King Kevin, kicking his feet against the restraints of the Tansad as he tried to climb out, brought Nancy back to her toddler. Instead of getting control back into her life, she'd only made things worse by quarrelling with John and wondered where their life together was going anyway. Wee Billy didn't seem any closer to accepting that his mum had been seeing John Brannan, let alone sleeping with him and her dream of living in the house in Albert Street, was also fading fast.

"C'mon," she said, sitting the bairn in his high-chair, "let's get us fed and watered and let tomorrow do what it will."

Lexie wandered through to the kitchen and glanced at the clock, before picking up Annie's note. Shopping all morning, she read, frowning? Her mum must be stocking up to feed an army. Usually, the thought of food turned her stomach, but for the first time in what seemed an eternity, she realised her stomach felt settled and even her appetite that had deserted her, now seemed to be returning.

Tentatively, she put an egg on to boil and cut a thick slice of bread for grilling. She filled the kettle and spooned tea into the teapot, her whole body sensing that sustenance was, at last, on the way. The fear of confronting Nancy the day before, had left her distraught, but she knew she couldn't hide away forever. The thought of people pointing and staring at her as the baby grew inside her was bad enough, but the knowledge that Bo had coldly used her to get his revenge, before leaving for Canada, had cut deep.

This wasn't how she'd envisaged her future, to be back in Dundee, pregnant and without a father for her bastard bairn. She shook the thought from her head; pride comes before a fall, she told herself, sadly, and what had made her think Bo McGhee had still been in love with her after all she'd put him through, when she'd jilted him and married Robbie Robertson?

The egg, rattling against the side of the pot as it boiled, reminded her body that it wanted to eat. Almost automatically, she toasted the bread and filled the teapot with boiling water, even in distress, Mother Nature was looking after the new life being nurtured out of sight in her womb and despite the bleakness of her future, Lexie ate.

The drive to Forfar was taken in apprehensive silence, neither Billy nor Annie noticing the signs of Spring blossoming all around them.

"We're here," Billy announced as they pulled up outside the stone-built villa, with bay windows and an impressive front door. "Let's hope they're in," Annie said, "maybe we should have telephoned them....you know, let them know we were coming?

"Too late now," Billy countered, opening the motor car door and helping Annie to step out, "let's just hope that Isabella is still a Christian!"

It was John Anderson who opened the door to them, his eyes

lighting up at their presence. "Isabella," he called out excitedly, "look who's here!" His wife came scurrying to the door, "look who is here?" she queried before spotting Annie on her doorstep.

"Annie?" she gasped, reaching out her hands to welcome her, "and Billy," she added, "come in, come in." She ushered them into the front room, while John was despatched to the kitchen to put the kettle on. As Isabella and Annie began catching up on the years they had missed, Billy slipped away to find his way to the kitchen. John Anderson and the Salvation Army had saved his life when he'd returned from fighting in the First World War, shell-shocked and barely alive. Had it not been for him, Billy would have ended up living on the streets destitute, till he died of cold and hunger.

"It's great to see you both," John said, as he set out the teacups on a tray, "there's a lot of water flowed under the bridge since we last met." Billy nodded, "but we're all still here and, God willing, we'll be here for a long time yet."

"Is everything alright?" John asked, pouring the water into the teapot: never one to indulge in small talk and sensing that Billy and Annie hadn't just dropped by this early in the morning to chat about old times.

"No," Billy replied flatly. "It's Lexie," he said, "she left her job at the RAF Base at Montrose two months ago and Annie received a letter from her when we were in Ireland saying...... .well, maybe we should let Annie tell you and Isabella all about it and see if you can help."

John picked up the tray and indicated to Billy to lead the way back to the parlour.

"Tea first," was all he said, as he followed Billy into the room and set the tray on the small gate-leg table beside the fireplace.

Isabella quickly filled the cups and passed them around along with the plate of biscuits, but no one seemed to want to eat. "How's Lexie, Annie?" John asked, quietly, forcing her to respond, "Billy tells me she's left her job." For the next hour, Annie tried to explain about Lexie's distress, without revealing her secret and how she seemed to have sunk into a black depression, refusing to speak to either of them about what was troubling her and could Isabella perhaps try to get through to her, please?

"We should tell you," Billy interrupted Annie's flow of platitudes, "that Lexie is pregnant and not married." Annie blanched visibly, but here was no point in hiding the truth, "and she's ashamed and quite ill with it all," Billy continued, "but it's more than that," he added, "and that's what we can't seem to get to the bottom of."

Isabella looked shocked. Lexie, PREGNANT and unmarried! She'd understood when it had happened to Nancy, her flirtatious nature was always getting her into trouble, but not Lexie, 'she was a good girl', she'd told Isabella, 'not like her sluttish cousin'. Then she remembered the shame that Annie and felt at giving birth to her bastard son in the Poor House in Belfast and the distress she'd felt when she'd had to tell Lexie the secret about her own past: no wonder Lexie couldn't speak to Annie about any of it without opening up deep wounds that were best forgotten.

Isabella leaned over and took Annie's hand. "Of course I'll help," she said, she'd seen enough pain in her own life to know how it felt to be alone and frightened, but she had her faith, Lexie, it seemed, had none.

"Does Lexie know you're here?" John asked. Billy shook his head, "she thinks I'm at work and Annie's shopping."

"Then we can't just come back with you both and descend on her unexpectedly," he counselled, "why don't I telephone later this evening and arrange to visit you, that way the contact will come from us." Billy readily agreed, but Annie was hesitant, "she may not come out of her room," she said, "Nancy called after work with Mary Anne and Kevin, but she point blank refused to see them and......" she looked at Billy as the possibility sank in, "she may do the same thing again."

"Let's cross that bridge when we come to it," John said, "whatever it is that's causing Lexie this deep unhappiness, will come to the surface when she is ready." "Meanwhile," Isabella added, helping Annie with her coat, "pray for guidance and keep the faith."

Back in Dundee, Billy headed to Baxters while Annie scurried from shop to shop in Albert Street filling her basket with provisions before climbing the stairs back home, her nerves tingling with fear at what she might find. But, to her surprise, Lexie was up and about, seemed to have had breakfast and was tidying the kitchen!

"Tea?" Lexie asked, flatly, as Annie set her shopping basket down on the table.

"You seem.......better," Annie said, warily, feeling guilty about involving Isabella and John when Lexie seemed to be much improved, but when Lexie turned to face her, she could still see the emptiness in her blue eyes. "I've stopped being sick," she stated, "that's all!"

"Good," Annie said, cautiously, "then maybe a little walk later?............." But before Annie could say another word, Lexie's voice hardened, "I don't want a little walk," she said, harshly, "nor anything else for that matter, I just want to be left alone."

The door slammed behind her and Annie could feel tears of hurt and rejection filling her eyes. Lexie may have stopped vomiting, but the sickness that enveloped her heart and mind remained. "Pray for guidance and keep the faith," Annie muttered to herself, dabbing her eyes and glad now that Isabella and John had agreed to help.

Whatever it was that had happened to Lexie was too painful for her to speak of and Annie knew she could do nothing to change that. Lexie was lost to her.

——oOo——

Chapter 6

John Brannan was still rankling after his spat with Nancy the night before. He'd never been married, nor had he been a father and hadn't realised that the bond a mother had with her bairns was so strong, even when they were grown up. Nor had he realised the bond a son had to his father could still be strong, even after the pain he had caused his family and especially now that Billy Donnelly was dead.

He heaved a sigh of relief when he spotted Nancy and Mary Anne coming into the Weaving Flat and heading for their looms. He'd have to be careful how he trod in future, or he could find himself alone again and he didn't want that. The key to his dilemma, he surmised, was wee Billy, he had to befriend him and win his trust....but how to do that, he had still to figure out?

The weaving looms sprang into life and the racket they created prevented any chance of conversation with Nancy. He'd have to bide his time till the end of the shift, when his grovelling to Nancy would begin.

"Wait up!" he called to her, as she made her way to the Mill Nursery to collect Kevin, "Please," he emphasised, "slow down." Nancy clenched her fists, wee Billy had come home last night smelling of beer and smoke. He was still underage for buying drink, but one of the other two that John had seen him go off with, plainly weren't.

Images of her husband Billy Donnelly flooded her mind with fear that her son was going to follow in his father's footsteps and end up a hopeless drunk. But wee Billy hadn't been in the mood for apologising last night and instead, accused his mother of being a 'hussy', willing to go to bed with any man who took her fancy! There was no mistaking who he was meaning, but Nancy had no answer for him. She knew that Billy had made a good job of turning their son against her, but had hoped that time would have healed the wounds.

"Blood's thicker than water," she muttered to herself as she turned to face John Brannan.

"I'm sorry," John began, "really, I mean it," he said, emphasising the words and kicking a wee stone off the pavement and into the road, his eyes avoiding contact with Nancy's. "Huh!" Nancy huffed, as she kept walking briskly towards the Nursery door. "C'mon Nancy," John pleaded, "I made a mistake, right, but it won't happen again."

You're right," Nancy retorted, holding out her upturned hand, "it won't happen again and I'll have my key back!"

John felt his blood run cold; surely, Nancy wasn't serious? But Nancy was serious and waited in silence while John dug the house key out of his trouser pocket and handed it back to her. Without a backward glance, Nancy disappeared through the Nursery door, leaving John Brannan alone in the street.

Di Auchterlonie smiled to herself as she watched the scenario play out from the darkness of the close leading to her 'single end.' She'd been Nancy's best friend during the war when Nancy had bedded Jim Murphy while Billy had been fighting in France. It was always easy for Nancy to attract men and she'd made the most of the freedom from her marital constraints, in the dance halls of Dundee. But, for Di, despite being available, she'd never even gotten close to walking up the aisle and had began resenting Nancy more and more, especially when John Brannan had come to work at Baxters and immediately made his interest in Nancy obvious, ignoring all of Di's attempts at 'flirting' with him.

"All's fair in love and war," she murmured to herself as she emerged from the close, falling into step with John Brannan as he walked down the street, alone. "Going my way," she trilled, wishing she wasn't still in her working clothes, with her chestnut hair, her best feature, hidden under the jute-covered head-square?

John Brannan glanced at the woman by his side; Di Auchterlone, he winced, what did she want? "Not feeling the joys of Spring?" Di continued, determined to elicit some response to her approach. John sighed, "sorry Di," he said, "it's been a long day and I just want to get home."

Di's lips tightened; she couldn't lose this opportunity to get John's attention and desperately sought for the words to keep him from walking away.

"You look as though you could use a drink," she urged, "I know I could?"

John's eyes met hers. At least someone wanted his company, he pondered, bleakly... Di Auchterlonie wasn't Nancy, but the alternative of sitting alone in his two-roomed flat swayed his mind towards the pub.

"Why not," he said, shrugging. Di immediately linked her arm into his, "the Snug at the Thrums?" she suggested, hoping that there would be plenty of Baxters workers there on a Friday night to see her walking in on the arm of John Brannan!

Di's grip tightened as they entered the Snug, making sure she loudly greeted the knot of women already there, all the while, beaming at John Brannan's back as he ordered their drinks at the Snug's hatchway. He handed Di her glass of Stout and set his own pint down at the tiny table and wooden bench, where Di had cleared a space for them to sit, together.

He was already regretting his decision as he took a long draught of his ale, but his stomach tightened as he looked around at the faces of the silent women staring back at him... Weavers all! He knew how it must look and could have kicked himself for being so stupid as to let himself be seen in the pub with Di Auchterlonie on his arm.

Quickly downing his pint, he rose to his feet. "Sorry Di," he said, pointedly, "things to do," before striding out of the Snug and into the coolness of the street.

The cackling of female laughter followed him till the pub door swung shut behind him and he breathed in the smell of the jute that always hung in the air. By Monday, he realised, every Weaver in the flat would know about him and Di

Auchterlonie in the Snug. John leant against the wall and gazed up into the darkening sky, his future with Nancy disappearing with the daylight, one mistake she may have been able to forgive, but being seen with another woman, albeit innocently, would be deemed unforgivable.

Despondently, he turned into the Cowgate and home, crossing the road to avoid the trio of lads pushing and shoving the smallest one around. "Beer money!" one of them shouted, pulling at the other's jacket pocket, "hand it over, NOW!"

"I telt you, I dinna hae ony money!" the youngster squealed, "you've took it all."

John Brannan squinted into the gloom as a hard fist knocked the lad off his feet and two pairs of boots began to kick him as he lay helpless on the ground.

"Hoi!" he shouted, running towards the melee, his army training and physical build giving him the advantage over two scrawny lads. "Leave him be, or you'll have me to answer to!" Realising they couldn't take on a man, the ringleader gave a final kick to the prone figure on the ground, before running off down the street.

John Brannan knelt beside the battered youth. "C'mon laddie," he said, turning him over, "let's get you to your feet." The bruised face and bloody nose of wee Billy Donnelly met John's eyes. So much for wee Billy's pals, he thought. "Can you walk?" he asked, helping Nancy's son to stand and beginning to guide him to the close. "I'm fine," wee Billy murmured, shaking off John's supporting hands, "I dinna need your help," adding angrily, I dinna need anybody!"

John watched as the stumbling figure of wee Billy disappeared into the darkness of the close. There would be Hell to pay when Nancy saw the state he was in. "Join the club," he whispered to himself, "I'm in your mum's bad books as well." For the second time that night, he leant against a wall and gazed at the now dark sky, speckled with twinkling stars. Sometimes, you've just got to accept your fate and stop trying to win, he shrugged. "Tomorrow is another day," he reminded himself, but John Brannan knew tomorrow would be worse than today, once

Nancy got wind of Di Auchterlonie's antics.

Nancy felt the colour drain from her face when her son stumbled through the door, blood dripping through his fingers as the fought to hide the mess that was his nose.

"What the Hell...?" she began, steering the lad to a chair and sitting him down. "Here", she said, anxiously, "put this under your nose and put your head back." Nancy handed him a dishcloth and dabbed at the blood on his hands and jacket with a wet facecloth. There was no point in asking her son what had happened, as she knew there would be no answer and her fear deepened. Wee Billy was becoming just like his father?

Her confidence in being an independent woman, capable of living life on her own terms, slowly wilted and Nancy felt empty and alone. All her dreams of happiness with Billy Donnelly had long gone and she'd just given John Brannan his marching orders.

"Sorry mum," she heard the mumbled voice of wee Billy, "I fell." Nancy's lips tightened, "FELL!" she echoed, "is that all you've got to say for yourself?"

Bruising was forming under her son's eyes as she looked. Tomorrow his face would be purple and black, but his nose looked straight enough, so didn't seem broken.

"Get out of my sight," she rasped, turning her back on him to hide her own tears.

The chair scraped across the floorboards and she listened till wee Billy's footsteps stopped with the shutting of the back room door.

Nancy flopped down at the kitchen table, her head in her hands, would she ever be happy again? Kevin started grumbling for his tea and Nancy picked him up. "Don't you turn into a bad'un as well," she chided her bairn, "and give some other poor lass a life of misery." King Kevin grinned and Nancy hugged her toddler to her breast. "C'mon," she whispered, "tomorrow is another day."

—·—oOo—·—

Chapter 7

It was Lexie who picked up the ringing telephone. "Dundee 102," she said, "Lexie speaking." Her training at answering telephones in the WAAF came automatically to her, but when she heard Isabella's voice, she almost dropped the receiver.

"LEXIE!" Isabella almost shouted, "it's Isabella.....you remember me don't you?"

Lexie heard herself stammering, "mmmum's not here just now..... I'll tttell her you rang," before slamming the telephone back to its cradle. Her heart was racing and she could feel her whole body shaking a she fought to steady her breathing. "No, no, no," she repeated; she mustn't know of my shame, not Isabella with her Christian beliefs. Lexie felt a wave of nausea hit her, but it wasn't morning sickness this time, it was panic. She had to get away from here, grabbing her coat and slinging her handbag over her shoulder, she ran out of the door, down the stone stairs and out into the street and straight into the arms of Charlie Mathieson.

Many moons ago, Charlie and Lexie had been engaged to be married, but she'd called the engagement off, believing Charlie wasn't 'man enough' for her when she'd became besotted with Robbie Robertson. With his rugged good looks and romantic sailor's life, he'd swept her off her feet.

"Hey!" he said, holding her shoulders tightly, "where's the fire?"

"No fire," Lexie muttered, "just in a hurry."

"Wait a minute," Charlie said, "I recognise that voice." He tipped Lexie's head back and forced her to look at him. "Lexie", he said incredulously, "is it YOU?"

43

Lexie struggled to free herself. Why did the past keep haunting her she fumed inwardly, "let me past!"

Charlie tightened his grip. "NO," he said, "not in the state you're in, whatever it is, you need to calm down." Responding somehow to the sympathetic tone of his voice, Lexie felt herself fold into Charlie's arms, the fight suddenly leaving her. "C'mon," he said, "let's get you a cuppa and you can tell me all about it."

Lexie allowed Charlie to guide her down Albert Street to a teashop in Princes Street. "There," he said, pulling out a chair and easing her into it, "now let's get you some tea and you can tell me what's wrong."

She watched as the tea was poured and the sugar and milk added, wondering what twist of fate had arranged this encounter. She hadn't been over the door in weeks and in her panic to avoid Isabella, she'd ran straight into another 'ghost' from her past, Charlie Mathieson.

"You don't look well," Charlie said, his forehead furrowed with concern.

Lexie gripped her teacup with both hands as she guided it to her lips.

"I heard about Robbie, by the way," he told her, "his ship torpedoed in the Atlantic and all hands lost!"

Lexie nodded; remembering the telegram telling her that he'd been killed in action and now look at her, alone and pregnant with Bo McGhee's bairn. How the mighty are fallen, she thought, helplessly, as the pain of her shame washed over her again.

"Does Sarah know you're back in Dundee?" he asked. Lexie looked at him quizzically and shook her head. "She'd love to see you again, Lexie," he said, "she speaks about you all the time."

"Speaks about me?" Lexie queried, "to you?"

"All the time," Charlie grinned, "it's what man and wife do," he said, "talk about things."

Lexie could hardly believe her ears. Sarah McIntyre, mousy Sarah, who wouldn't say' boo to a goose', MARRIED!

"Don't look so surprised, I guess we saved one another's lives," he continued quietly, "I'd been jilted by you and Sarah had been forced to give up the Irish doctor she was sweet on."

Lexie was so stunned at the news, that she almost forgot her own problems! Since joining the WAAF in 1943, she'd lost touch with Sarah and had always imagined her as the 'auld maid' living her life in quiet desperation teaching English to the pupils at Morgan Academy.

"So," Charlie continued, leaning closer, his worry increasing the more he took in Lexie's wan appearance and thinness. "How about we surprise Sarah with a visit?"

"Visit?" Lexie asked, the anxiety edging back into her system at the thought of facing her old friend, "but she might be busy... .or something," she added lamely, wishing she'd never left the house. But Charlie wasn't going to take 'no' for an answer and signalled for the bill. "C'mon," he said, "Sarah would kill me if she thought we'd met and I didn't bring you home."

Lexie felt caught between 'the devil and the deep blue sea', to go back to Albert Street would mean confronting her mother and perhaps, alarmingly, Isabella Anderson. Lexie nodded agreement, where else had she intended to go when she rushed out of the house in panic with no thought and little money!

Charlie guided her up Pitkerro Road, past Baxters Park to a stone built house fronted by a small garden that boasted a stone bird bath and a border of shrubs and Spring flowers. "Here we are," he said, holding open the front gate for Lexie to enter. Lexie felt a sharp pang of loneliness and regret, this should have been her life with Robbie, happy and married and pregnant with his bairn, but fate had decided otherwise and she had become his widow. She felt Charlie nudge her forward, as the front door opened and Sarah blinked in surprise at the sight of her.

"Lexie?" she queried, "is that really you?" Lexie could feel tears forming in her eyes. Sarah was coming towards her, her hair swept up in a cascade of waves, elegant in a summer frock and open sandals and wearing the smile that Lexie remembered from long ago. She glanced at her husband as she wrapped her arm around her friend; what had happened to Lexie since they'd last met, she wondered, anxiously, all of her energy and enthusiasm for life seemed to have been drained from her and left behind this shadow of her friend. Whatever was wrong with Lexie, Sarah knew instinctively, she would talk when she was ready, but in the meantime, her experience of dealing with her own mother's anxiety and dark moods had taught her to be patient and to just wait.

"It's so lovely to see you Lexie," Sarah said, sitting on the armchair opposite the sofa where Lexie now sat. "I've so missed you," she added, wistfully, "when you joined the WAAFS I wanted to join too, but with mum....you know....she needed me here, so that was that." Lexie sat in silence, she'd spent so much time alone with her hurt and rejection by Bo McGhee, that she felt frozen in the face of Sarah's obvious happiness with her life.

"Do you remember when we'd walk through Baxters Park" Sarah continued..., "or feed the swans at the Swannie Ponds... ...or when we went down to the Ferry and had our sandwiches on the beach?" Her eyes glistened with the memories of a time before the war parted them and now, so much had changed, especially her friend.

I do," Lexie said, her chin quivering as her emotions began to surface, before spilling over into a flood of tears and sobs.

Sarah flew to her side. "It's alright, Lexie," she whispered, "I'm here and I won't let you go." Charlie came into the parlour but was hushed away by Sarah, this wasn't the time for anyone else to be around, her wonderful friend had come back and Sarah thanked God that Charlie had brought her home.

"I know you're unhappy," Sarah ventured into the quietness that had followed the tears, "but whatever it is you have to face......you don't have to face it alone." It was a simple statement of fact and Lexie knew it. Even after all those years, it was as though Sarah had waited, patiently, for this moment to just be here when Lexie needed her and she'd no intention of letting her down.

"I'm going to have a bairn," Lexie said "and the bairn's dad doesn't want to know."

Sarah felt her heart ache for her friend, all she'd ever wanted was to be loved and find happiness in her life and it had all come down to this moment. All the plans they had made when they were young and innocent, for Lexie, had come to nothing, but for Sarah, fate had brought her Charlie Mathieson, a wedding ring and a lovely home.

Sarah knew how much courage it had taken for Lexie to speak of her shame and hopelessness, but now it was out in the open, she was more determined than ever to stand by Lexie and the bairn, when it came along.

"Does your mum know?"

Lexie nodded, "only that I'm pregnant but not about........Bo McGhee."

Sarah winced at the strange-sounding name. "Do you want to tell me about it?"

For the next hour, Lexie unburdened her soul to Sarah, safe in the knowledge that she wouldn't be judged or become the subject of gossip. "So," Lexie sighed, "like a fool, I believed that he'd forgiven me for marrying Robbie and jilting him and the night he was to return to Canada, we........" Lexie's lips tightened as she took a deep breath, "we made love....under the Christmas stars........and I really believed he loved me like before, but........I've heard nothing from him since Christmas and now it's April and......" Lexie turned her blue eyes to face Sarah. "Tell me you understand," she whispered "and that you don't think I'm........a slut!"

"Oh! Lexie!" Sarah exclaimed, "NEVER......you're the most wonderful person in the world, you're loving and generous and honest and if this......Bo person, had tricked you into believing that he loved you, then it's him who should be ashamed, not you."

The sound of gently knocking on the parlour door broke into the 'heart to heart.'

"Can I come in yet?" Charlie asked.

Sarah looked at Lexie and saw the beginnings of a smile crossing her lips, "I think that would be fine," Lexie said, taking Sarah's hand in hers "and I think it's time for me to go home and face the music with mum and Billy, but whatever happens, I'm so glad you're my friend and that you love me for who I am...not who I've become."

47

For the first time in months, Lexie felt a lightness in her steps as she returned to her Albert Street home to face her mum and Billy.

Chapter 8

Breakfast in Nancy's household was a silent affair. Mary Anne, usually chatty and full of energy, supped her porridge while stealing glances at her brother's battered face and her mother's angry one. Whatever had happened wasn't good.

"Make sure you tell Ernie Griffiths about your 'fall'" Nancy grimaced, as wee Billy pushed his chair away from the table, "don't want him thinking you were in any kind of trouble and you lose your apprenticeship." Wee Billy turned his black eyes toward his mother. He knew she was right, there were plenty of hard working young lads who would quickly take his place, if Ernie thought he was doing anything to sully the painter and decorator's hard-earned reputation.

"Nag, nag, nag," Billy muttered under his breath, making Mary Anne's eyebrows raise and Nancy's eyes to flash dangerously. "Get to work," she spat "and don't think I don't know what you're up to........." she shouted, as the door slammed shut behind her son's departing back.

"What was that all about?" Mary Anne asked quietly as she began to clear the table.

Nancy sighed and lit a cigarette, blowing the smoke into the air above her head and shrugging. "He's been drinking," she said, before adding, "just like his dad."

Mary Anne looked at her mother quizzically. She knew the lads wee Billy had been hanging out with, trouble-makers all of them and none of them working, meaning wee Billy would have been the only one earning any money and if he was drinking, so were they and wee Billy would have been buying the beer.

"You do know he's been seen in the company of the Kelly brothers?"

"No!" Nancy exclaimed. "The Kelly family are a bunch of thugs and thieves, aren't they? Wee Billy's not that daft to be running round with them.......is he?"

Mary Anne nodded: If only her dad had still been alive, he would have sorted them out and wee Billy wouldn't have any more 'falls' she told herself. But her dad was dead and, despite everything, she still loved him.

Nancy stubbed out the cigarette. "We'd better get off to the Mill now," she said,

"we don't want to get the sack for being late." Mother and daughter pulled their coats on and hurried along the Cowgate to Baxters back entrance, braced for another day of hard graft. John Brannan watched the women fanning out into the Weaving Flat from his Supervisor's desk and breathed a sigh of relief when he saw Nancy set up at her looms. At least she was here and not taken off to another Mill where she'd be out of his reach, maybe forever. The thought chilled him to the bone and he knew that, somehow, he had to get through to her, make her understand that he loved her.

When the 'bummer' sounded the end of the shift, Nancy glanced across to John Brannan's desk. Maybe I've been too hasty, he told herself, blaming him for her son's behaviour when it was maybe, just maybe, that wee Billy had only himself to blame. But John was nowhere to be seen. Perplexed, she made her way out of the Weaving Flat, she had secretly hoped that he'd pursue her and was left deflated as she took the lonely walk to the Nursery to pick up Kevin.

"Hello Nancy." John's voice sounded in her ear as she came out of the Nursery with King Kevin holding on to her skirt as he skipped alongside of her. "Hello John," Nancy responded, pleased that he'd been waiting for her. He took hold of Kevin's free hand. "Who wants a swing then?" he said, sweeping Kevin into the air and 'birrling' him around, as the bairn giggled with delight. "Put him down," Nancy chided smiling at the sight, "you'll make him dizzy."

John lowered Kevin back onto the pavement. "Like you make me dizzy, Nancy Donnelly," he said, longing to hold her but keeping his distance, "dizzy with love for you." Nancy felt her heart skip a beat and a flush of colour rushed to her cheeks. "Huh!" she said, confident now that John was back at her command, "fine words indeed John Brannan, but that won't get you my key back."

But Nancy was smiling at him and his spirits soared. He'd waited long enough for the chance to be with her, he would wait forever to share her bed again, if that's what it took.

"I know that," John said, "and I'm sorry I upset you and wee Billy, I just thought that you'd be happy I'd made the mince and......" Nancy held a finger to his lips to stop him speaking before lightly kissing him, right there in the Cowgate in full view of her neighbours, nattering at the ends of their closes. "You're forgiven," she whispered, slipping the key back into his hand.

She knew that wee Billy was out of control, but after May Anne's revelation about the Kelly brothers, she knew she needed a man to deal with them, and that John Brannan was strong enough to handle himself around bullies, hadn't he saved them all from a drunken Billy Donnelly. But not only that, she'd found that she missed him and he was right, it was time wee Billy grew up.

"Come round later tonight," she told him when they reached the close leading to her home, "we need to talk." King Kevin went bounding into the darkness of the pend and jumped onto the first step, looking back for his mother to follow him, but Nancy was held in the arms of John Brannan, as his passion for her overflowed into an urgent kiss. "I'll come by at 9 o'clock," he breathed into her hair, "and you can talk all you want," he added, releasing his hold and stepping back into the street and turning for home.

Nancy knees felt weak and her breathing had quickened with the encounter as she followed her son up the flight of stairs to home. Whether wee Billy accepted him or not, she now knew for sure, she wanted John Brannan back in her life and tonight she would prove it to him.

Annie jumped when she heard the key turning in the lock. "She's back," she whispered to Billy, glad that Lexie was home, but worried about where she'd been.

They both pretended to be doing 'other things' when their daughter came into the parlour, Annie knitting furiously and Billy re-reading the same page of his newspaper.

"Does anyone want a cuppa?" Lexie enquired as if nothing had changed and she wasn't about to expose the name of her unborn bairn's father.

"Where have you been?" Annie blurted out, trying to gauge Lexie's mood and remembering that she was a grown woman and not her little girl any more.

"With Sarah Dawson," Lexie told them, "or should I say Sarah Mathieson as she is known now." Billy frowned, as Sarah's father he should have known that his daughter had married, but realised that her mother, Josie, had made sure he'd been cut out of the lives of his girls when he'd left her to be with Annie. The silence that followed, told Lexie that neither of them knew of Sarah's marriage.

"Well......I think we all need some tea," Annie finally said, as she made her way to the parlour door, "and maybe her dad has a question or two to ask about it all."

She cast a glance at Billy, who remained silent as his guilt reminded him of how he'd given up everything to be with Annie and although he had no regrets about leaving Josie, to hear that his favourite daughter had married and he never knew, cut like a knife through his heart.

"She lives on Pitkerro Road, across from the Ponds, with her husband Charlie Mathieson," Lexie related, quietly, to Billy. "You remember Charlie, don't you?"

Annie had been married to Euan McPherson when Lexie had become engaged to the young Draughtsman from Baxters, but Billy only knew from the Mill gossips that the engagement had been called off by Lexie.

Billy nodded, almost automatically, but it all seemed so long ago now and so much had changed for all of them that he no longer felt part of it, but somehow, fate kept dragging him back into the lives of his female off-spring, but who seemed to be further and further away from him instead of closer. The one place where he wanted to be was Ireland with their son, John and his wife Mary, but the chances of that happening any time soon, had gone.

Nancy, Billy realised, was a law unto herself now and he just hoped that some decent man would turn up to look after her and her brood, but it would take someone stronger than she was and they were in short supply since the war ended. And as for Lexie, he wondered, looking at Annie's wounded daughter, what had become of her fire and zest for life. This was the girl who'd won an Empire Medal for bravery during the conflict but now... Suddenly, Billy felt very old and useless. It seemed that everything he'd tried to do in the past to protect the women in his life had been turned on its head by the fickle hand of fate.

The return of Annie with their tea broke into his reverie. They both watched as she poured their tea, placing a biscuit in each saucer before handing the cups to Billy and Lexie and taking one for herself. There was so much Annie wanted to ask Lexie, but feared she might push her further away. "Did I tell you that Isabella and John Anderson are living at Forfar?" Annie asked, hoping that this would generate further conversation. Lexie ignored the question and put her tea back onto the tray.

"I've something to tell you both," she said, instantly getting the undivided attention of her mother and Billy. "As you know," she continued, "I'm going to have a bairn, a bastard, as it will be called." Annie flinched at the name but said nothing. "But I'm going to love the bairn just as I loved its father, with or without the approval of the rest of the world."

"We're not judging you Lexie," Billy told her, sincerely. "Neither your mother nor me, nor anyone else for that matter, can 'cast the first stone.' There it was, Lexie grimaced, the 'holier than though' of the church and chapel goers of Dundee that forgot their Christian values when an unmarried mother was amongst them. And she had been as bad as they were when

Nancy became pregnant to Billy Donnelly, out of wedlock.

"I know," she said, but there's more to it than that." The whole story about Bo McGhee and his supposed love for her that had made Lexie forget all her moral virtues and agree into letting him bed her before he returned to Canada with Louie. The sorry tale of her infidelity continued. She knew Bo was married, she knew that she should have said 'NO' but after the loss of Robbie that had left her so lonely, she had pushed all thoughts of right and wrong from her mind and behaved like a 'slut' as she called herself and deserved the shame that engulfed her.

"Does this 'Bo' know you're pregnant with his bairn?" Billy asked, feeling anger and guilt at his own behaviour when he'd done the same thing to Annie and her sister Mary, before leaving Ireland and them, behind: But Mary had been shrewder than Annie and had followed him to Dundee and demanded he marry her. Reluctantly, he had and Nancy was born within three months of their marriage.

Lexie clenched her hands together and shook her head: She'd written to Bo six times since he'd left for Canada, but had heard nothing back and as the pregnancy continued, she realised that she never would. He'd not only bedded her, but had duped her into believing that he loved her, when all he'd wanted was revenge for her treatment of him, when she'd married Robbie aboard his ship and jilted him on the dock at Halifax.

Annie felt her shoulders sag. The one thing she'd feared most of all was that her daughter would repeat the same mistake she'd made and bring an illegitimate bairn into the world, with no husband to support her. It had almost happened to Nancy, but Billy and Euan had seen to it that Billy Donnelly had stepped up to the mark and married her, but the union had ended in tears, when he'd turned to the prostitute, Gladys Kelly for love, instead of his wife. And now he was dead and Nancy was alone again. Annie shivered. What was going to become of them all, especially Lexie, when the gossips found out!

Billy felt a cold anger grip his insides. Whether to make up for his own past behaviour in Ireland or to stop Lexie from going through the same anguish that Annie had had to endure for years, he determined to somehow, find Bo McGhee and force him to face up to his 'mistake' and marry Lexie. And he knew just where to begin his search.

—-—oOo—-—

Chapter 9

At 9 o'clock on the dot, Nancy heard the sound of gentle knocking at her door.

She'd changed from her working clothes into a cotton frock and brushed her hair till it shone. After that kiss at the end of the close, she wanted John Brannan more than ever before. There would be time to talk later, but first of all......she wanted more of John's kisses. "It's open," she called, seductively, "come in."

The door swung open and John Brannan entered. He too, had made the effort to impress the other, wearing a clean, white shirt under his waistcoat and boots that shone with polishing. "Are we alone?" John asked, not wishing another confrontation with wee Billy. Nancy touched her lips with her finger. "Sssshhhh!" she said, "Kevin and Mary Anne are asleep in the back room and wee Billy's at some Boxing Club he's joined and won't be back till late."

"Then we don't have time to waste on talking," he said, hoarsely, quickly crossing the room and sweeping Nancy into his arms and, meeting no resistance, laid her fully across her bed in the kitchen alcove, never taking his eyes of her. "Do you want this as much as me?" John whispered, slipping the straps of her dress from her shoulders. "Please say yes."

Nancy shivered, memories of the first time with Billy Donnelly swept over her. It had been a long time since she'd felt such deep desire for a man, but now, she knew she could do nothing but submit to this man's touch. "YES." The word was breathed out with force, as John's hand found the hem of her frock and swept the thin cotton uparound her waist, with no petticoat nor underwear to hinder him, he knew in that moment, that Nancy was truly his......at last.

The clock on the mantelpiece chimed ten, but neither of them wanted to move from the bed. John wished he could just fall asleep with Nancy in his arms, but the imminent return of wee Billy, forced the issue. "Wee Billy will be home soon," he whispered into the darkness, "do you want me to stay?" But Nancy was sound asleep and gave no answer.

John eased out of bed and pulled on his clothes, there would be a time when he would stay, he knew that now, but not tonight, making love to a willing Nancy was enough for one day and there was always tomorrow, he told himself, as he slipped out of the sleeping household and into the night air. "Yes," he told the moon, "there's always tomorrow."

When Nancy awoke early next morning, her initial feeling was one of panic as she realised that she was naked. Then she remembered the night before and John Brannan's body pressing down on her own. She reached over for him, but he was gone, but the desire for him to make love to her again had not!

She threw back the bedcovers and pulled the crumpled frock over her head. The last thing she needed was for wee Billy to wander through to the kitchen and see his mother naked in bed. The kitchen was cold as she set a kettle of water on to boil. She'd have to wash away any trace of their sexual coupling before her brood woke up, especially wee Billy and started asking questions. She looked at herself in the mirror over the mantelpiece, fluffing her hair to shake loose the curls and leaning forward to see if anything was different about her that would tell the world she'd been bedded.

If wee Billy or Mary Anne noticed anything about their mother, none of them said a word and breakfast was eaten in the usual haste as getting to work dictated their day. "Are you going to the Boxing Club again tonight?" she asked her son, trying to keep her voice steady and disinterested in the answer. "Probably," he told her, smiling to himself as he headed for the door. His mother had believed the lie, but he wouldn't be spending the night at the Boxing Club, he'd be with the Kelly brothers and the drink.

Nancy felt her heart quicken, as soon as she had the chance to speak to John, another night of passion could now be arranged. King Kevin was dropped off at the Nursery and she linked her arm into Mary Anne's as they hurried to the Mill. Di Auchterlonie ran up behind Nancy as she made her way to her looms, her eyes sweeping the Weaving Flat for sight of John. And there he was, at his usual spot, but there was nothing usual about the look that passed between them!

"Penny for them" Di Auchterlonie said, as she drew alongside Nancy?

"What!" Nancy exclaimed, unaware until she'd spoken that Di was so close. "Well you were either gazing at nothing or...... perhaps it was our handsome Overseer?" Nancy felt her face colour with embarrassment, surely, she wasn't that obvious!

Di Auchterlonie's smile vanished, so there was still something going on between John Brannan and Nancy Donnelly and that look said it all. "See you at dinner-time," Di said sweetly, dropping the subject as quickly as she'd brought it up, "I've got so much to tell you."

Nancy set her looms on, keeping her head fixed on the warp and the weft. What did Di Auchterlonie want to tell her she wondered, knowing what a gossip her friend used to be? Surely, she'd know if any of the other weavers had got wind of her involvement with John Brannan, but she'd have to wait until dinner-time to sound Di out.

The wail of the dinner-time 'bummer' silenced the looms as the Weavers quickly knocked off, hungry for the soup and pies served up at the Canteen. Metal trays clanged and scraped along the counter rails past the Servers, who ladled the hot soup into bowls and flipped the pies onto plates, their eyes always on the next tray. Nancy carried her dinner to a table in the corner of the canteen and waited. If Di Auchterlonie was on the lookout for her, she'd be easily spotted.

She didn't have to wait long, as Di manoeuvred herself toward her between the tables, finally plonking her tray down across from Nancy. "I could eat a horse!" Di mumbled through a mouthful of meat pie, taking her time chewing it before biting into the pie again. Nancy felt her temper begin to simmer; was Di going to eat the entire meal before she told Nancy her 'news'?

"So, what's new?" Nancy asked, casually, nibbling at her pie but not tasting anything. Finally, Di nodded vigorously, as she swallowed the last meaty mouthful, a grin spreading over her face. "Well," she said leaning forward so Nancy wouldn't miss a word, "you're not the first to hear my news," she said, looking around the Canteen, "half the weaving flat saw the two of us together drinking in the Snug at the Thrums last Friday, but as my friend, I wanted to tell you my wonderful news, before the gossips put 'arms and legs' on things....." Nancy was growing impatient, wishing Di would get on with it so she could quiz her about what the gossip mongers were saying about HER. ....."but it's common knowledge now anyway"..." Di's voice filtered through again, "that the handsome Overseer of ours............you know, John Brannan...............? Well...," Di was now grinning from ear to ear, as she watched Nancy's eyes widen, "we're courting."

Nancy felt a mixture of emotions hit her, disbelief, confusion, anger and jealousy, as Di 'rabbited' on. "Of course, we had to leave the Snug separately, you know, keep the gossips at bay, but after the pub, we went back to my place and ....ooooh, Nancy! We couldn't keep our hands off one another and........." Nancy pushed her chair back, her heart pounding and her face scarlet with hurt and shame, as she rushed from the Canteen, not stopping till she was back in the Weaving Flat.

"You're back early," John said, amiably, his arms open to welcome the figure of Nancy running towards him. The slap that landed on his face was filled with such venom that he almost fell over. "NEVER AGAIN" Nancy hurled the words at him, her eyes blazing, "NEVER KNOCK AT MY DOOR AGAIN, OR I'LL KILL YOU WITH MY BARE HANDS."

Dangerously close to tears, Nancy grabbed her things from beside her looms and rushed outside before John could stop her. "NANCY!" he called after her, "WHAT'S WRONG?" But Nancy was gone, along with her dream of happiness with John Brannan. All the way home she cursed herself for her stupidity in letting yet another cheating man bed her. "John and Di Auchterlonie," she kept repeating to herself, "John and Di Auchterlonie" and "all the time he was making love to her, he was doing the same thing with Di Auchterlonie!"

Nancy slammed the door shut behind her, threw herself onto her bed and wept.

How could she have got it so wrong AGAIN? First, Billy Donnelly, then Jim Murphy and now, John Brannan had ALL gladly taken her body, but each had left her heart shattered with their cheating and lies.

When the tears, finally, stopped flowing, calmness came into Nancy's soul and with it, the ice cold fingers of revenge. Tomorrow, she would see her father, glad now that he was back at the Mill and make sure John Brannan was sacked.

—·—oOo—·—

Chapter 10

Bo McGhee! Bo McGhee! Billy kept repeating the name to himself over and over again. So this was the man who'd had his evil way with Lexie and then dropped her like an old shoe to face the world alone...... and with his bastard bairn inside her!

Well, no man was going to do that to Annie's girl and get away with it. If it cost him every penny he had and every ounce of his strength, he'd find Bo McGhee and bring him back to face up to his responsibility and marry Lexie.

Early on Sunday morning, Billy drove to Montrose. Now that he had a name, he'd try again to find out if Squadron Leader Morris knew the man, or at least could point him in the right direction to find him.   James Morris was off duty when his telephone rang in his Quarters and the Guard told him that Mr Dawson would like a word with him, if that was possible. James lips tightened.

After Billy had left the base, James had contacted Wing Commander Kettlewell and advised him of Mr Dawson visit, but had been told, in no uncertain terms, that he was not to take the matter further and that Lexie had resigned her position as his Secretary for personal reasons and that was that.   His first instincts were telling him that the Wing Commander was hiding something, but his orders had been given and had to be obeyed.

"Direct him to the Canteen and I'll see him there," he said to the Guard, annoyed that his time off was being interrupted by Billy's visit and frustrated that he'd been told to ensure that the issue of Lexie Melville's sudden departure was closed, but without any explanation as to why.

The Canteen was open but only sparsely occupied and Billy found a table in the far corner of the room, hoping they would have some privacy there. The casually dressed young man approaching him was the Squadron Leader, out of uniform and not smiling. Billy stood as James approached and immediately apologised for bothering him on a Sunday, but for Lexie's, sake now that he had a name, he had to get things moving before the trail went cold.

"I have a name," Billy blurted out and I'm hoping that you'll know him."

James Morris waited. "I can't say much about all of this, but I must find Bo McGhee," Billy added urgently.

James frowned; the name meant nothing to him. "And you think I might know the man?" he said, raising his shoulders in confusion.

"He was a Captain in the Canadian Air Force during the war and, somehow, he was here at Christmas!" He leaned forward and grasped James Morris's arm......"can you tell me where to find him?" Billy added, desperation in his voice, "please."

This Bo McGhee must be known to Wing Commander Kettlewell, James surmised, but he had his orders. "Sorry," James said, "I've never heard of the man and when I spoke to Wing Commander Kettlewell about your daughter, his response was the same as the one I gave you at your first visit, Miss Melville left the Base for personal reasons and that's as much as he knew."

Billy's shoulders dropped. He'd pinned his hopes on, somehow, finding a lead to where Bo McGhee had gone, but he'd ran into a 'brick wall.' "Sorry," James said again, feeling a wave of pity for Billy, whatever it was that Bo McGhee was guilty of, Wing Commander Kettlewell knew something about it, but James was powerless to say any more. He stood up and extended his hand to Billy. "I hope you find this Bo McGhee," he said, "but now the war is over, it's very difficult to trace our own missing personnel, never mind someone from overseas."

Billy nodded, despondency weighing heavily on his shoulders, he'd failed almost at the first hurdle. "Thanks," Billy said, "I understand." James Morris felt caught up in something he knew nothing about, but sought to say something to give Billy at least some hope. "Have you been to Lossiemouth?" he asked, suddenly, his mind going back to the war: Pilots from large parts of the British Empire had been sent to Lossiemouth for training on Wellington Bombers to boost the number of flyers battle-ready for bombing raids over Germany.

"Lossiemouth!" Billy echoed, "of course," he said, "Lexie was based there during the war and maybe, just maybe, that's where I'll find Bo McGhee!"

James smiled, happy that he had renewed hope in the old man, but sure that he hadn't disobeyed Wing Commander Kettlewell. "It's quite a distance to Lossiemouth," James said, not holding out much hope that Bo McGhee was somehow there, "maybe better to get in touch with the Base first, before you make the journey." Billy nodded his head vigorously. He had no intention of telephoning the Base, he was going to go to Lossiemouth and bring Bo McGhee back with him and nothing was going to stop him.

With Mary Anne minding King Kevin and wee Billy still asleep after another Saturday night at the Boxing Club, Nancy donned her coat. "I won't be long," she told her daughter, "I just need to have a quick word with your Granddad before work starts again on Monday."

May Anne just smiled, she was used to her mother going off on a tangent when the mood took her, but she was a little huffed that she and Kevin were left out of the visit.

Annie and her Granddad had always been the people she could depend on to be there when they were needed, so instinctively, she knew her mum was in trouble....again!

Nancy hurried out of the Cowgate and into King Street, where the church bells of St Andrews Church were calling the righteous to worship. She pulled the collar of her coat up, hiding her face, she didn't want any of the women from the Weaving

Flat seeing her and wanting to stop and gossip about Di Auchterlonie and John Brannan.

Her temper rose again at the memory of Di's news and her step quickened as she hurried past the Mill and onward into Albert Street.

Muttering to herself about how she'd paint the blackest picture of John Brannan to her dad, leaving him no option but to sack him, quickened her steps. Then he'd see, she fumed, and Di Auchterlonie could have him, unemployed and out on the street. Nancy began to smile, "then we'll see how you like it, John Brannan," she whispered, as her knocking brought Annie to the door.

"Nancy," Annie exclaimed, "this is a surprise......is anything wrong?"

"Nothing much," Nancy replied, "is dad in?"

"No, no he's not," Annie said, still keeping Nancy at the door, giving Lexie time to get to her bedroom and hide.

Nancy looked perplexed. "Can I come in then?" she asked, trying to see past Annie and into the house. "If you're busy, of course...." Nancy's annoyance level was rising again, "I suppose I could come back." It was a 'Mexican Stand-off,' with neither wanting to give way.

"Do come in Nancy," Lexie's voice cut through the tension, "I've been hoping you'd call." If the devil himself had been standing there, Nancy couldn't have been more stunned. "LEXIE!" she gasped, "I don't believe it, when did you come home?" Annie felt her breathing quicken, the one person Lexie had dreaded finding out about her pregnancy, was leaning past her and reaching out her hand towards her daughter.

"Why didn't you let me know?" Nancy admonished Annie, casting a critical eye over Lexie; she'd certainly lost weight, her face was thinner but then..... Nancy's eyes settled on Lexie's waist line, with its tell-tale bump.....surely not!

"Can you make us some tea, mum," Lexie instructed rather than asked, "me and Nancy have a lot of catching up to do." Annie watched as the pair went into the parlour, with Lexie shutting the door, firmly, behind her. Whatever it was that she was going to say to Nancy, Annie wasn't to be part of it.

Nancy sat on the sofa and waited till Lexie settled herself opposite her. She'd already checked out her left hand for a wedding ring and found none. So the pure and virtuous Lexie had been bedded by someone, Nancy concluded, but who and more to the point, why wasn't he here?

"I see things have been happening," Nancy said, nodding in the direction of Lexie's abdomen; if Lexie thought her cousin was going to, politely, avoid the obvious, she was mistaken, but the memory of Sarah's support and acceptance strengthened her.

"I'm pregnant," Lexie stated without hesitation and I intend to give birth to the bairn, so, if you want to call me a slut, or my bairn a bastard, then go ahead", Lexie told her, defiantly, before adding in a whisper, "but I hope you won't."

Nancy was silenced by Lexie's words. She still remembered how Lexie had shunned her when she'd came to Annie in the same state all those years ago and now, the boot was on the other foot, but there was no gloating at Lexie's distress, just a wave of compassion for the girl before her, knowing what she was going to have to face from the gossips and 'holier than thou' church goers of the town.

"Is the father around?" Nancy asked, quietly, already realising if the man was around, he'd be standing beside Lexie. Lexie shook her head, her arms folding across her body, she didn't want to bring Bo McGhee into this, but if she was to expect Nancy to help her face the months ahead, she knew the truth was the only way. "His name is Bo McGhee," Lexie said, "and no, he's not around." She took a deep breath and told Nancy all of it, ending with her acceptance that she'd been used by the Canadian for revenge.

There was a gentle knock at the parlour door. "Come in," Lexie called, wondering how long her mother had been standing there, but feeling the weight of shame lifting from her shoulders. Nancy understood. "Is it time for tea?" Annie asked, putting the tray down on to the small table and trying to gauge the atmosphere. "It's time," said Lexie smiling at Nancy, "tea's just what we need."

Nancy was almost home, her mind full of Lexie's confession, before she realised that she hadn't done what she'd gone to do and get John Brannan sacked. "Men," she muttered to herself as she turned into the close, but shewas stopped in her tracks by John Brannan, who'd been waiting for Nancy's return, since he'd seen her leave earlier that morning.

"Speak to me, Nancy," he pleaded, "Tell me what I've done wrong?"

Nancy shook herself free from his hands gripping her shoulders. "Get out of my way," she hissed, "I don't hold with liars and cheats." John stood back, confusion blanking his thinking.

"What are you talking about?"

Nancy couldn't believe that she'd been fooled by his love-making when she'd, willingly, let John Brannan into her bed and all the time, he'd been doing the same to Di Auchterlonie! She felt her temper flare again.

"Ask the gossips," she spat, "I'm the hot topic at the Mill," she fumed, "so if you know what's good for you, you won't be there on Monday, especially once my dad finds out about you."

John Brannan was frozen with shock at the threat that Nancy had thrown at him and could only watch, helplessly, as she flounced up the stairs to her house, slamming the door shut on his future with a resounding BANG.

How had he got into this situation? John asked himself anxiously, as he turned back into the street. It was one thing trying to get Nancy to forgive him for doing, 'who knew what', but for Nancy to get Billy Dawson to sack him from his job, was quite another! Now the war was over, orders from the Military and the Navy were drying up and it wouldn't be long before people would start being paid off by Dundee's mill owners. A chill ran through his bones, no matter how much he'd been of assistance to Mr Dawson in the past, he knew it would count for nothing, if Nancy went through with her threat.

Di Auchterlonie knew she'd hit Nancy's Achilles Heel, with her 'elaboration on the truth' about John Brannan and their 'romance,' and the look of dejection on his face as he came out of Nancy's close told her all she wanted to know. She'd been keeping her eyes and ears wide open since her 'talk' with Nancy and was now in no doubt that Nancy was history.

Quickly, she crossed the Cowgate's cobbled road and, like before, fell into step alongside John. "Lovely day for a walk," she said, coyly, glancing up at the sky, "mind if I join you?" John's eyes focussed on Di Auchterlonie, this was the second time she'd approached him, seemingly, from nowhere; had she been watching him, he wondered?

"I'm not going for a walk," he told her, firmly, "so you'll have to walk on your own."

Di gave him a look of mock surprise. "Oh!" she said, "it's just you were looking so fed up, I thought you'd enjoy a little stroll, maybe down to the Sea Braes....clear your head."

"There's nothing wrong with my head," John told her, "so if you don't mind...."

"Is it Nancy who's got you upset?" Di asked, innocently, before he could disappear into his close. John turned to face her, "'cause if it is," she continued, "you know I'm her best friend..... so if you want me to try to find out what's wrong, you've only to ask."

Much as he didn't want anyone to know his business, John realised that if Di had Nancy's ear, then she might be able to find out what was turning Nancy against him.

"Maybe I need a walk after all," he said, conscious of the neighbours' twitching curtains' in the narrow street. Thrusting his hands in his pockets and keeping his arms tight by his side, to ensure Di kept her distance, this time, he strode ahead, with her hurrying feet trotting behind him.

"Slow down," Di gasped, trying to keep up the pace John had set, as he turned down St Andrews Street heading for the Harbour. But they were at Dock Street before he eventually slowed down. Di had been right about one thing, the walk had cleared his head and he was ready to use any means open to him to win Nancy back and that included Di Auchterlonie.

—·—oOo—·—

Chapter 11

Annie picked up the ringing telephone. She still didn't know why Nancy had wanted to see her dad, but was just so glad that there was now no need for Lexie to go into hiding any time anyone came to the door.

"Dundee 102, Mrs Dawson speaking."

"Annie," Billy said, "is Lexie there?"

"She's in the kitchen, washing up the tea things," Annie smiled, "shall I get her?"

"NO!" Billy said, quickly, "I'm just telephoning to let you know that I won't be home tonight, I'm going to RAF Lossiemouth to find Bo McGhee."

"Bo McGhee's in Lossiemouth?" Annie asked, incredulously.

"I don't know for sure," Billy told her, "but Squadron Leader Morris at Montrose thinks that Canadian pilots were there during the war, so he might still be there now!"

Even as he said it, Billy knew it was a long shot, but for Lexie's sake, it was a trip he had to make.

"So I don't want Lexie to know.....raise her hopes," he added, "just in case I'm wrong, so keep this under your hat till I get back, probably in a couple of days."

"But, what if she wants to know where you are?" Annie asked, "you know I'm not good at lying."

"Tell her it's something to do with the Masonic Lodge," Billy said, thinking quickly, "and that's all you know."

Annie replaced the receiver just as Lexie came into the parlour.

"Who was that?" she asked, now feeling able to face even Isabella and John Anderson.

"It was just Billy," Annie told her hurrying out of the parlour, knowing her face would give away any lie. Lexie frowned, "what did he want then?" she called after her mother, "and did he say when he'd be back?"

"He's gone to the Lodge," Annie told her, gazing out of the window to keep her back to her daughter "and might be very, very late......in fact, he won't be home till tomorrow!" But Lexie wasn't fooled, she knew her mother was lying, but what she didn't know was why?

"Did you tell him Nancy had visited?" Lexie asked, forcing Annie to turn around and look at her. Annie's neck was flushed red and her eyes were watering. "Questions, questions," she flustered, rushing out of the kitchen before Lexie could say any more and leaving her in no doubt, Billy was up to something, but her mother wasn't about to tell her what it was. She'd just have to wait till Billy returned home

Billy boarded the Milk Train to Lossiemouth in the early hours of Monday morning. He'd found a bed for the night in the Lochside Inn at Montrose and paid the owner to keep an eye on his motor till he returned. All he could now do was to hope and pray that it wasn't going to be a wasted journey. Surely, someone would remember the Canadian pilots and the whereabouts of Bo McGhee in particular.

The taxi cab dropped Billy off at the gates of the Base, guarded by two armed airmen, who asked for identification. Billy patted his pockets, cursing to himself that he hadn't thought of bringing any papers to prove who he was.

"Sorry," he said, "I don't have any identification with me, but I was sent by Squadron Leader James Morris at Montrose, who will vouch for me."

The guard's eyes narrowed. "Wait," he said and disappeared into the Sentry Box.

After what seemed an eternity, the guard came to the gate and opened it, indicating that Billy should enter. He pointed to a low building at the far side of a concrete drilling square. "Wing Commander Duncan will see you," said the guard, before returning, smartly, to his post.

The Wing Commander was much younger than Billy had imagined he'd be, in such an important role, but his welcome was friendly enough. "Come in Mr Dawson," he said, "and sit yourself down." Billy shook his offered hand.

"I've just spoken with Squadron Leader Morris, the Wing Commander said "and he tells me you're trying to trace a Canadian pilot?"

Billy sat forward in his chair. "His name is McGhee," he said eagerly, "Bo McGhee."

The expression on the Commander's face was blank. "He would have been here during the war," Billy quickly added "and it's imperative that I find him."

The whole story of Lexie's plight unfolded, while Robert Duncan listened. He showed no surprise, he'd heard the sorry tale many times before. When the war was on, men and women fought together and the knowledge that tomorrow could be their last, meant that caution was often thrown to the wind. This man's daughter was just another 'casualty of war.' "So, if you have any way of finding out where he is....?" Billy pleaded, before lapsing into silence.

"The Official Secrets Act prevents me from saying too much," the Wing Commander said, as he linked his fingers together and focussed his full attention on Billy. "But I can say this much. I'm afraid I wasn't in charge here during the war, it was a Wing Commander named Johnny Johnstone. Unfortunately, Johnny died a month after peace was declared and that's when I took over." Robert Duncan sat back in his chair, before continuing. "There was a lot of confusion towards the last few months of the war," he said, "but I can tell you that the records of any visiting personnel would have been returned to their home country, along with the men's details."

Billy felt his heart sink, not only was Bo McGhee not at Lossiemouth, there was no record of him even having been there!

"I'm sorry," said Robert Duncan, "that I couldn't be of more help, but I wish you luck in your search." The meeting was over, Billy realised, with no progress being made.

"Thanks," he said, despondently, "I'll not take up any more of your time."

The Wing Commander watched from his window, as the figure of Billy Dawson merged into the distance. How many more fathers had been left to pick up the pieces of their daughter's lives, while the perpetrator of their distress got off scot- free? War was a nasty business, Robert Duncan shuddered, and for Billy Dawson and Lexie Melville, it looked like the peace could be just as bad.

Wing Commander Kettlewell thanked James Morris for letting him know that Billy Dawson had visited again, but this time, giving Bo's name as the father of Lexie's baby. He slowly replaced the telephone receiver. So, Lexie Melville was indeed pregnant and now, if Billy Dawson was to be believed, his nephew, Bo McGhee, was the father. When Bo and his son Louie had spent Christmas at the Montrose Base, he believed that Bo was in love with Lexie Melville, after all, he'd flown from Canada as soon as he'd heard from Martin that Lexie was working there as a civilian and was now also a widow. So, it was possible, Martin pondered, but what had gone wrong that Lexie Melville's father was now searching for Bo?

Keeping the news of Lexie's pregnancy to himself, he picked up his fountain pen, unscrewed the top and started writing.

Dear Bo

It's been a while since I've heard how things are with you and Louie. I'm not at Montrose at the minute as the War Office has sent me to England to sort things out at RAF Wilmslow, so any correspondence you may have sent, is probably at Montrose and unread.

So, you may not know that Lexie is no longer working at Montrose, she left a couple of weeks before I was posted to Wilmslow and I must admit, I was surprised, but she seemed determined to go, so that was that.

Hope the Canadian Winter at Moose Jaw wasn't too long and bitter and I'm sure Louie built the biggest snowman at the Base. He's a terrific lad Bo and it's a pity you're both so far away.

Keep your old uncle in mind now and then and I hope all is going well.

Uncle Martin

Martin Kettlewell replaced the lid of his pen. It looked like Lexie Melville had got herself into trouble and was pregnant, but he still found it hard to believe that his nephew had anything to do with it. He sealed the letter in its envelope and put it for posting in his Out Tray. Only time and Bo's reply, would tell.

Bo and Louie's mother had parted long ago, with Angela Lafayette returning to the night-life she loved, leaving Bo to bring up Louie alone. But Angela was no fool and the guilt money she demanded from Bo since their breakup, kept her married to him and refusing to agree to a divorce.

Billy crept into the house in the early hours of Tuesday morning. The journey back from Lossiemouth to Montrose had left him disheartened and weary, but another night away from Annie would only cause her more worry, so he drove through the night back to Dundee and home. All was quiet as Billy flopped down onto the sofa and kicked off his shoes, there would be plenty of time later to tell Annie what had happened at Lossiemouth, but right now, all he wanted was to sleep.

But it was Lexie who roused him with a cup of tea and a worried look.

"What are you doing sleeping here?" she whispered, taking in the crumpled state of his clothing. Billy rubbed his eyes and pulled himself up into a sitting position, every muscle groaning and aching. "Just got home late," he said, taking the teacup and gulping down the hot liquid, "car problem," he added, by way of an explanation.

"You've been gone two days," Lexie said, quizzically, "where were you when the car broke down?"

Billy sighed, he'd hoped he'd have been able to return home with Bo McGhee in tow ready to beg forgiveness for what he'd done and immediately marrying Lexie, but he'd come home alone.

"I went looking for Bo McGhee," Billy stated quietly, not wanting to waken Annie.

He could tell by the look of horror on Lexie's face that this news was not what she'd wanted to hear.

"Where!" Lexie exclaimed, sharply, "where did you go looking for him?"

"Montrose on Sunday and Lossiemouth on Monday," he said, quickly realising there was no point in trying to lie his way out of this one.

Lexie's lips were a tight line across her face. "What did you tell them?"

Billy felt his stomach tighten with anxiety. The very thing that Lexie had wanted kept secret, he'd blabbed to Squadron Leader James Morris at Montrose and Wing Commander Robert Duncan at Lossiemouth. "The truth," Billy said, "hating himself more with every moment that passed.

All the confidence that Lexie had built up, thanks to Sarah and Nancy's support, evaporated. Before the week was out, the whole of her world would know she was a whore who'd been bedded by the Canadian before leaving her to 'stew in her own juice' while laughing all the way back to Canada and his French wife and son.

"I was only trying to help," Billy called to the disappearing back of Lexie, as she swept from the room. The slamming of the front door resounded into the silence as Lexie ran from the house, tears of shame flowing from her eyes.

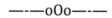

———oOo———

Chapter 12

Nancy headed straight to Baxters Office on Monday morning. She had to see her father before facing John Brannan in the Weaving Flat, but his Secretary, Joan Kelly, had bad news for her. "Mr Dawson's not coming in today," she said, waving a written message at Nancy. "Reception got a telephone call early this morning."

Nancy cursed inwardly. She wanted John Brannan to lose his job, not her to get into trouble for not turning up for work. There was nothing else for it, but to face him and the gossips and, particularly, Di Auchterlonie's smug face.

Neither Nancy nor John Brannan made eye contact as Nancy knocked on at her looms, but she spotted a few of the weavers nodding, knowingly, to one another as she got down to work. The gossips were getting ready for the dinner-time bummer when they'd digest more than their 'pieces' she winced and the main course would be HER.

John kept his head down at his desk, tallying the yardage and wondering if he'd made a mistake in asking Di Auchterlonie to intervene, on his behalf, with Nancy.

He'd had no option, he told himself, for if Nancy carried out her threat and got him sacked he would lose everything. At noon, the dinner-time bummer sounded and he crossed his fingers that Di would find out what was wrong and how he could sort it before it was too late.

Nancy sat at a corner table in the Canteen and placed her glass of milk and Spiced Ham roll in front of her, keeping her eyes fixed on the roll as she ate. Cackles of laughter along with the sound of her name, filtered into her ears, reinforcing her determination that John Brannan would pay for this humiliation with his job.

"I know I'm probably the last person you want to see," Di Auchterlonie said, her voice laced with concern, as she came over to Nancy's table, "but as your best friend, I hope there's no bad feelings about me and John, you know, getting together. Obviously," she continued, pulling out a chair to sit down, "had I known you were interested in him, I'd have told him just what to do with his advances......"

Nancy smiled to herself. "Best friend, eh," she said coldly, aware that the whole Canteen had gone quiet and all eyes were fixed on her, "you're no friend of mine Di Auchterlonie" Nancy hissed "and don't pretend otherwise." Slowly, Nancy picked up her glass of milk and poured it over Di's hair, smiling as the milk cascaded down her face and shoulders. "Sorry!" Nancy said, sarcastically, banging the empty glass back onto the table, "I mistook you for the alley cat you are!" She looked around the Canteen at the shocked faces. "Anyone else thirsty?" she shouted, her eyes flashing with anger, or have you all had enough?" Murmurs and hoots followed Nancy out of the Canteen. John Brannan was welcome to Di Auchterlonie, she decided, vehemently, and tomorrow, she'd make sure he too paid, but for him it would be with his livelihood.

"What the Hell happened to you?" John asked, as Di stood before him at his desk, milk still dripping from her hair. Di sniffed, "I was only trying to find out what was bothering her, like you asked me to," she emphasised, "when she did this, in the canteen, with everyone watching!"

John hurried Di out of the Weaving Flat into the corridor. "Go home," he ordered her "and get cleaned up." Di nodded, crocodile tears forcing themselves from under her eyelids. "I'll come by later on," he added, "make sure you're alright." Di smiled to herself; Nancy's fit of temper had worked in her favour and when John Brannan came to her single-end after work, she'd have him........ all to herself.

The weavers were buzzing with excitement at Nancy's outburst, as they came into the Flat. "She always was a feisty little bitch," Ada White commented, "jist 'cause her bloody father runs the mill, she thinks she can dae whit she wants." There were murmurs of agreement. "If it had been ane o 'us," she declared, getting into her stride, "we'd hae been secked!" The Green Eyed Monster had always followed Nancy and the Ada White's of this world, never missed a chance to 'take her down a peg or two.'

John Brannan felt his face heat up with embarrassment and anger. He hadn't counted on Di approaching Nancy in public and making matters worse, but the damage was done now and with no results. He still didn't know why Nancy was so angry, but tonight, he'd make sure he ended this stupid game he'd started with Di, once and for all. "Back to work," he shouted, to the cluster of weavers, reluctant to give up their fun at Nancy's expense, "or I'll sack the lot o' you."

Reluctantly, the women began to disperse, but not without a final 'sting' from Ada White, loud enough for John Brannan to hear. "Of coorse, Nancy Donnelly's always had men chasin' her," she grinned, winking theatrically at John Brannan, "and we all ken whit happened to the last Overseer" she added, casting around for agreement... "Jim Murphy wasn't it?" With hands on hips and a gleam of victory in her eyes, she moved closer to the now silent John Brannan.... "SECKED!"

John felt his fists clench. "Get back to work, Ada," he rasped, his temper just holding, "you've said enough." The weaver shrugged, "If you don't believe me," she whispered, with a sly backward glance, "ask Di Auchterlonie, she can tell you ah' aboot Nancy and Jim Murphy."

The racket of the looms starting up brooked no further talk, but John was certain that as soon as the shift was over, the gossip mongers would really get into their stride.

But Ada White's story of Nancy and Jim Murphy was clawing at his heart. Di Auchterlonie would be visited that night and he'd make sure, she told him everything.

—·—oOo—·—

Chapter 13

A bleary-eyed Charlie Mathieson, summonsed from his bed by the frantic knocking, opened his front door to the distraught figure of Lexie. It was obvious that something was far wrong with her, as he ushered her shaking figure through the door.

"Who is it?" Sarah's anxious voice sounded from the bedroom, as she pulled on her dressing gown and squinting at the bedside clock, realised it was only half past six in the morning.

"LEXIE!" she exclaimed, hurrying towards her friend, "what on earth has happened?" while at the same time indicating to Charlie to put the kettle on. "Come in," she said, guiding Lexie into the parlour, "whatever it is, we'll get it sorted." The sound of Sarah's steady voice and quiet assurance that everything would be alright, calmed Lexie's soul and slowed down her breathing and by the time Charlie had dressed and brought through the tea, she felt drained, but calmer.

"Do you want me to go into school and tell them you'll be late?" he whispered to his wife. Sarah nodded, "Tell the Head Master, I'll be there after lunch," she said, "in time for the English Period." Charlie gave a quick nod of understanding, before leaning towards Sarah and kissing her goodbye. "See you later dear," he said, "and I hope you feel better soon Lexie," he added; glad now that she had broken off their engagement leading him to end up marrying Sarah.

Once Sarah heard the closing of the door, she wrapped an arm around Lexie's shoulder. "C'mon," she said, "let's get some breakfast and you can tell me what's happened." Lexie followed her into the spacious kitchen and while Sarah busied hesrelf with scrambling eggs and cutting bread for toasting, Lexie gazed at the everyday objects of life, dotted around the warm room. The clothes horse above the range, draped with Charlie's shirts and Sarah's blouses, the glass-fronted dresser, where the crockery was stored. A full dinner and tea set made Lexie blink away a stray tear, Sarah would use them when they entertained visitors and lay them out on her dining room table along with the silver cutlery and crystal glasses.

A frisson of envy touched Lexie's heart, for her, life would never be that of a normal wife, for her it would be struggling alone with a fatherless bairn.

Although not knowing what the future held, the developing new life inside her needed food to grow and as Mother Nature had given her back her appetite and despite her unhappiness, Lexie ate everything that Sarah placed in front of her.

"The sun's warming up," Sarah said, opening the kitchen window that overlooked the back garden, "let's sit out for a while and you can tell me all about it," her gentle smile making Lexie smile too. The two women sat side by side on the cushioned chairs, breathing in the warm air and watching the sparrows flitting in and out of the hedges till Lexie found the words to speak about Billy and his visits to Montrose and Lossiemouth.

"I had hoped that if I came back to Dundee, then no one at the Bases would ever know about my shameful behaviour, especially, Wing Commander Johnstone at Lossiemouth!" Lexie hugged herself and began to tremble again at the thought. "The Wing Commander would have been so disappointed and ashamed of me and Wing Commander Kettlewell at Montrose who had been so kind to me and welcomed me into his family that Christmas, what would he think of me now, the type of woman who led his nephew on, knowing he had a wife in Canada?"

"STOP IT!" Sarah said, firmly, "what's done is done, and you're no more to blame than Bo McGhee and as for feeling ashamed of yourself, feel proud of who you are and I only wish I was able to have a bairn......!" Lexie blinked into the silence.

"Sarah?" Lexie reached out and took her hand, "I didn't

know.....I'm sorry....I've been selfish, as usual, telling you all about my problems and never asking how you are." Sarah sniffed back a tear. "There's nothing you can do about some things," she said, "but all I'm saying is, having a bairn isn't something to hide, but something to be proud of, so be proud Lexie and it doesn't matter who knows, what you will have is a beautiful child to love for the rest of your life."

Lexie felt a surge of compassion enter her heart. What fate had decided that Sarah would have a husband but could never be a mother and Lexie was to become a mother, but would never be a wife?

A new resolve began to form in her mind. If she was going to be a mum, then she'd be the best mum she could be and from now on, she'd face the gossips and 'bible-thumpers' on her own terms. "No more shame," she vowed to Sarah, "no more hiding away and when the bairn comes into the world, it will be just as much yours as mine, to love and bring up."

The two friends hugged on the doorstep as they said goodbye. "Charlie's a lucky man to have you in his life" Lexie said, "and so am I."

"Just remember to be happy and proud," Sarah smiled "and everything will be alright in the end." "And if it's not alright," Lexie quipped back, remembering their old catchphrase, "then it's not the end." The tears had dried and laughter had returned to Lexie's life, thanks to her wonderful friend and it was a very different woman who returned to Albert Street to face Billy and her mother.

Annie felt her shoulders relax when she heard the front door opening and Lexie's footsteps in the hall. "At least she's back," Annie whispered to Billy, "maybe she's calmed down and forgiven us." Billy raised his eyebrows. "Maybe," he said, "maybe not."

Lexie entered the kitchen and went straight to Billy, placed her arms around his neck and whispering in his ear, "I'm sorry, Billy," she said, "I've been so wrong about myself and everything else. Can you forgive me?" For once, it was Billy who was lost for words, but Annie wasn't. "Of course he forgives you," she gushed, "don't you Billy!"

The dark cloud that had been hanging over the kitchen lifted. As far as Annie was concerned, whatever it was that had brought about the change in Lexie's mood, it didn't matter, her daughter was back and whatever the future held, they would face it together.

"You're forgiven," Billy said, smiling, as he checked his pocket watch. "But it's time for work," he added, relief easing the tension in his neck, "time and tide wait for no man."

Lexie nodded, slowly, as Billy's words found their mark. If she was to look after her bairn, she couldn't rely on Billy and her mum forever and now that the morning sickness had stopped, there was no reason for her to stay hidden at home. Her first step in facing the world, with pride, would have to be to get back to work and earn her own money again. Sarah was right and a feeling of exhilaration swept over Lexie, despite never having wanted to come back to Dundee and her old life, now she was back, she was going to make the best of it, for her sake and the sake of her unborn child.

"Can I come with you," Lexie asked, suddenly, "see the old office again?"

Billy looked at Annie for an explanation, but she was as confused as he was.

"If you want," he said, "but nothing much has changed, so I'm not sure......"

"Good!" Lexie exclaimed, "some things should stay the same," she told him, "except people that is, it's people that need to change," she added with a wink.

"Change," Annie murmured, now alone in the kitchen. The mood of the morning had changed on the 'turn of a sixpence,' whatever it was that had caused the change in her daughter, Annie thanked God for it. She must telephone Isabella later and tell her the good news.

The rattle of the letterbox brought Annie's reverie back to the 'here and now'.

The Postie had been and a large, brown envelope lay on the doormat. She picked it up and turned it over, recognising the writing immediately. The postmark was Belfast, the letter was from their son, John. A twinge of guilt niggled at Annie's heart, she'd been so caught up with Lexie's problems, that she'd put off writing to let John and Mary know how things were. The letter was addressed to both Billy and herself, but she decided she'd wait till Billy came home from work and they would open it together. Annie smiled, now that Lexie was in a better frame of mind, they'd have some happy news to tell John.

Billy and Lexie walked through the entrance to Baxters and climbed the carpeted stairs leading to Billy's office. The faint sound of the clacking machinery from the Weaving Flats and the smell of the jute, brought back the past in an instant.

Joan Kelly's eyebrows arched in surprise at the sight of her boss and Lexie Melville.

Joan had taken over the role of Office Manageress when Lexie had joined the WAAF and through hard work and perseverance, she had mastered the filing system, the typewriter and the many secretarial duties required by Mr Dawson.

"Can you rustle us up some tea, Joan?" Billy asked, blindly unaware of the anxiety that Lexie's appearance at the offices had created in his Secretary. When Joan had started work at the Mill, Lexie had been the Office Manageress and in charge and had made it plain that her dowdy appearance had been frowned on by the stylish and snooty Miss Melville. But Lexie was 'family' and Joan's fears grew, that her sudden appearance at Baxters, could only spell trouble for her.

Lexie sipped her tea, the feeling of 'belonging' in this place growing as she heard the familiar sounds of office work happening in the connecting office. The ringing telephone, the sound of the typewriter and the metallic screech of the filing cabinet drawers being opened and closed, as Joan Kelly went about her business, unwittingly, bringing the past back into the present for Lexie.

"Can I speak honestly," Lexie said, returning her teacup to the metal trolley Joan had wheeled in. Billy was buoyed by how quickly Lexie seemed to have forgotten about his visits to the

Bases and leant back in his chair, lighting a cigarette. "Of course," he said, "fire away."

Lexie took a deep breath, "I want to come back to work," she said, "here, with you!"

The match almost burned Billy's fingers, as Lexie's words sank in. What was Lexie up to now, Billy wondered, anxiously, there was only one job in the office and that was already being done..... by Joan!

"But......is that wise?" Billy said, searching his brain for an excuse to put Lexie off the idea, "in your condition?" Lexie laughed, "I've survived a world war," she said, "so I think I can manage to battle my way through some paperwork." He was pleased that Lexie was taking control of her life, but Billy had deep reservations about making way for her return at the expense of Joan Kelly. He knew Baxters wouldn't pay two wages for working just one job and he could just hear Annie's voice rounding on him if he refused Lexie's demand, but the unfairness of sacking Joan, who had worked damn hard for the past three years, wouldn't let Billy give in to Lexie's demand.

"I'm sorry, Lexie," Billy heard himself say, "but there's no vacancy here. As you can see, Joan Kelly is the Office Manageress now, and with her old mum to look after, it's only her wage that's keeping her from ending up in the Poor House."

Lexie felt her enthusiasm vanish like a deflated balloon; what had made her think all she had to do was ask and it would be given to her. She glanced through the glass panel of the office door, the gauche girl who'd taken over her job in 1943 was no more, Joan moved efficiently around the office, her hair in a neat bun on top of her head, wearing a navy and white dress and navy shoes and exuding competence from head to toe. Once again, Lexie's 'instant' solution to her problem was flawed. If she wanted to make her own way in the world, she would have to think again.

When would she ever learn to think things through before springing into action, she chided herself. It had been the same that Christmas when she'd thrown caution to the wind and gave in to her neediness for the love that Bo McGhee had seemed to offer, that had got her into the shameful state she was in.

"I understand," she whispered, "I didn't think about Joan and her mum, just myself...as usual." Billy felt his heart ache for Annie's daughter, he remembered seeing her off at the railway station, when she'd set out on her great adventure to be an independent woman in the WAAF, vowing never to be tied down in Dundee again. But her search for freedom and happiness had now been ended by fate returning her to where she had begun, but now with a bairn on the way and no man to love and support her. Billy shook his head, sadly, being independent may be fine for the women of the upper classes, but for working girls, a man was still their only option for security.

"C'mon," he said, gruffly, guiding Lexie to the office door, "best you get on home and now that I know you want to be a working girl again, I'll keep a lookout for any jobs that might suit you." Lexie nodded, solemnly, as the first door she'd opened in her quest for a new life had been slammed in her face. "It's alright," she said, "I think I need to walk for a bit, clear my mind and think again."

The dinner-time bummer wailed in her ears as she left the offices, but instead of going home, Lexie headed for the Canteen. Maybe Nancy or Mary Anne would be around to talk to and anyway she was feeling hungry again, not just for food, but for company and for an end to her despondency.

The Canteen was a mix of clanking trays and savoury aromas, making Lexie's mouth water, as she took her place amidst the swarm of Weavers queuing to be served. Nancy spotted her immediately. Lexie stood out like a sore thumb amongst the other turbaned and apron-clad women. "Over here," she mouthed, waving to catch Lexie's attention and wondering what on earth she was doing there.

"This is a surprise," Nancy said, "is everything alright?"

Lexie shrugged, "not really," she said, plonking her tray of food on the table and sitting down. Nancy wasn't in the greatest of moods herself, after her encounter the day before with Di Auchterlonie and the 'glass of milk,' but she could see that Lexie was quite miserable.

She watched as Lexie began to eat ravenously. "That bairn of yours has quite an appetite," Nancy quipped, attempting to bring a smile to Lexie's lips, but failing. "Well," Nancy continued, patiently, "I'm glad to see you out and about," she said, "hiding away wasn't doing you or the bairn any good."

Lexie nodded agreement as she cleared her plate. The emptiness in her stomach had been filled, but not the emptiness in her soul. "I was just with your dad, asking for my old job back," she told Nancy, "but Joan needs the work more than me and so I'm back to square one."

"You want to go back to work?" Nancy asked, surprised at the turn-around she saw, "good for you," she said, "I'm sure dad will find you something."

The news that Billy was back at work heartened Nancy. At the end of the shift she'd try again to have John Brannan sacked. The thought of the retribution she was about to bring down on his head, flushed her cheeks with heat. He'd be sorry he treated her like some 'street-walker.'

"I have to get back to the Weaving Flat soon," Nancy said, "but meet me later if you like at the Nursery when I pick up Kevin and you can tell me all your worries over a cup of tea at home." Lexie nodded, "I'd like that," she said, hoping Nancy would have some answers by that time, on finding work.

"You might want to have a look at the place actually," Nancy added, "after all, if you're going to be a working mum, you're going to need someone to look after the bairn when it's born, just like the rest of us."

Lexie hadn't even considered how she'd manage after the birth, assuming that Annie would look after the child while she worked, but as she strolled down the cobbled road she realised that, as usual, she was expecting everyone else to change their lives to make way for her needs. First it was Bo McGhee, then Joan Kelly and now her own mother, whom she'd, unthinkingly, expected would give up her own life with Billy, to mind her bairn.

So much for being an independent woman, Lexie chided

herself as she walked, beginning to realise how selfish she had been all of her life, by always expecting everyone else to come to her rescue when things went wrong and never seeing the damage she was doing to others, when she'd pushed them aside to suit her own desires. She'd been thoughtless to so many people over the years, she realised, and by the time she'd reached the Nursery, she was feeling sorry about everything in her life and feeling more alone than ever. She was about to change her mind about meeting Nancy when the sound of children laughing and squealing reached her ears.

The door to the Nursery was open to let in the cool air and Lexie could see the hive of activity inside, as the nurses went about their business of feeding the babies and keeping an eye on the toddlers, Kevin included.

"Can I help you?" the nurse who seemed to be in charge called out, as Lexie realised she'd strayed into the large room. Lexie stepped back, "I'm sorry," she said, "I didn't mean to intrude." The nurse smiled, "you're not intruding," she told her, "come in."

Lexie inched into the room. "I'm Kevin Donnelly's Auntie," she said, pointing to Kevin shovelling sand into a small bucket in the sand-pit and oblivious to Lexie's presence

The nurse grinned. "He's a proper little boy," she said, "never happier than when he's making sandcastles or building a tower with the wooden bricks."

The nurse signalled to the others that she was ready for a cup of tea. "Come and join me," she said to Lexie, "by the look of things you'll be in need of our services before too long," she added almost casually, as she reached for the teacups from the shelf in the tiny scullery. Lexie looked down at the burgeoning bump. There was no pretending that no one would notice anymore. "It's a wee while to go yet, but in the meantime, I just need to find some work."

The nurse handed over a cup of tea to Lexie, noting the absence of a wedding ring on her finger: Poor lassie, she thought, left holding the baby while the dad disappeared out of her life. She'd seen it more and more since the war ended, women left on their own to struggle with bringing up their bairns and trying to keep 'the wolf from the door.' Whether widows or fallen women, the problem was the same, with no man to support them, their lives were one of poverty and loneliness.

"It'll be mighty hard work in the Mill, if that's where you're looking for a job," she said, "and if you don't mind me saying so, you've not got the hands of someone who's used to handling the jute." Lexie held up her soft hands and polished nails. 'Typists hands', Mrs Fyffe had called them, when Lexie first went to work at Baxters Office and she had gifted her a pair of Kidd Leather gloves to keep them protected from the Scottish weather. Lexie smiled at the thought; what would Mrs Fyffe think of her now.

"I'm actually a Secretary," she said, "but there's no work for me at Baxters, so I'll just have to keep trying." She handed back the empty teacup, "Kevin's mum won't be long," she said, "so I'll let you get on with your work and wait outside till she comes."

"Just a minute," the nurse said, "tell me your name before you go and how I can get in touch with you. We might be requiring an Auxiliary Nurse soon, when Elsie leaves to go back to Dumfries to look after her dad....."

Lexie stopped in her tracks. "But, I'm not a Nurse," she said, "I learned first aid in the WAAF, but it had nothing to do with minding bairns!" The nurse smiled, "you wouldn't be a proper Nursery Nurse," she said, "more a nurse's helper, you know, do the jobs needed to keep the bairns happy and fed and it'll be good experience for when your own little'un comes along."

Lexie felt her spirits soar, and to think she'd almost gone home, but somehow the fates had led her to the nursery door and given her fresh hope that she could cope with the future for herself and her bairn, without help from anyone. Nurse Williams wrote down Lexie's name and telephone number, "I can't promise anything," she said, "but let's just wait and see."

Lexie almost hugged her. All thoughts of meeting Nancy and telling her all her worries were forgotten, as Lexie almost skipped from the Nursery and into the Cowgate. Billy would be home by the time she'd walked home to Albert Street and she couldn't wait to tell him and her mother her news.

—-—oOo—-—

Chapter 14

When the shift ended, Nancy hurried from the Weaving Flat to her dad's office. Joan Kelly was just locking up as she reached the top of the stairs. "I thought Mr Dawson was in today," she said. "He was," Joan said, "but he left soon after Miss Melville, so it looks like you'll have to wait till tomorrow." The key turned in the lock and clicked. "There," Joan said, drained by the worry of Lexie's arrival that morning and relieved that the day was over and she was still in a job, "time to go home."

Nancy fumed all the way to the Nursery and her meeting with Lexie, determined to visit her dad at home over the coming weekend; surely he would be around by then! She now wasn't in the mood of listening to Lexie's worries, so was glad to hear that she had left a wee while ago, after chatting to Nurse Williams.

Nancy sighed with relief as she took Kevin's hand; sometimes fate worked in her favour and this was one of those times and she could only hope that her luck would hold till the weekend when, finally, she'd get John Brannan sacked.

She knew that Mary Anne would have the tea started by the time they got home and smiled at the thought of a peaceful evening ahead. Nancy was proud of her daughter, Mary Anne was a good girl, always happy and the first to lend a hand when it was needed and never giving her a moment's concern. She just wished she could say the same about wee Billy, since he'd joined this Boxing Club, he seemed to be getting home later and later and despite trying to stay awake till he got home, she'd invariably have to go to bed herself, if she was to be fit to go to work in the morning.

The potatoes were boiled and the sausages cooked through by the time wee Billy came into the kitchen. "You're a bit late aren't you?" Nancy queried, glancing at the clock before filling another plate and putting it in front of her son, "maybe an early night is in order."

"Maybe," he replied, "but not tonight."

"Why not tonight?"

"Boxing."

Nancy frowned. "All this boxing," she said, "is it going anywhere?"

Billy felt his teeth clench; why did his mother have to keep asking questions all the time, he was 17 now and old enough to do what he liked and what he liked was to drink. He had a longing for it, just like his dad and if he wanted to be like anyone in the world, it was to be like his dead father.

He shrugged his shoulders in answer to his mother's question but said nothing.

The quicker he ate his meal and got out of there the better, he was meeting the Kelly brothers outside the Thrums Bar and he had the money they needed to buy him his alcohol. And he couldn't wait!

"Don't be late," Nancy called to her son's disappearing back, as the door slammed and he was gone. "Do you know anything about this Boxing Club?" she asked Mary Anne, who was holding Kevin on her knee while he munched into half a sausage.

"Not really," her daughter said, "but there's a crowd of lads always hanging around outside the new Premierland Stadium in William Lane since it opened and there's boxing goes on there."

Nancy had heard of the place, but it was nowhere a woman would want to go, unless she was a prostitute and 'on the game.' She started clearing the table while Mary Anne began to get Kevin into his pyjamas and ready for bed. If only she knew someone who could sort out wee Billy. What he needed was the firm hand of a man, but that option had already been ditched, when John Brannan had bedded Di Auchterlonie behind her back and it wasn't something she wanted to talk to her own dad about, at least, not until he'd sacked John Brannan.

By 8 o'clock, King Kevin was tucked up in his cot and Mary Anne had gone to her pal Amy's house, to try to make themselves beautiful with Ponds Cold Cream and a pot of Rouge, Amy's mum had bought for her. Nancy let her thoughts drift through her mind, most of which started with 'if only.' If only Billy Donnelly had been man enough for her, if only Jim Murphy hadn't been married when she let him stay the night, if only the war hadn't happened and if only her husband hadn't died a waster and an alcoholic, leaving her to soldier on alone. But her main 'if only' was, if only John Brannan hadn't bedded Di Auchterlonie, they might still be together and she wouldn't be feeling so alone and desolate.

But Di Auchterlonie couldn't wait till John Brannan knocked at her door. She'd washed the curdled milk out of her hair and brushed it dry before the fire. Her working skirt and jute-scented 'Pinnie' had been discarded in favour of a sleeveless blouse and floral cotton skirt and half a gill of rum was already warming in two glasses on the sideboard.

At 7 o'clock John Brannan came a-knocking. Di fluffed up her hair, for the final time, and unbuttoned another button at the front of her blouse before opening the door. With eyes blinking like a fawn looking for protection from its mother, she ushered John inside. "I'm so glad you've come, John," she whispered, "I've been so upset since....well, you know......since Nancy poured her milk all over me...." She raised her eyes to meet John's, but they held no look of love or longing for her, just a cold, hard stare. Confused, Di shrunk away from him and hurried to the sideboard. "Rum?" she said, hoping it would soften the grim expression on John's face.

"No thanks," he said, grasping her arm, "now sit down and start talking and if you lie to me, I'll know it and it'll be the worse for you." Di felt a wave of panic as John pulled up a chair across the table from her, she'd expected him to, at least, be grateful to her for 'doing what he'd asked', never mind the humiliation she'd suffered at Nancy's hands.

"Tell me about Jim Murphy!" he demanded. Di frowned, "what's he got to do with you and me?" John clenched his fists beneath the table, he'd realised of late that Di would have turned their two brief encounters into her idea of something 'romantic,' but he'd deal with that later, right now, he needed to know about Jim Murphy and his involvement with Nancy.

"I'll ask you again," John said, this time, bringing menace into his voice, "tell me about Jim Murphy."

Di stood up and crossed to the sideboard, picked up the two glasses of rum and returned to the table with them. She'd known that she was always going to be second best to Nancy, but if she couldn't have John Brannan, neither would Nancy Donnelly..

She pushed one of the glasses of rum over to John and swigged her own down in one swallow. "You want to know about Jim Murphy do you?" she said, carefully returning her glass to the table. John nodded, never blinking, as he met her stare.

"You mean Nancy's fancy man?" John felt every muscle in his body heat up with anger. "Go on," he said, "and I want the truth."

"Well," Di began, "I don't think you'll like the truth very much," she said, her voice taking on a pretend sadness, "but now that you've asked me, the truth you shall have." "Get on with it," John told her through gritted teeth.

"Well," Di began again, choosing her words with care, "Jim Murphy was the Overseer at the Weaving flat...., a bit like you are now...., anyway, he caught Nancy Donnelly's eye and she was determined to have her way with him. Of course, he was married, as was she, but her husband;" Di hesitated and gazed at the empty rum glass, before continuing. "Poor Billy Donnelly," she said, "away fighting in the war and trusting that his wife was at home minding his bairns, when all the time she was out dancing at the Palais and fluttering her eyelashes at any man in uniform......." John banged his fist down on the table, making Di jump, "Jim Murphy," he repeated the name, "the Overseer."

Di nodded, quickly, "Sorry, John," she said, "but Jim Murphy was the unlucky one who was 'found out'.......and by his wife, no less, the others just 'came and went' shall we say." She could see John Brannan's temper increasing with every word; by the time she'd finished with her version of the truth, Nancy

Donnelly's name would be blackened beyond recovery.

Di was warming to her story by the minute, "Jim Murphy," she intoned, "well, he'd been seen by the neighbours, sneaking out of Nancy's house in the early hours of the morning, more than once..." she added, "till Nancy Donnelly and Jim Murphy were the talk of Baxters." Di waited till she was sure John Brannan was ready for her final verbal onslaught. "Then, Jim's wife found out about what they were up to and went to see Mr Dawson....... he's Nancy's father you know," she added, gleefully, knowing full well that John knew exactly who Billy Dawson was, "and she got him SACKED!"

Di sat back with a nod of satisfaction, before hammering the 'final nail in Nancy's coffin'. "But, Jim had left his 'calling card.'" John frowned, "calling card?" he repeated, "what calling card?" Di leant towards him, making sure John heard every word. "Nancy was PREGNANT!" John felt the colour drain from his face; no wonder Billy Donnelly had so much anger in him when he'd met him that night in the Thrums Bar. He felt all his resolve to expose Ada White as a bare-faced liar drain away. Nancy was a slut, nothing more, nothing less, and he was just the next 'victim' to be taken in by her sensual looks and enticing body. And now, he was at risk of losing his job over it, just like Jim Murphy had done.

He picked up the rum and downed it in one gulp, almost gagging as the raw alcohol rushed down his gullet. "Thanks," he said, coldly, standing up, "for the rum," he added, "not for the truth." Without another word, he turned towards the door. "Where are you going?" Di squealed, anxiously, "stay for another drink, at least!"

John turned to face her. "There'll be no staying," he said, "and no more drinking with you, either here or anywhere else. Now I'll bid you goodnight."

——oOo——

Chapter 15

When Billy returned from the Mill, Annie brought out the letter from Belfast and handed it over to her husband. "It's from John," she smiled wistfully, "and Mary, of course, but I wanted to wait till you came home before we opened it. Billy felt a surge of guilt that he'd failed to contact his son since he'd bade him farewell, but now that Lexie was finding her feet again, he was beginning to relax and was hungry for news from Belfast.

"Get us a pot of tea and scones," he told Annie, beginning to feel some normality returning to his life "and once I've had a wash and got these boots off, we'll read it together." The tea and scones were eaten and all thoughts of Dundee and Lexie were forgotten, as Billy opened the envelope with the butter-knife.

Dear Mum and Dad

I hope everything is going well for you both and that Lexie is also fine. Before you left, I spoke of buying a house where all of us could live….. Annie stopped Billy reading further. "Why didn't you tell me about this," she said, her chin quivering, I didn't know John was doing this……and for us?"

"Hush now, Annie, "Billy said, "he only talked about it, but nothing was certain and, anyway, we had things to do here and John decided it was best to say nothing."

Annie felt peeved. "So, it's my fault that he had to hide things from his own mother?"
Billy took her hand and linked it through his arm. "Let's just see what more he has to say"………*well, two weeks after you left, the offer I put forward was accepted, so, now your son is 'Lord of*

93

the Manor' so to speak. It's a pretty big house with lots of land around it for Mary's hens and pigs, not to mention a vegetable garden. You know Mary, she loves all things in nature and she can't wait to get started. I've enclosed a photograph of the house, that's Mary at the front door waving the key, so we'll be moving in at the start of July. Billy and Annie gazed at the large photograph. "So, he's bought it?" Annie asked incredulously. "But he doesn't say where in Belfast it is," Annie said. "Well, it doesn't look like it's in the city," Billy said, "more like in the countryside outside Belfast."

Annie felt a twinge of longing, "it takes me back to where we first met," she whispered, "do you remember the little farm with mammy, Mary and me, when you turning up to help with the flax gathering?" In that moment, time seemed to stand still, as Annie gazed into the eyes of her first love, the handsomest man she'd ever seen. "You're still handsome," she said, softly, as the years fell away and she was that young girl again, "I loved you then and I love you still," she told Billy, "and no matter what happens, I will love you till I die." Billy lay the letter down on the table and took Annie in his arms. "You were always my girl," he said, his voice breaking with the emotion of the moment, "and no matter how much water has flown under the bridge since that time and no matter what happens in the future, you always will be my girl, my Annie Pepper."

"Keep reading," Annie said, sniffing back a tear and handing Billy the letter again..... *Mary prays for you both every night and says to tell you she's keeping a candle burning in the window till you come back to us. I pray that Lexie is happy now and well on the way to recovery. Please say hello to her from us and tell her that she is always in my heart.*

Please find the time to let us know how things are in Dundee, but in the meantime, know that you are loved very much and we miss you every day.

Your loving son and daughter-in-law,
John and Mary

If Billy had his way, he'd have been making plans to return to Ireland as soon as humanly possible, but although Lexie seemed to be better, he knew that as the pregnancy progressed and the bairn was born, she'd need her mother more than ever. With a sigh, he returned the letter and photograph back into its envelope and set it on the floor beside the sofa.

"C'mon old girl," Billy grinned, standing up and reaching out for Annie's hands, "how about a nice walk in Baxters Park," he said, "there's still lots of warmth in the sun and you can look at it all again all you like, when we get home."

Chapter 16

Bo McGhee picked up his mail at the Canadian Air Force Base at Moose Jaw, Saskatchewan. It had been a long winter since his return from Montrose and his Christmas reunion with Lexie and his heart and soul were almost broken, when he had to leave without her and return to his life in Canada.

As soon as was humanly possible and the Canadian Air Force could allow, Bo had travelled to Quebec to convince Angela Lafayette that she needed to divorce him. Money would be no object, he'd told her, whatever she needed to set him free, he would hand over and, of course, he would continue to bring Louie to visit her as often as his job would allow. Sure that Angela would agree that their marriage was in name only and should be legally ended, Bo had knocked on the door of her upstairs apartment in the Artists Quarter of the city, but there was no answer.

She was probably sipping coffee or more likely Cognac, Bo decided, at the small coffee house on the pavement below. "Angela?" Mr Pascal at the Café Rouge pondered, "she moved away some months ago!" Bo hadn't been in touch with his wife since the previous Summer, although the money he paid her every month had still gone into her account at the Bank of Quebec, but when he asked them if she was at a new address, they were unable, or unwilling, to tell him.

Frustrated, but with no answers as to her whereabouts, Bo had returned to Moose Jaw only to find Angela Lafayette making herself at home in his Quarters, with Louie playing with the model airplane she had bought him for Christmas, albeit now three weeks late. Bo felt the beginnings of anger forming in his stomach, but knew not to show his feelings, whatever had got Angela here, it didn't matter, he could now get her to agree to a divorce and open the door for Lexie to return fully into his life.

"I've been to Quebec to see you, but was told that you'd left your apartment months ago," Bo said, giving her a quizzical look "and now, here you are in Moose Jaw?"

Angela lit a cigarette and blew the smoke into the air, watching it swirl and disappear before she answered. "I've been at Cap-de-la-Madelaine, if you must know," she said, "but what I have to tell you is not for Louie's ears, she added, as she waved an elegant hand towards her son. Bo crossed over to where Louie was kneeling, studying every detail of the model aircraft. "Hey, Louie, how about you take your new model over to Chuck's and let him see it?"

"OK Papa," Louie grinned, "he'd like that, he's going to be a pilot when he's older you know, just like me." Bo smiled at his son's enthusiasm. "Remember to kiss Mama, goodbye, before you go," Bo reminded him.

"It's alright, Louie," Angela assured him, stubbing out the cigarette, "I'll still be here when you get back."

Bo felt his blood run cold; what was Angela playing at; as soon as she agreed to the divorce, she'd be escorted off the base and onto the first train back to Quebec?

"Aren't you going to offer your wife a drink?"

Bo ignored her request. I went to Quebec to ask you to agree to a divorce," Bo said plainly, "not to have a friendly drink with you."

Angela's eyes filled with tears. "You haven't even asked me why I was at the Cape," she whispered, "don't you care about my feelings at all?"

Bo steadied his voice and sat down. He'd have to be careful not to be put off by Angela's 'crocodile tears.' "Alright then," he said, "why were you at the Cape?"

"Papa's dead."

Bo clenched his teeth. Angela's mother and father had lived at Cap-de-la Madelaine these past 20 years and the last time Bo had seen either of them, they were both healthy and full of life. "Are you sure?" he asked, foolishly, unwilling to believe anything Angela told him about her life. Angela's eyes flashed, "it's not something I'd make up, Bo," she said, coldly, "but if you want to see the grave, I'll show you where it is."

Bo flinched. "I'm sorry," he said quietly, "your dad was a fine man and your mother will miss him very much......"

A fresh wave of tears began to flow down Angela's face, but this time, Bo had to accept they were real and crossed over to where she sat. "Here," he said, giving her his handkerchief, "I'll get you that drink."

Bo poured two shots of Rye Whiskey, making his a double, and took them over to where Angela sat, handing her a glass. "I'm sorry," Bo repeated, ashamed of his callousness, "and if there's anything I can do to help, let me know." It was the sort of thing people say when someone has lost a loved one, but for Angela, it was all the opening she needed to shatter Bo's dream of a future with Lexie.

Angela downed the whiskey in one swallow. "I want to come back," she said, almost briskly, "be with you and Louie, as a family again, my family." Bo couldn't believe his ears! "I don't want to be like Mama," she continued, the tears welling again, "without Papa, she is all alone and will probably die alone and I don't want that future for me. I still love you Bo and Louie needs a Mama as well as a Papa....." Bo leapt to his feet, the blood rushing through his veins like wild fire. "STOP IT," he shouted, "I WANT A DIVORCE, NOT A REUNION!"

Angela's eyes narrowed as her composure returned. She dabbed her eyes with the handkerchief and lit another cigarette. "There's another woman," she said, into the silence, "isn't there?" Bo's eyes levelled with hers. "Yes," he said, "and I intend to divorce you and marry her." Without hesitation, Angela reached for her coat and hat. "I'm booked into the Imperial Hotel in town for now and when you change your mind, come and find me."

"I won't change my mind," Bo told her icily, his fists clenching. "Nor will I," Angela retorted, equally coldly, "I will be your wife till I die."

Bo stared at the closed door, a mixture of disbelief at what had just happened and the realisation that he could never make Lexie his wife, sinking into his heart. All his dreams of a future with Lexie had been shattered and all he had left was the memory of that one night of love they'd shared at Christmas. Unashamedly, Bo wept.

When Lexie's first letter had arrived, a few days after Angela's ultimatum, he couldn't bear to open it, then over the coming weeks, there were five more that also went unopened and then, they stopped coming. With nothing to offer Lexie and his marriage to Angela firmly in place, 'till death do us part', as he'd said when he'd placed the gold ring on her finger, Bo forced himself to stop thinking about Lexie and what might have been and focussed all his energy on Louie and his job, until the letter from Martin Kettlewell hit his desk in late April.

It wasn't a long letter, but the news that Lexie had left Montrose without giving a reason to his Uncle Martin, felt like a rejection of him and, despite never responding to her letters, he was now sure they'd have been nothing more than 'Dear Johns' anyway. Bo sat very still, finding it hard to understand why he felt so hurt that Lexie had disappeared again from his life, when it was he who had disappeared from hers!

He'd reply to his Uncle's letter that evening, keep it short, he decided, after all it was just a bit of Christmas madness to think he and Lexie had a future that was now well and truly over. He screwed Martin's letter into a tight ball and tossed it into the waste paper basket. There was work to do and Louie to look after and that was enough. He'd been crazy to think the fates would allow him any happiness; he just had to accept it.

The sun had long set when Bo put pen to paper.......

Dear Uncle Martin,

Your mail caught up with me this morning and I hope things are going well at Wilmslow Base, which is where I'll send this reply. We got through the Canadian Winter and Louie is well and happy,

There's bad news though, Angela's Papa died a few weeks ago and she turned up at Moose Jaw soon after, wanting to pretend we were a happy family. She said she was feeling lonely and wanted to be with Louie, but she's gone back to Quebec now and good riddance to her.

Sorry to hear about Lexie leaving. She's a sweet girl and I'm sure you'll miss her secretarial skills. If you see her sometime, say 'hi' from me and Louie.

Try to 'wangle' a flight to Canada later in the Summer, it would be great to see you and Louie would love showing you around the Base.

Your favourite Nephew,
Bo

He put the letter in its envelope and addressed it to the base at Wilmslow. Tomorrow he'd hand it to one of the girls for posting and with so many flights between Canada and Britain since the war finished, it shouldn't take long to get to Martin. Bo stretched and headed for bed, the visit from Angela and her ultimatum vying with images of Lexie and wondering if she ever even gave him a second thought.

Unable to sleep, he pushed back the covers and padded through to his Bureau and rolled open the lid where Lexie's unopened letters were in a drawer where he'd left them. With a heavy heart he tore each one into shreds, unable to bear to read her words of rejection. "There," he said aloud, when he'd finished destroying what remained of Lexie Melville, "some things are just not meant to be."

Bo returned to his bed, pulled the covers over his head and silently wept till sleep finally claimed him.

Martin Kettlewell didn't have long to wait for Bo's reply, but was even more confused when he referred to Lexie in such a casual manner. 'A sweet girl', he'd called her and to say 'hi' from him and Louie? Considering the lengths Bo had gone to at Christmas to meet her again, pretending to be Santa Clause while Lexie looked after Louie and surprising her, when he revealed himself from underneath the red suit and white beard and that Louie was his son.

After their Christmas Dinner, Martin had taken Louie into the other room in his Quarters and left Bo and Lexie alone and now he wondered if that had been a good idea. But, the following day, Bo and Louie had flown back to Canada and Lexie seemed fine, until she suddenly left the Base, that is, in February, without giving a reason. And now, her step-father had turned up at Montrose saying Lexie was pregnant and that Bo was the father!

Martin picked up his pen, whatever was going on only Bo could give him any answers. If Lexie was pregnant, and he didn't doubt it, then someone fathered that child, but only Bo would be able to tell him if it could have been him. He began writing.....

Bo, he began, *I have to be blunt with you. I've found out the reason Lexie left the Base. Her step-father spoke to Squadron Leader James Morris in my absence and told him that Lexie was pregnant. Not only that, he insists that you are the child's father and is demanding you be found and brought back to 'face the music.'*

I can't believe that you would have taken advantage of Lexie, but he also says that she has written to you several times but with no reply from you. You need to clear this matter up and quickly. Let me know how to proceed with this, as you know I was very fond of Lexie and can't believe she is lying about any of this, but I also can't believe that any nephew of mine would be capable of such behaviour.

I await your response with an anxious heart.

Uncle Martin

—·—oOo—·—

Chapter 17

Lexie was flushed with hope and excitement as she hurried up Albert Street, her confidence growing by the minute that she could be strong and independent and look after both herself and her bairn. After all, she told herself, Nancy brought up three bairns during the war while Billy was in the Scots Guards and she had to go back to work as a Weaver when their marriage broke up and Billy drank any money he earned.

Lexie stopped in her tracks. "Nancy," she said out loud; she'd forgotten about meeting her at the nursery, but was sure she'd be forgiven when she heard her good news. Nothing was going to get her down ever again, she decided, she'd have her bairn, work at the nursery and everything would be just fine. Lexie was even singing to herself as she ran up the stairs and into the house.

Having spent the afternoon strolling in Baxters Park and reminiscing about the old days and how much Lexie's health had improved, Annie had been surprised when Billy had told her of her daughter's intention to find work at Baxters to support herself and the bairn, when it arrived.

"Then she'll need me to look after it, if she goes out to work," Annie had said, immediately. Billy had frowned, the last thing he wanted was for Annie to be tied down in Dundee, especially now that he'd seen the house in Belfast and was renewing his hope of them all living there together. "Now, now," he'd cautioned, as they turned for home, "let Lexie make her own decisions about the future and keep in mind that she's a grown woman now and needs to be able to look after herself."

Both Billy and Annie had been lost in their own thoughts as they'd walked through the Park, but soon after they came home, Lexie's arrival changed any thoughts for the future either of them were considering.

"Lexie!" Annie exclaimed, on seeing the flushed face of her daughter, "what's happened?" She glanced at Billy, for confirmation. "You look......well.... excited."

Lexie slipped out of her coat and pushed her hair back from her hot forehead, before slumping into the armchair. ""Is there any tea left in that pot?" she asked, smiling like 'the cat that got the cream' as her mother would say, "I'm parched."

"Not anymore," Annie said, standing up, "I'll make a fresh pot." Again, she glanced at her husband, but it was obvious that he was as wise as she was about Lexie's glowing mood. "I'll help you," Billy offered, jumping up from the sofa, not wanting to be alone with Lexie till an explanation was forthcoming. He'd been expecting her to be disconsolate after being refused Joan Kelly's job, but she seemed positively delighted.

Alone in the parlour and imagining the looks of amazement on Annie and Billy's faces when she told them her news, she crossed to the sofa and picked up the envelope she'd spotted lying on the floor. Her brow furrowed as she withdrew a photograph of a large stone-built house and a smiling girl at its door holding a key. Compared with Albert Street, the house looked a world away from the greyness of Dundee and its country location, reminded her of the large farmhouses she'd seen around Lossiemouth during the war. Her curiosity aroused, she withdrew the single sheet of paper and slowly read it.

With every word, her confidence in being a new and independent woman began to disintegrate. 'Mary prays for you both every night' she read 'and says to tell you that she's keeping a candle burning in the window till you come back to us. I pray that Lexie is happy now and well on the way to recovery....' It was signed by 'John and Mary.' Lexie dropped the letter to the floor and ran to the safety of her bedroom: Did everyone know of her shame, even her half-brother and his wife, almost strangers to her?

All the excitement she had felt about her future suddenly felt like an illusion. The realisation that her mother and Billy were already planning to return to Belfast FOR GOOD, leaving her alone in Dundee with a helpless bairn to care for, shook her rigid! Working or not, she could only cope as long as Billy, but more importantly Annie, remained nearby to support her.

"Here's more tea," Annie called, merrily, as she pushed open the parlour door "and some scones for good measure......" Annie put the tray on the table and froze. There was no sign of Lexie and there, on the floor, was the photograph and John's letter and it was obvious that she had read it. She nearly knocked Billy over, as she hurried to Lexie's bedroom and knocked on the door.

"Lexie," she called, trying to keep the panic out of her voice, "can I come in?"

"Go away," her daughter called back "and leave me alone."

Annie felt her shoulders sag. Whatever Lexie had wanted to tell them, she'd now never know. She turned to Billy, who hadn't realised what had happened and shook her head. "She thinks we're leaving her," Annie whispered "and going to be with John and Mary in Belfast."

Billy flinched, just when it seemed that things were sorting themselves out and he was beginning to believe that their future in Ireland with his son was becoming a reality, Lexie had reversed all that and he was back to square one.

"She just needs time to come to terms with Belfast," Billy said, trying to assure Annie, as he guided her back into the parlour. He had to make sure the situation didn't come down to a choice for Annie, between staying in Dundee or returning to Belfast. If that happened, he knew what Annie would choose, with or without him.

The banging of the front door startled both of them, as Lexie made her departure.

Billy sighed. She was on the run again, he frowned and it would be almost impossible to predict her mood, if and when she returned.

As before, when she was beset by doubts and fears, Lexie made a bee line for Sarah's house in Pitkerro Road. The Morgan playgrounds were empty of pupils and Lexie prayed that Sarah would be home and not held up at school by marking or meetings. But Sarah was in and alone, preparing a meal for when Charlie came home from work at the Drawing Office at Cox's Mill.

Sarah had been putting Lexie's erratic moods down to the pregnancy, but it was becoming obvious to her, that her emotions were actually beginning to drain Lexie's energy. "I thought you were feeling better about the bairn," Sarah said, to start the conversation. Lexie hung her head, "I was," she whispered, "I even tried to find a job at Baxters, but Joan Kelly is doing a better job that I did and Billy says he's not for paying her off and taking me on again." Sarah frowned. "Is that the reason you're so upset?"

Lexie shook her head again and brushed the tears away with the edge of her sleeve.

"Mum and Billy are going back to Belfast to live there...... FOREVER! Sarah reached out and took her friend's hand. "Are you sure?" Lexie nodded furiously, "I read John's letter," she said, her voice beginning to tremble again, "he's keeping a candle burning in the window till they return."

"John wrote to you and told you this?" Sarah asked in disbelief.

"NO," Lexie said, "the letter was written to mum and Billy, but they left it out so I could read it," she added, not wanting Sarah to think she'd been snooping.

Lexie's distress was evident, but Sarah couldn't believe Annie and her father would just leave her alone to cope with the birth and a life of destitution, but she intended to find out. "Stay here," Sarah said decisively, "Charlie will be home soon and I'll be back as quickly as I can."

"Where are you going?" Lexie asked, wondering at Sarah's strength and ability to cope with life.

"Not far," she said "and I want you to remember, that whatever happens, I'll be here for you."

Annie opened the door to Sarah's knocking. "Sarah!" she exclaimed, panicking that something had happened to Lexie.

"Everything's alright," she assured her, "but I need to speak to my father." Billy appeared behind Annie at the door on hearing his daughter's voice. Since leaving Josie McIntyre to be with Annie, he'd lost contact with Sarah and, apart from now knowing she'd married Charlie Mathieson, he knew little else about her life.

Clear, brown eyes held his gaze as Billy stepped aside so that Sarah could enter.

"In private," she added, before turning to address Annie. "I'm sorry, Mrs Dawson," she said, "but what I have to say, is for my father's ears only." Annie felt crushed, if it had to do with Lexie, then she should know about it! As if reading her mind, Sarah assured her, that her father would talk with her, but only after she'd gone.

Billy and Sarah went through to the parlour while Annie took refuge in the kitchen, her mind unsettled, but reassured that Billy would explain everything after Sarah left.

"I don't have long," Sarah began, "Lexie is at my home and very distressed." Billy ran his fingers through his hair, before handing Sarah the letter from John. "She read this and disappeared," he told her. Sarah read the letter. "And, are you and Annie going to leave Dundee and live in Belfast?" Sarah asked bluntly. Billy lips tightened into a straight line, "I want nothing more," he said, honestly, "but since this business with Lexie, I can't see it happening."

Sarah nodded. "She's having a tough time of it," she said, "and without Annie around and no sign of the father turning up I dread to think what might happen."

Billy knew the truth of it and shook his head. "Then, we have to stay," he said, his voice thick with resignation.

"What if I looked after her," Sarah said, "she could live with Charlie and me till it's time for the child to be born, but then... ...... we would adopt it as our own and Lexie can return to her old life, wherever that may take her."

Billy couldn't believe his ears. "I can't have children of my own," Sarah continued, never flinching or avoiding her father's eyes and we could give the child a good life, better than the one

Lexie could give it, in trying to bring her bairn up alone." Billy was lost for words, he knew nothing of his daughter's life, nor of her longing for a child . "So, if you agree" Sarah concluded, "then I'll put my suggestion of living with us at Pitkerro Road to Lexie, when I get home and as to an adoption, well, that will be up to Lexie once the child is born. What you tell Annie is up to you, but it would mean you could both go to live in Belfast now, knowing all is well here."

"But, what if Lexie wants to keep the bairn?" Billy asked, already forming a plan to return to Belfast. "Then, there's no adoption," Sarah told him, quite simply, "but I think the reality of the future for both Lexie and her bairn, will convince her that adoption is for the best."

Billy sat very still after Sarah left, marvelling at the maternal urge that his daughter had expressed, leading her to speak of her longing for a bairn of her own and Lexie turning up on her doorstep, unmarried and pregnant, seeming like the answer to all her prayers.

Annie jumped up from the kitchen table as soon as she heard Sarah leave and hurried through to the parlour. "Well," she said, "what's going on?"

"Sit down," Billy said "and just listen before you say anything." Annie nodded and crossed her hands in her lap. "Lexie is at Sarah's just now, but it's looking like she may want to stay there......for a while anyway....."WHY!" squealed Annie... ."now, now," Billy cautioned, "let me finish."

"It's a wee while before the bairn is due to be born and with all this upset about Belfast and John's letter, Sarah thinks it would be best if Lexie stayed with her and Charlie for a while till she calms down and feels well again..... for the bairn's sake," Billy added, as he squeezed Annie's hands, "that's all."

Annie stared at her husband in disbelief, "she'd rather be with Sarah than her own mother?" Billy pulled her towards him, "c'mon now, Annie, you know that's not true," he told her, "Lexie loves you dearly, if anyone's upset her it's Bo McGhee," Billy said, tightly, "so, let's leave Lexie alone just now, if she's happy at

Sarah's and wants to stay there, then we shouldn't interfere."
"INTERFERE!" echoed Annie loudly, "if anyone's interfering, it's
SARAH!" Billy felt his control of the situation desert him, but
before things got worse, he put a stop to any further discussion
by walking out of the parlour and leaving Annie alone. "Mothers
and daughters," he muttered, pulling on his jacket and bonnet,
tired of the whole mess. He left the house and headed for the
Lodge, hoping that things would be calmer when he returned,
especially Annie.

—-—oOo—-—

Chapter 18

Bo McGhee read his Uncle Martin's letter with a mixture of shock and disbelief, "Lexie's PREGNANT," he read, his emotions ricocheting between his heart and his mind; her letters, the ones he'd shredded in the belief that they held words of rejection, would have told him differently, but now....! Lexie was pregnant and he was the child's father?

His mind went back to Christmas, when he and Lexie had made love before he flew back to Canada. She'd been willing, as was he and all thoughts of Angela Lafayette had been pushed aside by his desire for Lexie. At the visit from Angela when he'd asked her for a divorce, he'd truly meant to bring Lexie to Canada and marry her, but Angela had refused. But Lexie's pregnancy had changed everything. Now, he would have to return to Montrose and leave Louie behind with Angela till he, somehow, saw Lexie again and explained everything, especially everything about his wife and why he was unable to marry her.

Having shredded all of her letters, he had no idea where she was living, but words on a page, he knew, would have been useless anyway, he had to see her face to face and soon. His letter to Martin Kettlewell was brief. I will fly to Montrose Base as soon as you return to your duties there and will explain everything then. Bo

After her visit to Annie and her father, Sarah returned to her home in Pitkerro Road.

Charlie had taken over the abandoned preparations for their dinner and nodded towards the back garden where Lexie sat. "She's not saying much," he said "but, at least, she's stopped crying." Sarah sighed; her conversation with her father about the adoption of Lexie's bairn would remain secret, even from Charlie. There was too much at stake right now, but when the time was right, after the birth, she was sure Lexie would see sense and then she, Sarah Mathieson, would be a mum at last.

She joined Lexie in the garden. She loved her friend dearly, but her need to be a mother overrode everything and the first step she had to make was to convince Lexie that moving in with her and Charlie would be best for her and the bairn; but it would also mean Sarah could keep an eye on how Lexie's pregnancy was progressing, after all, in her heart, it was her child too!

"I've been to see your mum and my dad," Sarah began "and you were right, they are thinking of moving to Belfast.......not right now," she added, quickly, "but it's a possibility." Lexie felt her chin quiver. "Are you sure?" she asked. Sarah levelled with her, "no," she said, "but I think it would be better if you stayed with me and Charlie for a while...you know, let things settle down a bit. After all, you have the bairn to consider and all this upset isn't doing either of you any good."

Lexie blinked in disbelief. "You would do this for me?" she said. But, Sarah cut her short......"you're my best friend," she said, "and it's the least I can do." Lexie took Sarah's hand, "I don't know what to say," she said. "Just say YES," Sarah told her, "we have plenty of room and you won't have to worry about anything......I'll take care of you."

Lexie felt her body relax amazed, again, at how Sarah was able to cope with whatever difficulties she brought to her door. "I'd better tell mum that I'll be staying here for a while," Lexie said, "she'll worry otherwise." Sarah flinched. She didn't want Lexie going home and have Annie changing her mind. "Why not telephone her," she said, quickly standing up, "c'mon, I'll show you where it is."

Lexie dialled the number, but it went unanswered. "Try again later on," Sarah said, "but right now," she added, brightly, changing the subject, "I'm starving......how about you?" She linked Lexie's arm through her own, "Charlie will have these vegetables chopped by now, so I hope you have your appetite back."

Charlie seemed to be pleased that Lexie would be staying with them for a while. He had seen the longing in Sarah's eyes when Lexie had told her she was pregnant and hoped that by having her live with them, Sarah might somehow feel she could experience, at least, part of the joy of a new life coming into the world.

It was after eight o'clock that evening before Lexie telephoned again, but it was Billy who answered the call. "It's me," she said, "Lexie." Billy held his breath, "Hello Lexie," he said, indicating to Annie who was telephoning. Annie's hand flew to her throat, fearing why her daughter was telephoning instead of being there.

"Yes," Billy said, before listening again, "I understand," he said, "I'll tell your mother."

"Tell me what?" Annie asked, as Billy replaced the receiver into its cradle.

"Lexie says not to worry, she's fine and Sarah and Charlie are looking after her very well." Annie's eyebrows pulled into a frown. "Looking after her better than her own mother" she said, hurt surging through her heart? Billy sighed, "she also said that if we want to go to Belfast to live we should go and that John and Mary will be running out of candles to burn in their window, if we don't go soon."

Annie's hurt turned into a flood of tears. Her own daughter was telling her to go away, that she wasn't needed, not now, not ever. Billy hushed her in his arms, Lexie hadn't said the bit about the candles; he'd added that himself. Annie needed to break the tie with Lexie and especially about staying in Dundee if living out the rest of their lives in Belfast was going to become a reality. And anyway, he told himself, once the bairn was adopted by Sarah, Lexie would be able to go anywhere in the world to live, maybe even Belfast!

—·—oOo—·—

Chapter 19

Nancy was glad when the 'bummer' sounded for the end of the Friday shift. She'd managed to avoid eye contact with Di Auchterlonie, but had glanced up from time to time to see John Brannan, head bent over paperwork, at the Overseer's Desk. "Enjoy the time you have left Mr Brannan," she murmured, unheard over the racket of the looms, "for this weekend I'll make sure you're out of a job by Monday."

Nancy hurried to the Nursery to pick up Kevin, Mary Anne would have started to prepare their tea, she could depend on that, but it was wee Billy that couldn't be relied for anything lately, other than going to that Boxing Club he was so fond of. Every Friday and Saturday he'd go there, never coming home before midnight but, strangely, with never a blemish on his face? He must be a very good boxer, Nancy mused as she walked home, as no one seemed to be able to get close enough to throw a punch at him!

Nancy came through the door into the kitchen, but there was no smells of anything cooking and Mary Anne was slumped in the fireside chair, her hair flattened onto her brow and her face flushed and hot. Nancy quickly crossed the room and knelt down beside her daughter, her hand immediately finding her forehead. "You're burning up," she said, helping Mary Anne to her feet. "C'mon, into bed with you, you're in no fit state to cook the tea and if you're no better by morning, I'll get the doctor in." Mary Anne could only nod, as Annie helped her undress and get into bed. "Sorry mum," she murmured, "I'll be fine tomorrow."

The slamming of the front door signalled the arrival of wee Billy. It was Friday night and he couldn't wait to get out and spend his wages on the drink. He was meeting the Kelly brothers at Premierland Boxing Stadium, but until he was another year older, he couldn't get served in the pub, so had to depend on them to buy the drink he needed. But Billy was getting fed up of having to pay for their share as well as his own and tonight he'd determined to tell them they'd have to pay for their own drink.

"Where's Mary Anne?" he asked Nancy as she came through from the back room "and where's my tea?"

"Your sister's in bed with a fever, so you'll have to go to Capitelli's Chipper for some fish suppers for us," Nancy clipped "and get an extra single fish for Kevin while you're at it."

"Don't order me about," Billy shouted, "I'm not your 'lacky' like Brannan and you can get your own chips," he added, before pulling his coat back on and slamming out of the door.

Wee Billy was trembling all over, as he headed for Premierland Stadium. It was getting worse than ever and the only thing that stopped the shaking was alcohol and plenty of it. Going to work in the mornings was becoming more of a struggle and he had to make sure, there was a half-bottle of rum in his haversack to get him through the day and the Kelly brothers were his only way of getting it.

Nancy lifted Kevin onto her knee and sat rocking him, stunned at the vehemence of her son's words. Since his dad had died, it seemed like wee Billy was trying to copy his worst side. If things hadn't gone Billy Donnelly's way, his answer had always been the bottle or his fists and it seemed that wee Billy was fast becoming his dad's double.

With Mary Anne sick, Nancy had no option but to go to the chip shop herself and take Kevin with her.   Friday evening in Dundee, when the mill workers had been paid, always meant queues at the chip shop and it was while waiting for her turn to be served, she was tapped on the shoulder and heard the familiar voice of John Brannan.

"I just want to say," he said over her shoulder, "that Di Auchterlonie has explained everything...... and I understand." Nancy frowned, "understand what?"

"All about Jim Murphy..... and you!" Nancy froze: If Di Auchterlonie has told him anything about Jim Murphy and her, it was sure to be Di's version of the truth.

"Di Auchterlonie is a liar," Nancy retorted through gritted teeth "and if you believe her you'll believe anything." She swung Kevin into her arms, "you can have my place in the queue," she said icily, "I've lost my appetite."

Anger fuelled her return home, but Nancy burst into tears as soon as she closed the door behind her. Muttering to herself and sniffing back the tears, she buttered some bread for Kevin and made herself a pot of tea. "Bloody Di Auchterlonie," she shouted aloud, wallowing in misery at how her life was turning out and now, with no man to help her deal with wee Billy, she felt the cold fingers of revenge forming around her heart. She would deal with Di Auchterlonie in her own good time, but tomorrow, she would see her father and make sure John Brannan was sacked.

John Brannan bristled with annoyance at the sniggering and nudging of the women in the chip shop queue who had witnessed Nancy's put-down and it was with relief that he paid for his fish supper and hurried from the heat of the chipper. He'd expected to hate Nancy by now, knowing from Di that she'd got pregnant to another man while her husband was away fighting in France, but seeing her dark hair and the curve of her shoulders, had brought back that old feeling of desire that had first drawn him in.

Frustrated by his inability to forget about her, John ate his supper without tasting a thing and could feel the tension in his body growing by the minute. The clock ticked towards seven and the thought of another night alone in his room, forced him into action. "Walk," he told himself, "get out of here and walk away from all of this."

He pulled on his jacket and bonnet and strode into the Cowgate. The evening was warm and bairns were playing in the street, the mill workers were gathered at the end of their closes, gossiping as usual and the men would be in the Thrums Bar, drinking their wages down the drain. Everything was normal, but John Brannan was not. Somehow, he had to get over his obsession with Nancy Donnelly.

His feet took in the direction of the Stannergate, where the fresher air from the river cooled the heat in his soul. Bairns were scrambling amongst the rocks with their buckets, picking whelks that the outgoing tide had left along the shoreline while their mums watched from the shingle. The whelks would be boiled that night and be served at breakfast with their toast.

With no children of his own, as John watched them, his thoughts turned again to Nancy and Kevin, the toddler that Jim Murphy had fathered and his jaw tightened. It should have been him fathering Nancy's bairns, not Jim Murphy, nor any other man for that matter. He gazed out at the Tay, flowing endlessly by without a care in the world and knew, like it or not, he loved Nancy Donnelly and to be without her was killing him.

Chapter 20

Wee Billy was waiting at the corner of Todburn Lane for the Kelly brothers to get there. He opened his wage packet and checked the amount, £5. 10/-, that would be enough for tonight and tomorrow, but it would mean even more rum for him, if the brothers bought their own drink. With trembling hands he quickly pushed the notes back into the brown wage packet, and walked up William Lane, the nearer to get to their meeting place, as his need for the alcohol deepened.

"Billy!" he heard his name being called from amongst a group of men headed for Premierland for that night's Boxing Matches. The Kelly brothers were amongst them, now all Billy had to do was hand over enough money for the drink. The three of them turned into a close in William Lane and went through to the weed-covered back green. "Whisky for us and Rum for you," Mick Kelly said, his hand outstretched. Billy was torn between his need for the drink and his determination not to pay for the brothers as well. "Isn't it about time you two paid for your own drink," he said, trying to keep the fear out of his voice?

Mick Kelly's eyes narrowed. He knew all the signs of an alcoholic, after all, his father and grandfather were both in thrall to the demon drink and he could see that Billy Donnelly was as desperate for alcohol as them. He nodded to his brother and stepped away. "Well, that's just fine," Mick said, shrugging his shoulders, "and after all we've done for you," he added, with a sorrowful shake of his head. Billy flinched, he knew that without them, there would be no rum to stop the shakes......... "wait," he said, "I was joking, that's all, taking £1 from his wage packet and handing it over to Mick who, casually, flicked the

116

note with his finger. "I think another ten bob would be in order," he said, "and we'd like to see the boxing later," he added, "so maybe you could buy the tickets for that as well?"

Dumbly, Billy nodded. There was no way out, he either did as the brothers told him, or he'd become like the other out-of-work men he saw every night, shuffling along the streets, picking up dog ends and begging for money.

The light was beginning to fade as John Brannan walked back up Blackscroft towards the Cowgate, his feet slowing as he neared Nancy's close. He looked up at her window and saw that her light was on. Perhaps he should knock on her door and apologise for her missing her supper, maybe offer to fetch her another one, tell her he loved her, no matter what she'd done... ....But, John stopped himself with a slap on his forehead. "STOP IT" he told himself, "keep walking."

The orange glow from the Thrums window beckoned. If he was to face the rest of his life alone, then he might as well try to enjoy it. The heat and smoke from the bar almost made him turn away, but the barman had recognised him and was already pulling him a pint of beer.

"Mr Brannan," he said, placing the foaming glass on the bar, "we've not seen you for a while," he said with his well-practiced friendliness, "everything a'right?" John grimaced, "ach, you know," he said, "could be better." A loud roar of raucous laughter drew everyone's attention. "The Kelly brothers are at it again," the barman said, "I don't know where they're getting all the money from, none of the layabouts work, but they always seem to have enough to spend on drink every weekend."

John's eyes narrowed. The Kelly brothers were the same lads John had seen kicking wee Billy like a stray dog in the street a few months back. He'd sent them packing at the time, but although he'd then tried to befriend Nancy's son, he'd got nothing but cheek and told to mind his own business.

The barman returned to his duties with a shake of his head and John returned to his pint, keeping an eye on the brothers, lest they wanted to renew his acquaintance, tanked up as they were with drink and beginning to stagger. Mick Kelly drained his glass. "Goodnight all," he said, "we're for the boxing now and another wee drink with our great pal........ BILLY." A cheer went up from the other drinkers as the two brothers headed for the door of the Thrums, waving a half bottle of rum in one hand and a half bottle of whisky in the other. John Brannan pulled his bonnet over his eyes and turned his back to the departing brothers. "Thanks for the pint" he said to the barman, finishing his drink, "I think I may join them," he said, indicating the departing backs of the Kelly brothers, "I feel like a bit of boxing myself."

John stood on the pavement and lit a cigarette. He had a healthy fear of violence and the feeling of unease, that the Kelly's were up to no good, had started the adrenaline tensing his muscles. He'd seen the damage they had done to wee Billy before and didn't think it was any other 'Billy' they intended meeting but Nancy's son. But, there was no rush, he told himself, he knew where they were headed and the more the brothers drank, the less able they'd be to fight back if it came to fisticuffs.

The 'Leerie' was lighting the street lamps as John turned into William Lane. He could hear the cheering of the crowd coming from the Stadium and saw men gathered in groups outside the entrance, hoping to find a way to sneak in and get a glimpse of the action without paying the admission, but there was no sign of the Kelly brothers.

Slowly, he began walking up the steep slope of the Lane, keeping his eyes and ears open for any hint of trouble, then, as he passed the close leading to the run-down tenement homes above, he heard it! At first, he thought it was a cat mewing with hunger, before realising the sound wasn't coming from an animal, but from the mouth of a human being. He turned into the darkness of the close and waited till his eyes focussed. Then, in the filthy space beneath the stairwell, he saw two legs jutting out into the close covered in what looked like a white cloth, stained with dirt and what could only be... blood!

He listened for any other sound, but there was none. Getting closer to the figure, he realised that the white cloth was

Painter's overalls and his adrenaline began to race.

Kneeling down amongst the dirt and debris, he reached out for the arm of the victim and pulled him upright. Wee Billy Donnelly was battered and bruised and bleeding heavily from his nose and forehead and was very, very drunk.

"Billy!" John said, shaking the boy to try to bring him into consciousness, "it's John Brannan...can you stand up?" Billy's eyes flickered for a moment, then closed again, whatever had happened to him, John had no doubt the Kelly brothers had a hand in it, but right now, he had to get the lad out of the close and back home. But not back to Nancy's.

John half dragged, half carried the lad across King Street and down the steep flight of stairs leading to the Cowgate. The few men that saw them, just assumed another drunk being taken home and, luckily, the beat policeman wasn't around to ask any awkward questions. Finally, they reached John's home and he unloaded his burden onto the bed. There was nothing could be done till Billy slept off the effects of the alcohol, but John could see the damage to his face was worse than he'd first thought. Billy's eyes had swollen alarmingly and his nose looked broken, the skin on his knuckles was red with blood; at least he tried to fight back, John grimaced, but any further damage would only be revealed when wee Billy tried to stand up.

John switched off the electric light and sat in the darkness. The adrenalin ensured he wouldn't sleep any time soon, but thoughts of what to do about wee Billy Donnelly and his mother Nancy, would have kept him awake anyway.

Daylight was creeping into the window when John heard groaning and sobbing coming from wee Billy. He boiled the kettle and made a pot of strong tea. The clock showed ten past five as he took the mug of sweet tea to the bedside of Billy. "Drink this," he said "and try not to spew." Billy could barely register who was speaking to him, his face hurt and his mouth tasted of blood, as he squinted into the blur of the early morning. He managed to drop his legs over the edge of the bed, but couldn't get them to hold his weight and his hands shook so much, he spilt more of the tea than he managed to get into his mouth. John Brannan watched the wreck that Nancy's son had become. He'd seen plenty like him, both in the army and in the streets of Dundee, hopeless drunks who ended up sleeping in the closes and existing on handouts from the Salvation Army. But, it usually took years of a life of 'hard knocks' to get this bad, Billy had managed it in two.

"What time is it?" Billy mumbled, trying to focus his eyes on the mantelpiece clock.

"It's just gone five," John said, "and I think we need to get you to the Infirmary."

Billy physically recoiled. "NO," he said, "I'm fine......just need to get home before mum wakes up."

John sighed, "there's the door then," he said, "I'm sure she'll be pleased to see the state you're in."

John watched as wee Billy tried to stand up, but the spinning of the room forced him to drop back down onto the bed. "Bit dizzy are we?" John asked, kindly, realising that behind the bravado of youth, Billy was still a wee laddie and a damaged wee laddie at that. "I can help you," John told him, "if you'll let me."

Billy blinked away the water from his eyes, "no you canna'," he said, flatly, "naebody can help me." John got up and went through to the scullery, returning with a basin of warm water and a face cloth. "I can," he said, taking Billy's hands and silently washing the blood from his bruised knuckles. "Now, give your face a wash," John said, handing over the facecloth and I'll get you something clean to wear."

Gingerly, the blood stained clothing was removed and replaced with a clean shirt and old pair of John's trousers. Wordlessly, wee Billy was helped to the table and managed to eat some porridge and drink some more tea.

"Do you want to tell me about it....." John asked, as he cleared away the dishes, "you and the Kelly brothers that is, who beat you up and left you for dead." Billy hung his head, before stretching out his shaking hands. "I need the drink," he said, "to stop this."

John clenched his teeth, he'd seen it when he was a Sergeant in the Scots Guards, young lads, trying to be men before their time and terrified that they'd be seen for what they were, scared little boys. And, Billy Donnelly was no exception, he was a scared, wee laddie and John Brannan shook his head.

"Drink's not the answer, Billy," he said, "and being bullied by the Kelly brothers will only stop when you manage to face your fear and... grow up!"

"I'm 17," Billy said, trying to muster his courage and I'm no' scared o' the Kelly brothers."

"I'm not talking about fear of the Kelly brothers, Billy" John said, "the fear you have is having to face the world without your dad being around........that's why you need the drink." John's words hit home and for the first time, since his father had died, the dam of hurt broke and wee Billy wept.

"C'mon," John said, when his sobbing had eased, "let's get you fixed up at the Infirmary and you can tell your mum you're giving up the boxing after the pasting you got last night."

"And you won't tell her anything about......what really happened?"

"Scouts honour," John said, "and next time you feel like a drink, get out into the hills and walk the urge away." Wee Billy nodded, "my dad used to walk in the hills," he said, before adding "and maybe we could go for a walk together sometime Mr Brannan."

"I'd like that," John said, gathering up Billy's bloody clothes, "and make sure you get your overalls washed before Monday. We can't have a painter without his 'whites.'

Chapter 21

Sarah hurried home from school the following day, her mind still racing. Could it really be that her dreams of being a mother might actually come true? Now that her father knew her secret, she told herself, she'd just have to bide her time and keep Lexie close till the bairn arrived.

"It's only me," she called out as she came through the door, forcing herself to calm the excitement that had been bubbling in her chest since her talk with her father. Lexie hurried through from the kitchen to meet her. "Is everything still alright" she queried worriedly, "have I to go back home again?"

Sarah put her arm around Lexie's shoulder and guided her back to the kitchen where Charlie was reading his newspaper. "Everything's fine and your mum is pleased about you wanting to stay with us.......for a while, for the bairn's sake. Lexie frowned; didn't her mother care about her at all? Was she just waiting for the chance to go off to Ireland with Billy and forget all about her?

Charlie noticed the frown, but Sarah didn't. "So, you can stay with us" she sparkled....... "until the bairn is born, if you like," before adding, almost triumphantly, then we can both look after it." Lexie silently nodded, she was grateful for Sarah's help, but it was only meant to be for a few days, then her mother would assure her they weren't going to Ireland and she'd go back home, but it seemed that the dice had been rolled and whether she liked it or not, fate had decided that Lexie would have to remain at Sarah's and bring up her bairn alone.

Annie sat for a long time after Billy had gone to the Lodge, everything seemed to be happening so fast, one minute Lexie was thinking of finding work, but the next all that had changed after she'd read John's letter from Belfast and stormed out of the house. The sound of the telephone ringing in the parlour forced Annie back to reality. Perhaps it was Lexie, she thought, wanting to come home, but it wasn't Lexie it was Isabella Anderson.

"Annie?" Isabella sounded full of beans as usual. Unlike Annie, her zest for life never seemed to diminish. As long as she had her faith, she seemed able to rise above any problems life threw at her and there had been many.

"Annie?" she said louder when there was no response, "can you hear me?"

Annie cleared her throat, "yes, yes, I can hear you," she said, "just a wee frog in my throat, that's all." But already, Isabella had picked up on the sadness in Annie's voice. She had seen her sister-in-law through many a hard time and knew her moods like the back of her hand. "What's wrong?" she asked, anxiously, "and tell me the truth," she added, "don't try to pretend you're alright when you're not."

Annie held the telephone receiver tightly. "It's Lexie," she said, "she's gone."

Isabella flinched. "Gone!" she echoed, "gone where?" Between tears and sobs, Annie told Isabella the whole sorry mess, "so you see," she ended, "she doesn't want me with her, she wants Sarah, and doesn't care if I go to Belfast with Billy... ..and never see the bairn.....EVER!"

Isabella sighed. "Oh Annie," she said, her compassion for her soul mate rising up from her heart. "I'm sure that's not true."

"But it is," Annie assured her, "and I don't know what to do?"

"Where's Billy," Isabella asked, her practical side surfacing to meet the demands of Annie's distress. "At the Lodge, I think."

"When he comes home, I want you both to get into the motor car and come to Forfar," she instructed, "we don't want you getting ill again and until Lexie sees sense, you need to stay here, with me and John and let us look after you."

Annie looked around the room. Fretting in this house would make her ill again she knew, especially while Billy was at work at the Mill and she was alone with her thoughts.

"Alright," she whispered, "if you think that's best."

"I do," Isabella told her quietly, "so put a few things in a bag and try not to worry, everything will be alright."

When Billy came home that evening, Annie's bag was sitting in the lobby and Annie was sitting in the parlour, coat and hat on and ready to go.

"Going somewhere?" he asked, wondering what was going on. Annie told him about Isabella and her suggestion about going to her and John's house in Forfar..."just till Lexie sees sense," Annie said, repeating Isabella's words with tight lips.

"Let's get you into the motor car then," Billy said with relief: With Annie at Forfar and Lexie with Sarah, he could let himself relax. He'd write to John and Mary soon and with a bit of luck, would be able to let them know that they'd both be coming to Belfast to live.

Isabella welcomed them with open arms. "Come away in," she smiled, "let's get you settled." Very soon, soup and sandwiches appeared, followed by a fine Fruitcake and a large pot of tea and Isabella was pleased to see Annie managed to eat a bit of everything. "I've made up a bed for you in the spare room," Isabella told her, "and for you too Billy, if you want to stay?" But Billy was not for staying and after kissing Annie goodbye, he returned to his motor car and Dundee.

Tomorrow is another day, he told himself, settling in behind the wheel, but tomorrow he would begin again his search for the whereabouts of Bo McGhee. Although he was happy that Lexie was with Sarah, he feared for Lexie's future if she decided to keep her bairn and the only one who could make a difference to her future security was Bo McGhee.

That evening, Sarah sang to herself as she washed the dishes. Lexie had retired to her room to try to sleep, after the last few days she'd had it was no wonder she was exhausted, but for Sarah is was quite the opposite. She'd not felt this good for a long time.

Charlie watched her as he dried the crockery. "You seem

happy," he said, eyeing his wife, quizzically, "with all that's been happening, I'd have thought you'd have been exhausted."

Sarah tipped the dishwater down the sink and turned to face her husband. "I am happy," she said, "Lexie's here and she has me to look after her......." before adding, "and anyone else that comes along," as she folded the dishcloth and placed it in the basin.

Since their marriage ten years ago, he had watched his wife become more and more despondent, as each month had passed with no sign of a pregnancy. The doctor had been consulted, but could give no reason for Sarah's inability to conceive. You are both healthy young adults, they'd been told, so just keep trying and it will happen. But ten years up the road, there was no sign of Sarah getting pregnant and, despite Charlie assuring her that it didn't matter to him if they didn't have children, he could see the longing in her eyes every time she saw a new born being wheeled out in its pram by its mum.

And he had seen it again, when Lexie had turned up at their door that morning and Sarah had insisted she stay with them. At first, he'd believed it would be for a few days, but now, it looked like Sarah intended for Lexie to stay till the birth of her bairn.

He felt a shiver of fear run through him as he wondered how Sarah would cope when Lexie went back to Albert Street with her bairn and she was needed no more.

"You do know that when Lexie has this bairn," he said, choosing his words carefully, "that she'll be moving back home and Annie and your dad will be looking after things again?"

Sarah felt a pain of anguish shoot through her. "Maybe she won't want to go back," she said, firmly, "maybe the bairn will want to stay with me forever, and then Lexie can go back to her old life at Montrose."

Charlie turned his wife to face him. "That's not going to happen, Sarah," he said, just as firmly, "Lexie and her bairn will be going back to Albert Street to live when this is over, BOTH of them."

Sarah shook herself free. "We'll see about that," she said, "she doesn't want this bairn, BUT I DO" she retorted, her eyes flashing with defiance and if you don't like it, you know what to do."   The air around Charlie whooshed as Sarah slammed the door behind her.   Since Lexie's arrival back into their lives, it seemed that their peaceful existence had been shattered and what had started as merely helping her friend, had turned Sarah into a zealot, releasing all the pent up longing for a child of her own into her very soul and Charlie fearing for her sanity when Lexie's bairn came into the world.

—-—oOo—-—

Chapter 22

Wing Commander Kettlewell's telegram to his nephew was short and to the point.

'WILL BE BACK AT MONTROSE ON JULY 20, STOP, TIME THINGS WERE SORTED, STOP, MARTIN.

Bo folded the printed page and placed it in his wallet. The die was cast, it was time to face the music and pray that Lexie understood. Bo walked to the Comms. Room at Moose Jaw and scheduled a seat on the weekly flight to the Montrose Base before handing the Teleprinter Operator his reply.

To: WING COMMANDER M KETTLEWELL.
ARRIVING MONTROSE BASE SUNDAY JULY 21. ETA 15.00 HRS.
From: WING COMMANDER R MCGHEE.'

Bo returned to his Quarters and placed a long distance call to Angela at Cap-de-la-Madelaine where she had gone when she realised that Bo had no intention of taking her back as his wife. "Bon jour," he heard her say, when the Operator had connected his call. "It's me, Bo and please, speak English." There was silence on the other end of the line.

"Can you hear me?"

"I can hear you," Angela replied, hoping Bo had now seen sense and was telephoning to ask her to come back to him.

"I need you to look after Louie for a week or so," Bo said, "something's come up and I have to return to Montrose."

Angela felt her lips tighten. "Hah!" she said, "she just tweaks her little finger and Bo goes running back like a little puppy dog."

Bo's fist gripped the Receiver. "Nobody's tweaking anything," he said, "now can you look after our son or not?"

Angela's mind was racing. "Only if you bring him here to the Cape before you go."

Bo flinched at the idea, but there was no option, if he wanted to get back to Montrose, then he'd have to take Louie to Angela. "I'll bring him mid-week," he said, "but I won't be staying, just dropping him off."

Reluctantly, Angela agreed, she'd hoped for at least one night with Bo, but he'd have to come again for Louie on his return and then......

Bo returned the Receiver to its cradle, his eyes misting over at the thought of seeing Lexie again and with a hundred questions running through his mind: Would Lexie even agree to see him, would she still feel the love she'd shown him that Christmas night, would he be able to walk away from her again? He reached for the bottle of Scotch he kept in his desk drawer and poured out a double measure. "Here's to the future," he said aloud, "and to you, Lexie, my Scottish Sweetheart."

Billy returned alone to Albert Street, the sound of his feet echoing through the deserted rooms and wondered if life would ever run his way again. He picked at some cheese and oatcakes, washed down with a dram of Whisky and thought of Annie. The year they'd met, the years in between when he'd had to love her from afar and then that wonderful time when she'd told him that she'd had a son and that he was the father. The beautiful Christmas they'd all been together in Ireland when John and Mary had married and now.......now Lexie had came back into his life, bringing with her the prospect of giving birth to Annie's first grandchild and that's when all his dreams of living out his life with Annie in Belfast crumbled.

"Bo McGhee," he murmured as he poured another dram. "I'll find you and make you face up to what you've created with Lexie, if it's the last thing I do."

"I'm sorry," Charlie whispered into the darkness of their

bedroom, while Sarah pretended to be asleep. She pulled the bed covers around her shoulders, "go to sleep," she murmured, "I just want to sleep."

Charlie turned onto his back and stared into the gloom. "I just don't want you to be hurt," he said, "if things don't work out as you've planned." With a sigh, Sarah threw back the covers and sat up, switching on the bedside lamp. "Nothing's PLANNED!" she told him, pointedly, "but if it works out that Lexie can't or won't look after the bairn, then there's no reason why we can't adopt it, now is there?" Sarah had switched on her reasonable, school teacher voice. "I know what I'm doing," she added, turning to face her husband, "you're worrying about nothing," she assured him, as she snuggled down into his chest. "Now, kiss me goodnight and we'll say no more about it," Sarah whispered. But it was an hour later before they both fell into a deep sleep, their pent up anxiety gone, as they made love for the first time in many weeks.

Billy slept fitfully, without Annie by his side, but by morning he had decided to return to the Base at Montrose and, this time, he wasn't going to leave without an answer as to Bo McGhee's whereabouts. The drive to Montrose was taken quickly as Billy, now familiar with the twists and turns of the road, made good time. Squadron Leader James Morris was still in charge when he arrived, but he had good news for Billy.

"Wing Commander Kettlewell is returning to Montrose Base on Saturday 20th July," he told Billy "and will be returning to duty the following Monday, so if you want me to tell him you still wish to see him, I'll get word to him and, I'm sure, he'll get in touch with you."

Billy felt his spirits lift. "And you think he'll know the whereabouts of this Bo McGhee?" James Morris shrugged his shoulders, "I'm afraid I don't know that," he said, "you'll just have to wait and speak to Wing Commander Kettlewell yourself."

Billy nodded. "Of course," he said, writing his telephone number down on a page from his notebook and handing it to the Squadron Leader. "He can contact me on that number," he said, "and thank you for your patience; I just hope the Wing Commander can help me find Bo McGhee."

James Morris watched Billy walk, purposefully, away before picking up the telephone and dialling Martin Kettlewell's direct line at Wilmslow. "Updating you, Sir, as you requested," he said, "regarding Miss Melville. Mr Dawson has just left the premises and will be expecting a call from you on your return to Montrose."

Martin wrote down Billy's telephone number. "Thanks James," he said, "Wing Commander McGhee will be arriving at Montrose on July 21 at 15.00 hours, make sure Quarters are prepared for him and James," Martin added, "thank you for your discretion in what is a very personal matter."

Billy hummed a tune to himself as he drove back to Dundee. Only ten days to wait and he'd, finally, find out where Bo McGhee was hiding, but right now, he'd have to speak with Sarah, find out how Lexie was coping and whether it looked like she would keep her bairn, or make Sarah's dream of motherhood come true.

Once back in Dundee, he lost no time in telephoning his daughter to find out how things were, but it was Lexie who answered his call. For a split second Billy thought about hanging up the telephone, but what would that have achieved? Nothing, he decided.

"Lexie!" he exclaimed, uneasily, "it's Billy, just telephoning to speak with Sarah, is she there?" Lexie felt a sweep of emotion on hearing her step-dad's voice, but that was quickly followed by resentment: He wanted to speak to Sarah, she told herself, not to her and the memory of reading John's letter reset her anger.

"She's out," Lexie told him through tight lips, "try again later.."

"WAIT," Billy shouted, realising that she was about to hang up the receiver, "your mum is missing you very much, and so am I," before hastening to add "please come home." But there was only silence followed by the sound of a 'click' then the purr of the dead line as Lexie slowly replaced the receiver. But, her mood had softened and she smiled as a tear formed in her eyes, she would go back home in a few more days, her mum would welcome her with open arms and all this talk about going to live with John and Mary in Belfast would be forgotten.

Billy stared at the telephone, he'd not worry Annie about Lexie's snub, he decided, as it would only bring her running back from Forfar. "Patience Billy," he told himself, "time enough to speak up when Bo McGhee is 'brought to book' and marries Lexie, then it will be the first boat to Belfast."

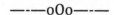

Chapter 23

Mary Anne's fever broke at midnight and Nancy breathed a sigh of relief when her daughter fell into a deep, healing sleep. She glanced over at wee Billy's empty bed, a frisson of unease causing her to shiver, "surely he should be home by now?" Wearily, she rubbed her aching shoulders and determined that, tomorrow, she would get to the bottom of this Boxing Club nonsense he'd gotten himself into and make sure he gave it up. But, right now, she just needed to sleep.

As she tiptoed from the room, she knew fears for their future had grown during the hours she had sat with Marry Anne, cooling her with wet cloths and soothing her agitation when the fever was at its pitch, but with no husband to lean on and worrying that Kevin may have picked up the infection, Nancy only slept, fitfully, and by five o'clock the following morning, she staggered from her bed and crept through to the back room to check Mary Anne's temperature.

She laid a hand on her daughter's forehead, relieved to find it cool to the touch, Mary Anne was going to be fine, but as her eyesight became accustomed to the gloom, she realised that wee Billy's bed still hadn't been slept in and a bolt of fear brought her to instant wakefulness.

"Mary Anne," Nancy whispered, shaking her daughter from her sleep, "where's Kevin?" Mary Anne opened her eyes and tried to sit up, unable to understand what her mother was talking about. "He's in bed, isn't he?"she said. "NO," Nancy told her, her agitation rising with her voice, "his bed hasn't been slept in!" Nancy crossed the room and pulled back the covers, "see," she said, shakily, "he's been out all night!"

Even as Nancy uttered the words, a deep foreboding gripped her, wee Billy had been acting strangely for weeks now, flying into rages, spending every weekend at that damn Boxing Club of his and staying at the tea table just long enough to eat his food before disappearing back out onto the streets.

"I need to go look for him," Nancy said, urgently, pushing the covers back over Mary Anne's shoulders. "Stay here in case he comes home," she instructed her daughter, as the memory of wee Billy's father being, found frozen to death outside Bell Street Jail, filled her with terror, that history was going to repeat itself. She hurried through to the kitchen and pulled on her shoes and winter coat over her nightgown before returning to the now, fully awake, Mary Anne. "Give Kevin some hot milk when he wakens up" Nancy told her thankful that, at least, her daughter could be relied on to help "and I'll be back as soon as I can."

She glanced at the kitchen clock before setting out in search of her son, "nearly six o'clock," she murmured, "God help me, please, let me find him safe," she prayed, hurrying down the stairs and out of the close into the near- empty street. A stray dog barked at her as she hurried past heading for the boxing stadium in William lane, the only place she could think of, where someone might know where she could find the Boxing Club and her son. But Premierland Stadium was closed and bolted shut with only the empty beer bottles remaining, left strewn on the ground by the Saturday night drunks.

"Billy," Nancy called out into the emptiness of the morning, "Billy," it's mum, can you hear me?"

"I think half the town can hear you."

Nancy swung around and was met by the stout figure of the beat bobby who'd been standing in a nearby close, waiting for the day shift Constable to turn up to hand over his duties report. Nancy almost fainted with relief. "My lad's been out all night," she gasped, "have you seen him?"

"Now, now," the bobby said, "calm down and let me get some details. What's your name?"

"Mrs Donnelly," Nancy said, "Nancy Donnelly and it's my son

Billy," she repeated, "he's been out all night."

The policeman frowned. "Donnelly, you say?" Nancy nodded.

"Would that be the Billy Donnelly who was found at Christmas outside Bell Street Jail," he asked, "frozen to death?"

Nancy flinched as the memory reinforced itself. "It's my son I'm looking for," she said, grimly, I know where his father is."

The bobby nodded. He'd been on duty that Christmas when Billy Donnelly had been found. "Another drunken layabout," they'd said, "tried to kill his wife and spent all his money on the drink and whoring with some 'prossie' fae Lochee." He could see why Nancy was so scared for her son: what was it they used to say, 'like father, like son!'

"Go home, Mrs Donnelly," the bobby said, kindly, "there's been nothing reported during Saturday night, so I'm sure he'll turn up some time today, feeling sorry for himself and promising to be a good laddie in future."

Nancy didn't know whether to laugh or cry. "You think so?" she said. "I know so," the bobby replied, "lads will be lads you know and he's not the first to stay out on a Saturday night... probably chasing some lassie or other." Nancy smiled, of course the bobby was right and annoyed at herself for getting so anxious, she turned to go home."Thanks Constable," she said, "I don't think we mums ever stop worrying about our bairns." The bobby shook his head, "neither do we dads."

With anger replacing fear, Nancy made her way back home just in time to see wee Billy disappear into their close. With every step her anger built, "that's the last time you'll be at that Boxing Club," she muttered to herself as she ran up the stairs after her son.

"Where the Hell have you been?" Nancy shouted, slamming the door behind her, "and out all night!"

Billy turned to face her and Nancy's hands flew to her mouth in shock. She could barely see his face for the white strips of bandaging taped across her son's nose and his two eyes, black and swollen so much he could hardly see out of them.

Mary Anne was standing beside the room door, holding Kevin's hand tightly, weak and trembling and unable to speak.

Whatever had happened to her brother?

She knew the Kelly brothers would have had something to do with it. She'd tried to talk to Billy the last time they'd beaten him up, but had been told to mind her own business, but now..

"Who did this to you?" Nancy demanded to know, gathering her wits together again, "and don't lie to me."

Billy clasped his hands together to stop the trembling that had begun at the Infirmary as the drink wore off. "You're a bit young to have the 'shakes'" the Doctor had said, spotting the signs immediately, but John Brannan had whispered something in his ear and the questioning stopped. "I met my match at the Boxing Club last night," he mumbled, "big lad from the Overgate belted me and broke this." Billy pointed to his nose. Nancy's eyes narrowed: from never having a mark on him, to looking like this, almost beggared belief! "Is that the end of this stupid Boxing Club then?"

Billy breathed a sigh of relief as his mother seemed to believe the lie, "it's the end," he said, hoping that John Brannan would keep his word about what really happened. "And I'm sorry I've worried you," he added, his damaged eyes blurring with real tears.

"Get some sleep," she said, realising any further questioning would be pointless and that Mary Anne needed reassurance. "You've got your work to go to tomorrow," she told her son "and you'd better not be late, God knows what Ernie Griffiths will say when he sees you." Nancy shook her head, before noticing what wee Billy was wearing, as he walked towards the back room.

"Whose shirt and trousers have you got on?" she queried, remembering he had still been wearing his painter's overalls when he'd stomped out without his tea the night before. Billy felt his blood run cold, he'd stashed his blood-stained clothes behind the bins at the back of the tenement, but now......."they took them off me at the Infirmary," he garbled, "I've to get them later on," he added, closing the door before any more questions could be asked.

Nancy hadn't the energy to probe any deeper and lifted Kevin into her arms.

"Let's get some porridge down you," she told him, hugging him tightly before setting him down in his high chair and beckoning Mary Anne into her arms. She could feel her daughter shivering, with fright more than the cold and took off her winter coat and wrapped it around her. "Sit yourself down," Nancy said, "everything will be alright, now that brother of yours has learned his lesson, things will get back to normal." But Mary Anne wasn't so sure, when she'd asked the neighbours about the Boxing Club, no one seemed to know anything about it.....wee Billy had been lying, she was sure of it.

"We're off to get the tram to Baxter Park," Nancy called into the gloom of the back room around mid-day. Every Sunday, she'd take Kevin and Mary Anne away from the grime and smell of jute at the Cowgate and breathe in the fresh air at the Park. She was answered with a 'grunt' from the depth of Billy's bed and shrugged. "Looks like he'll be sleeping for hours yet," she said, "best thing too"

Billy waited till he was sure his mother had gone before trying to raise himself up from his bed. His face felt like it was on fire and his body ached with every movement, but he had to retrieve his overalls and clean them of blood ready for work tomorrow, or the game would be up. He got as far as the kitchen sink and promptly vomited. His gut was in spasms of cramp and his legs felt like rubber, as sweat rolled down his back. If only he had some rum, he knew he'd feel better, but there was none and Billy gritted his teeth. Somehow, he had to get those overalls.

After what seemed like an eternity, he managed to get down the stairs to the bins where he'd hidden them and pushed the bloody bundle inside John Brannan's borrowed shirt. "Help me Mr Brannan," he muttered as he stumbled to the end of the close and into the street, no one was about and he thanked God it was Sunday. With the last dregs of his strength he made it to John's door before collapsing.

Wee Billy fell inside as John opened his door. "Billy!" he exclaimed, shocked at the frailty of the youngster, before man-handling him into the kitchen and through to the bedroom.

Gingerly, he rolled Billy onto the bed and removed the bundle from under his shirt and realised why he had came to him for help. Wee Billy needed help alright, but washing his overalls wasn't going to be enough to keep his drinking secret. Nancy was going to have to be told the truth.

For the next three hours, John watched the street for sight of Nancy, while Billy slept in his bed, then there she was, Nancy, with Mary Anne and Kevin skipping alongside of her. He ran down the stairs, his heart in his mouth and his mind racing.

"Nancy," he called out as she neared the close, "please," he said, his voice sounding hoarse in his ears, "I need to speak to you...." But Nancy held up her hand to stop him going any further. "I told you before, there's nothing you have to say that I want to hear, so leave me be."

"It's about WEE BILLY!"

Nancy stopped in her tracks and eyed him warily. Surely, he wouldn't use her son as a ploy to wheedle his way back into her affections?

"Take Kevin home," she told Mary Anne, quietly, becoming aware of the strain in John Brannan's face, "I'll be with you in a minute."

"Follow me," John said, leading the way to his home. Nancy hesitated, "talk to me here," she said, "I'm going nowhere with you." John took hold of her arm. "Your son needs you," he told her, grimly "and you need to know the truth about him."

Nancy shook her arm free and walked ahead of him. She'd known in her heart that something had been wrong with Billy for a while now, but he was leaving the Boxing Club now, wasn't he? Everything was going to be alright.

"He's in my bed," John said indicating the door to the back room, "sleeping off the drink."

Nancy frowned. "He was beaten in the ring at the Boxing Club," she said, "nothing to do with drink and, anyway, he's never going back, so everything is fine now." She flung the words at John before spotting her son's blood-stained overalls on the bunker.

"Go and see him for yourself," John said, steadily, "then when you're ready, come back and listen to the truth."

Nancy sat on the chair beside the bed and let her eyes become accustomed to the dimness. Wee Billy was sweating and muttering as his muscles went into spasms and he tried to relieve his itching skin by tearing at it with his nails, drawing more blood. Nancy tried to hold his hand, but it shook so much she had to let go. Tears filled her eyes as she watched her son in the grip of the 'horrors.' She'd watched while his father had gone through the same thing, time and again, but would always go back to the drink whenever trouble hit, which was often.

"I'm ready," Nancy said, returning to the kitchen and sitting down at the table, her fingers laced together and her eyes downcast. She'd been expecting John Brannan to tell her about Billy's drinking, but the full story of his involvement with the Kelly Brothers and his lies about the Boxing Club shook her rigid. What had her son turned into!

"He misses his dad, Nancy," John said, quietly, "despite everything, he loved him and he's scared of the future without him in it." Nancy nodded. She knew how upset wee Billy had been at his dad's death and how he'd turned his anger onto John Brannan, when he'd found him in the kitchen making the Mince and Tatties; he wasn't his dad, he was his mum's 'fancy man!' Nancy grimaced at the memory, was this when wee Billy had turned to drink? She felt lost and unable to help herself, never mind wee Billy and John could see that the shock of seeing her son and the state he was in, had shaken her rigid.

"I'll look after him till the worst is past," John said, tentatively, "if that's alright?"

Nancy nodded, any fight she had in her heart had gone, along with her intention to have John Brannan sacked, instead she assured him that her father would keep his job open for as long as it took till wee Billy recovered.

"Thanks John," she whispered, as she picked up the blood-stained overalls, "I'll get these washed for whenever he needs them and let Ernie Griffiths know he's not well."

How could she have got this man so wrong, she asked herself, before wondering what else she'd gotten wrong about him?

"I'm sorry," she whispered, "for everything."
"So am I, Nancy" John replied, "so am I."

Chapter 24

Sarah noticed the change in Lexie's mood the following morning at breakfast, putting it down to her getting used to living with her and Charlie and allowing her to hope that Lexie would stay till the birth.....and then.....her dream of being the bairn's mum may just come true.

"You're in a good mood... isn't she Charlie?" Sarah quipped, brightly, as they all sat down to breakfast. "I am," Lexie told her, "and before I forget, your dad telephoned yesterday when you were out and said he'd call back...."

"You spoke to him?" Sarah cut in, her fear that Lexie would change her mind and go home, stirring in her gut. "Not really," Lexie told her, "he just said mum was missing me and when was I coming home and that's when I disconnected his call."

Sarah fixed her eyes on Lexie, "and are you?" she asked, holding her breath and trying to keep the urgency out of her voice, "going home, I mean?"

But Lexie just shrugged and bit into her toast. "Why would I want to go back there when I have everything I need here," she finally, said "and anyway, I only have Billy's word for it." Sarah tried to relax, everything was going to be fine, she told herself, but she'd go and see her father after school, make sure he still planned to go to Belfast to live.

After the meal, Charlie walked his wife to the front door. He'd seen the glimmer of a smile on Lexie's lips when she'd repeated Billy's words to them. "Have a good day Sarah," he said, kissing her on the cheek before adding, "everything with Lexie will work out for the best." Sarah nodded goodbye, everything would work out for the best she told herself, decisively, one way or another, Lexie's bairn would be hers.

With too much time on her hands and the house to herself after Charlie had left for work, Lexie's thoughts began to wander back in time, before Bo McGhee, before her marriage to Robbie Robertson and his untimely death, before the war had happened and Euan MacPherson had still been alive. She'd been part of a family then, along with her young brother Ian and the security of two parents looking after them. Life had been carefree then and she thought it would be like that forever, but fate was teaching her a hard lesson and she was struggling to cope with the responsibility.

Lexie sighed, her hand resting on the burgeoning 'bump' that seemed to be getting bigger by the day. Soon, her bairn would be born and she tried to imagine what kind of a world she was bringing it into. Not like Sarah's world, with its comfortable house and well-tended gardens, no money worries and a loving husband, not like Billy and her mother's carefree existence, able to go where they wished and leave Dundee and Lexie behind... just like she'd left them behind when she'd joined the WAAFs.

How the tables had turned.

She sat down on the garden seat and felt utterly alone. Bo McGhee, wherever he was now, had held out so much promise of marriage and building a home and life together in Canada but... Lexie felt a wave of self-pity wash over her, it had all crumbled to nothing, when her letters had gone unanswered and she'd returned to Dundee, only to find that Annie and Billy had gone to Belfast. The little girl inside the woman, longed to be held and soothed, longed to be loved, but Lexie also knew that, more than anything, she longed for the security of her mum's love.

So why didn't she go and tell her, she chided herself, she didn't really want to live with Sarah and Charlie, constantly reminded of the life she couldn't have no matter how much she prayed for it. Decisively and with no hesitation, Lexie marched back into the house, pulled on her jacket and picked up her handbag. This wasn't where she was meant to be, she knew now beyond any shadow of doubt, much as she was thankful to

Sarah for all her kindness, she would go back to Albert Street, tell her mum how much she loved and missed her, and vow never to leave home again.

With every step down Pitkerro \Road, Lexie's heart quickened, how stupid she'd been, believing for even a minute that her mum would desert her and go back to Belfast with Billy. Her mum loved her more than anything else in the whole world and as she quietly turned the key in the lock of her home, she tried not to giggle as she anticipated the look of joy on her mum's face when she told her she was coming back home and, this time, for good.

But Annie wasn't in the kitchen, as usual, baking the scones and cakes to fill the tins, nor was she in the parlour having her elevenses and listening to the Wireless. Lexie began to panic, what if her mother was ill and in bed? She opened Annie's bedroom door, but the bed had been made, the quilt and pillows plumped up with no sign that anyone had slept on them the night before.

"Mum" she called out into the silence, before her eyes took in the dressing table where her mother kept her hairbrush and her pot of cold cream. None of her things were there! The panic was increasing as Lexie crossed to the wardrobe and flung open the doors, but only the empty coat hangers jangled inside, the few clothes that Annie kept for 'special occasions' were gone, as were her coat and shoes. Lexie opened drawer upon empty drawer before bursting into tears.

There was no disputing it, her mother was no longer living at Albert Street and the only place she could possibly have gone to was Belfast! She replayed the telephone call from Billy in her mind, asking to speak to Sarah....Lexie felt herself cringe, he'd at least had the decency to try to tell his daughter he was leaving!

When the tears of shock and hurt had dried, Lexie took her key and laid it on the kitchen table. She wouldn't need it any longer, her mother and Billy had seen to that, from now on, she was dependent on Sarah and Charlie Mathieson till the bairn was born, but she dreaded to think what the future held for them both, a fallen woman and a Bastard bairn, alone in a world that didn't care.

Sarah lost no time in telephoning her dad the instant the school day was over. But the telephone rang and rang without answer. There was nothing else for it, but to try again later as she made her way home, her fears growing with every step that Annie had managed to change Billy's mind about moving to Belfast. It was the only thing that could ruin her plans and she was too close to succeeding to allow that to happen.

The change in Lexie's mood was so striking that it took Sarah by surprise. She was sitting bolt upright on the garden bench and staring into the void that was her future.

Sarah took the seat beside her, dreading to hear the news that Lexie was going back home, but stunned into silence as Lexie told her of her visit to Albert Street.

"They've gone," she stated flatly, "gone to Belfast to be with their precious son."

"But didn't you say my dad telephoned just yesterday?"

"To say goodbye, I expect," Lexie pronounced.

"And your mum has gone to Belfast as well?" Sarah said in disbelief at Lexie's news.

"Didn't even leave a note," was the blunt reply.

Sarah sat back in the chair. So, that was the reason for the call, she realised, to say everything was working out fine and they were on their way to Belfast. Only, Lexie had answered Billy's telephone call and heard what she wanted to hear, that Annie wanted her to come home.

"And I've left my key there" Lexie added, turning to face her friend with a sigh, "so it looks like you're stuck with me," she said, "at least till the bairn's born." Sarah felt like dancing Lexie round the garden, but instead she put her arm around her shoulder and guided her back into the kitchen. "You can stay as long as you want," she said, "and that includes when the bairn comes along."

Charlie could hardly believe his ears that evening, when Sarah told him the news. "LEFT!" he exclaimed, "both of them... ..without even saying goodbye to her?"

"Don't sound so surprised," Sarah said, annoyed at Charlie casting doubt on her story, "Lexie's here with us, and now that Annie and my dad have gone to Belfast, she's here to stay."

The sound of the telephone ringing in the hall interrupted what was turning into an argument between husband wife. "I'll get it," Sarah said brusquely "and don't say anything when you see her tomorrow morning at breakfast."

"Dundee 172, Mrs Mathieson speaking."

"Sarah, it's dad." Sarah held the receiver away from her face in disbelief, before covering the speaker with her hand and moving as far away from Lexie's bedroom door as possible.

"Where are you calling from?" Sarah asked, confused, "you sound as though you're next door!"

"I'm calling from home," Billy said, "and I need to speak to Lexie."

"By home," Sarah asked, "do you mean Belfast?"

"No," Billy told her, becoming irritated with Sarah's questioning. "I've just come in and Lexie's key was sitting on the kitchen table. Has she been here today?"

Sarah felt the blood drain from her face. "So, you're not in Belfast?"

"No Sarah," her dad replied, getting more exasperated with his daughter, "now can I speak to Lexie?"

"Is Annie with you?" Sarah demanded to know.

Billy hesitated at the mention of Annie's name: Had Lexie come to make peace with her mother, found she was no longer there and thought that she'd gone to Belfast?" Billy could have kicked himself, if only he hadn't insisted on Annie going to Forfar to be with Isabella, while he sorted the mess out with Bo McGhee, mother and daughter would be reunited by now and Annie would be happy.

But Billy didn't answer. Fate may have worked in his favour this time, as long as Lexie stayed with Sarah, the better were his chances of moving to Belfast and the more likelihood of Sarah becoming the mother she craved.

"I have to go," Billy lied, "there's someone at the door.....I'll telephone you later."

Sarah gazed at the 'purring' telephone. If Billy was home in Albert Street...then where was Annie?

She tried to calm her thoughts, as long as Lexie believed her mum and Billy were in Belfast, she'd remain with Sarah and now that she'd locked herself out of her old home, there was no reason she'd find out the truth. She only had to keep Lexie and Billy apart till the birth and by that time, if everything went to plan, the bairn would be hers.

Chapter 25

John Brannan watched over wee Billy for three days, while he sweated and screamed through the horrors of the cravings for alcohol, while he clawed at his skin believing he was covered in ants and while he called out his dad's name again and again.

Then, when the alcohol had left his blood, John fed him soup and hot milk sweetened with sugar, never questioning him, nor berating him for his stupidity, just being there for Nancy's broken laddie. Then, shakily, he'd eased him out of his bed of pain and walked him around and around the small kitchen, till he was able to stand alone.

"How about a guid wash before you go home?" John asked, a full week since wee Billy had collapsed at his door. "I'll boil enough water and get the tin bath out from under the bed and there's that shirt and trousers you came here with to put on, all newly washed and pressed."

Billy nodded and wondered at the patience of the man. He'd hated him from the first time he saw him, sitting with his mother in their kitchen, laughing and making himself at home. A "fancy man" he'd called him, trying to take the place of his dead dad and his mother letting him. He shuddered at how he'd felt betrayed and hurt and had drunk even more rum to blot out the memory. But now.....

The warm water felt wonderful on Billy's sore skin and he soaked the bandage over his nose, finally, releasing the dressing into the bath. It felt strange to the touch, but the swelling had gone down and his eyes were focusing again and for the first time in a long time, he was truly sober.

Sitting face to face with John Brannan, drinking tea,

wondering if all of his kindness was to impress his mother and not to help him at all, wee Billy blurted out the question. "Are you doing this to get back in mum's good books?" he said, not sure that he wanted to know the answer.

John smiled. "I wondered when you'd ask me that," he said, "and to tell the truth I'd like your mum to see me as, at least, her friend, but whatever it was that we had, it's over and done with, thanks to Di Auchterlonie so, no, Billy, I did it for the laddie who was grieving for his dad, just like I'd grieved for mine, when he was killed at Loos, during the world war that was to end all wars, only it didn't."

Chastened by the reply, Billy got to his feet and extended his hand, feeling, instinctively, that this was a man he could trust. "Can we go walking in the hills sometime?" he asked, "if you're not too busy that is. John shook his hand, "I'll be here for you, Billy, whenever you need me, especially when the Kelly Brothers are around," he added, "they won't give up their free whisky easily." Billy nodded, grimly, "I won't give up easily either," he said, "especially when I know you're here."

His mother was stirring the pot of soup she always made at the weekend and Mary Anne had taken Kevin to Johnny the Italian's ice cream shop for a cone as a Saturday treat. Everything was as normal, except for wee Billy. Thanks to John Brannan not only had he survived the beating from the Kelly Brothers and the horrors of his body ridding itself of the drink, but he'd found a man he could go to for help when he needed it. He wasn't his dad, but John Brannan was alright.

For a minute that seemed like a lifetime, mother and son stood still, Billy scared to speak and Nancy scared to hear what he had to say. John Brannan had told her the sordid truth but she needed to hear it from her son. But the apology, when it came, was all that was needed for a smile break out across Nancy's face. There would be time later to hear wee Billy's side of the story and to try to accept how it had all gone so wrong for her son, but not now, now that he was back and safe once more, that was all that mattered.

"I suppose you'll be wanting some soup?" Nancy said, happily "and maybe an 'Aberdeen Buttery' with a bit o' your favourite cheese?" Wee Billy, pulled up a chair and looked around the roomy kitchen, compared to John Brannan's tiny room, this was huge. His mother's soup was second to none and with his appetite now back, Billy soon cleaned his plate and asked for more. "Did Mr Brannan not feed you then?" Nancy asked, wondering how long it would take for him to talk about it all, but just glad he seemed back to normal.

"Mr Brannan's alright," Billy said, solemnly, "if it hadn't been for him finding me last Saturday night," he added, "I might be dead by now." Nancy flinched visibly, "DEAD," she echoed, feigning disbelief, "but surely the Referee would have stopped the fight before any real damage was done?"

Billy ran his hands through his hair, just like his dad used to do, before telling his mother the truth, the whole truth. Nancy sat transfixed as her son told her about his drinking, the Kelly brothers and the non-existent Boxing Club he'd used as a cover to fool her into thinking he was involved in the sport. If anything, John had minimised the horror. "And when Mr Brannan found me in the close in William Lane, I'd been beaten up by the Kelly brothers and was so drunk I couldn't stand up." Billy's chin quivered at the memory, "so you see, mum, Mr Brannan saved my life and made me realise that rum wasn't the answer to what I couldn't fix by myself. The problem was.......I was scared of life without my dad in it, just like Mr Brannan had been when his dad had been killed fighting at Loos."

Nancy felt a wave of guilt hit her. She'd known wee Billy wasn't his usual self, but had put it down to his being young and headstrong, when all the time, he'd been grieving for his dad and like his dad, had taken to the drink to numb the fear of facing the world alone. And wasn't that what Billy Donnelly had done, when he'd had to face going to war, never knowing if he'd come back and when he did come back, finding she, Nancy, had been bedded by Jim Murphy and was pregnant!

Nancy clasped her hands together. Her son had been in distress, yet he couldn't come to her for help, she thought bleakly, but he'd been able to talk to John Brannan, a man he hated, but who took him in and looked after him till he was able to come home again. She felt guilt hit her again. This was the man she was determined to have sacked and for what? Being in love with her!

"Did you let Ernie Griffiths know anything?" Billy asked, breaking into her guilt.

"Only that you'd fallen and wouldn't be able to work for a wee while," Nancy told him, "but he'll be expecting you back next week......if you're able to climb the ladders, that is." "I'll be able," her son said, "and from now on, you don't have to worry about me getting drunk again, Mr Brannan's going to take me hill walking with him, just like dad used to do, if I get the cravings."

Nancy nodded and pointed to Billy's overalls hanging on the horse, white again. "They'll be ready for you," she said, "now let's try to forget the past and look to the future, our future together."

Nancy busied herself with the usual Saturday household chores, but her mind wouldn't settle and by evening time, she knew she had to face John Brannan and thank him for everything he'd done for wee Billy, before they returned to work on Monday. She knew she had an enemy in the shape of Di Auchteronie, so wanted to get the meeting with John over with away from her prying eyes, so it was with an anxious heart, she knocked at his door early on Sunday morning.

Unshaven and barely awake, John opened his door to Nancy. "I just wanted to say thanks for everything," she said, her eyes avoiding his, "and give you this." A freshly baked Apple Tart was offered on a plate and accepted.

"Has wee Billy told you everything then?" John asked. Nancy nodded. "Everything," she murmured, her mother's guilt returning and I'm sorry for......." But John stopped her from saying anything further. "Please," he said, "there's no need for you to be sorry about anything, it's me who should be saying sorry to you for wanting more than you were able to give."

Nancy didn't understand what he was meaning, she'd given herself to him, hadn't she, there was no more she could give, but it hadn't been enough and he'd chosen to also bed Di Auchterlonie! "Well," Nancy said, backing away from the door and shaking her head in confusion, "whatever it was I gave you, it seems that Di Auchterlonie gave you more, so let's leave it at that," she added, hurrying back down the stairs before any more could be said, leaving John and the Apple Tart behind.

"What was she talking about," John muttered to himself, as he closed the door and set the tart down on the table. He'd never laid a finger on Di Auchterlonie, in fact, he'd made it clear to her that even their 'tenuous friendship' was over, the night she'd told him about Jim Murphy being the father of Kevin, shattering his dream of a future with Nancy completely. He took a knife, sliced into the tart and began eating it, his early morning hunger ignoring his racing thoughts: could it be that Di was spinning a web of deceit to both of them? Telling Nancy that he had bedded Di and telling him that Nancy was no more than a slut and Kevin the result of her lust for Jim Murphy?

John washed and shaved and ate the last slice of tart. He had to pay a visit to Di Auchterlonie and, this time, he'd make sure she was telling him the truth about Nancy.

——oOo——

Chapter 26

Bo McGhee's flight touched down at Montrose Base at 15.00 hours on Sunday afternoon. He'd acted as co-pilot on the overnight journey, so needed coffee and then sleep in that order.

"There should be someone on duty in the Canteen," one of the ground crew told him, "and I'll let Squadron Leader Morris know you've arrived."

"Acknowledged," Bo said returning the salute, before making his way to the Canteen, shaking the stiffness out of his limbs as he walked.

It had only been seven months since Christmas, but it felt like an eternity for Bo. He looked around the near empty Canteen and remembered the last time he'd sat there with its Christmas decorations and balloons everywhere and smiled as he remembered his surprise appearance dressed as Santa Clause arriving in the snow. But now, there were no decorations and no snow and the drabness of the painted metal building echoed his mood.

And Lexie, he thought, what of Lexie? But before he could begin to imagine seeing her again, James Morris came into sight, his hand outstretched in welcome. "Wing Commander McGhee," he said, "we've been expecting you and your Quarters are ready." The men shook hands. "Wing Commander Kettlewell is looking forward to seeing you tomorrow, but in the meantime, if there's anything I can do, just ask."

Bo raised the empty coffee mug. "More of this would be good," he said, "then sleep."

James brought him a fresh mug of coffee. "Your old Quarters, next to Wing Commander Kettlewell's" he said, "are ready for you. Sleep well." James saluted Bo and left, if he'd understood correctly why Wing Commander McGhee was at Montrose, he'd kept it to himself, but if what he thought was true, the man was in for a rough ride.

Billy had received the phone call from Martin Kettlewell on the Saturday afternoon and couldn't wait. Bo McGhee was on the way from Canada and Billy would be at the base to confront him on Monday. Everything was coming together and once he understood his responsibilities to Lexie, the marriage would take place and the couple would become proud parents when the bairn came into the world. He felt sorry for Sarah, as the return of Bo McGhee meant that Lexie no longer needed to consider an adoption, but it also meant that he and Annie could go off to Belfast with a clear conscience knowing that Lexie would no longer be alone with her bairn.

Whether it was the time difference or the coffee or his uneasy mind, Bo couldn't sleep and by early evening, hunger had been added to the list. He washed and shaved and pulled on his 'civvies' and headed for the canteen. Once fed, he would knock on his Uncle Martin's door and try to gauge the warmth or otherwise of his reception. Martin Kettlewell knew very well the temptations of the flesh, but he was an honourable man and his ex-secretary made pregnant by his nephew wasn't sitting too well on his shoulders.

The Canteen was busier, with more civilians than air force personnel and Bo was glad he wasn't in uniform. But in or out of uniform, Winnie Adams recognised him at once. She had been with Lexie at the Christmas Party when Santa had revealed his true identity, surprising both his son and Lexie and it hadn't taken a genius to see that the handsome Canadian couldn't take his eyes off her.....then Billy Dawson had turned up at the Base in April, looking for the man who'd made Lexie pregnant! There was no doubt in Winnie's mind, Bo McGhee was that man.

She felt her temper rise as she watched him casually eating his meal, remembering when she'd feared she'd been made pregnant by Jack Forsyth, the Pilot Officer she had fallen for when she'd been a young WAAF. Lexie had stood by her then and although it turned out to be a false alarm, Winnie never forgot her friend's staunch support and understanding. Billy Dawson needed to know the man was here at the Base and as soon as her shift was over, she'd telephone the number he had left with her in April.

"Won't be a minute" she told her mum when she got home, "just need to make a telephone call." Clutching Billy Dawson's number, she hurried to the telephone box and making sure she had enough sixpences, she dialled the number.

"Dundee 102, Mr Dawson speaking." Winnie pressed the button and connected the call. "Mr Dawson," she said loudly, "it's Winnie, Winnie Adams from Montrose."

"This is a surprise, Winnie," Billy said, "is everything alright?"

"He's here," Winnie shouted, "the man you've been looking for. He's at the Base at Montrose and I thought you should know.....what with Lexie and all..."

Billy almost whooped with delight. Although he knew about Bo McGhee's arrival, it was a relief to know that he'd actually landed and that the meeting would definitely go ahead.

"You're a good girl, Winnie," Billy told her, "I will be at the Base tomorrow and we'll get this thing sorted out once and for all."

The telephone began to' beep', indicating that the call was about to be disconnected unless Winnie put another sixpence in; but before she could do so, the line went dead. Winnie took a deep breath and replaced the receiver. If Bo McGhee thought he'd got away with what he'd done to Lexie, tomorrow he'd find out he hadn't!

Martin Kettlewell had just finished eating his Supper and was savouring a measure of Scottish Whisky and Canada Dry when he heard the knock at his door. There was only one person that it could be, as no one on the Base knew he was back except Squadron Leader James Morris and he would have telephoned.

"Come in Bo," he called, "it's open."

Bo tried to gauge the warmth of his uncle's welcome, but Martin Kettlewell was giving nothing away.

"Good flight?" he asked.

"Long," Bo said, "got in this afternoon, but couldn't sleep......
so, here I am."

"Do you admit it then?" Martin asked into the tension. "Are
you the father of Lexie's child?"

Bo's lips tightened. If he thought his Uncle would have been
easy on him, he was wrong.

"We did make love, once, before I flew back to Canada at
Christmas," Bo said, "so provided there was nobody............"
Martin felt his anger rise and silenced Bo from going any
further. "If you're trying to tell me that Lexie Melville is a slut
and that she could be pregnant to anyone, then you disappoint
me, Bo and if you want to remain a nephew of mine, you'll stand
up like a man and do what's right by her."

Bo felt ashamed of himself for trying to throw doubt on
Lexie's claim. "I'm sorry, Uncle," he said "I didn't mean that, I'm
just at a loss as to what to do about it all."

"Well, you'll have a chance to deal with it tomorrow. Lexie's
step-father, Mr Dawson, will be here to make sure you face up
to your 'mistake' and I will be backing him up to the hilt." Martin
drained his glass, "now, I'd advise you to get some sleep,
tomorrow is going to hard for all of us, but especially for Lexie's
stepfather."

Bo was being dismissed by his Uncle and his shame
increased. If only Angela had agreed to divorce him, all of this
could have turned out so differently, but she wouldn't, leaving
him with nothing to offer Lexie but apologies and money if she'd
take it, but no marriage.

Back in his Quarters, Bo took out his hip flask and drained
the contents dry. Tomorrow he'd face whatever fate threw at
him, but it wasn't meant to be like this, not like this at all. Bo
closed his eyes and fell into an uneasy alcohol- induced sleep
and dreamed of Lexie and what he'd done.

—-—oOo—-—

Chapter 27

Di Auchterlonie felt a rush of colour flush her cheeks as she opened the door to John Brannan. The last time he'd been with her, he'd made it plain that he wanted nothing to do with her, but here he was and hope returned to her breast.

"You've caught me unawares," she flustered, trying to pat her hair into some sort of shape, "but you're very welcome," she added, demurely, stepping back to let John enter, "very welcome."

John removed his bonnet and rolled it into his pocket. "We need to talk," he said, pulling up a chair, uninvited, before nodding towards the other kitchen chair, indicating she should sit down. Di could see he was in no mood for the social niceties and she did as she was bid.

"I'll get right to the point," John said, "and depending how you answer my question will indicate where we go from here." Di's eyes widened, he'd said 'we', she told herself, did this mean he wanted to be with her after all? But her hopes were dashed when he uttered the next 'three little words.'

"It's about Nancy." Di felt her eyes narrow a she let the words sink in: she'd told him all about her 'old friend', albeit with a little varnishing of the truth, but it was Nancy's word against hers. But he'd now rejected Nancy, so what else could he want to know?

She crossed her arms defensively. "Whit aboot her?"

John crossed his arms in return. "Did you tell her that you and me were 'together'" John asked, "as in...together in bed?"

Di felt the colour drain from her face. She hadn't exactly said as much to Nancy, but she'd made sure that the other Weavers did the job for her. "NO, I DIDNAE," she spat, "but I'm no' responsible for whut the ither wimmen might have telt her."

"Other women?" John asked, "what other women?"

"The ither Weavers, of coorse", Di sniffed, "everybody kens Nancy Donnelly's a man eater, and when they saw me and you in the Thrums, they just put two and two thegither and lost nae time in tellin' her, that you fancied me. Espechlly, efter she'd covered me wi' mulk in the Canteen in a fit o'jealousy!." Di concluded her speech with a 'humph.'

John felt his knuckles form into fists. Every time he'd been seen out with Di Auchterlonie, trying to get her to act as 'go between' on his behalf, she'd been feeding her fantasies to the other Weavers to goad Nancy and do her dirty work for her. How could he have been so stupid!

"I've one more question," John said keeping his voice unemotional while his insides were in turmoil. "Is Jim Murphy Kevin's dad?"

"Everybody thinks so," Di blurted out, "ask onybody aboot Nancy's last fancy man, they'll tell you Jim Murphy was in her bed when her man was in France and the next thing we ken, she's gonna hae a bairn! An' Nae prizes fir guessin' who's the daddy!" she quipped, knowingly, fixing him with her watery eyes and gap-toothed grin.

John clenched his teeth. Di was sticking to her story and he felt his heart break again. Was he just the next 'fancy man' to be used and then dropped when someone better came along? "You'd better not be lying about this Di," he told her, "if I find out Jim Murphy isn't Kevin's dad, I'll be back and you'll be the sorriest lassie in Dundee."

Fearfully, Di jumped up and with hands on hips, screamed at him. "I'm only tellin' you whut abody else is sayin' aboot yir precious Nancy," she said, "and you can believe it or no' if you like." She knew now there would be no happy ending for her, but she was still determined that there would be no happy ending for Nancy and John Brannan either.

Wee Billy was sitting on the stairs to his flat when John returned from his visit to Di Auchterlonie. The lad was looking better and John shook his hand. "Glad to see you again, Billy," he said, "are you coming in for a while?"

Billy nodded. "I'd like that," he said, "and I need to speak to you about mum," he added, "there's something you need to know."

"Sounds serious," John said, opening his door and leading the way into his kitchen.

"It's about Kevin." John held up his hand to stop him going any further, "I know about Kevin," he said and about Jim Murphy being his dad too," thanks to Di Auchterlonie.

"Is that what she told you?" wee Billy gasped.

John's eyes narrowed. "I've just come from her house and asked her that very question and she was adamant that Kevin's dad is Jim Murphy."

"I think you might need a cuppa' tea when you hear what I have to say," Billy said, "so you'd best put the kettle on."

"I love my dad," Billy began when the tea had been poured, "but he was weak, not just when it came to drink but also when it came to women and one woman in particular.....a prostitute called Gladys Kelly. Long before dad went to war, he'd began spending any spare time and money he had on the woman, leaving mum broken-hearted and there was nothing anyone could do to stop him.

Then, when the war broke out and dad joined the Scots Guards, mum tried to make the marriage work, but dad was having none of it and would spend his leave with Gladys Kelly and not at home." John stared at the teacup in front of him, scared to take a sip lest Billy stopped speaking. "Go on," he said. "Well, during the war, mum and Di Auchterlonie began to go dancing, at the Palais I think, and that's where Jim Murphy met mum and convinced her that they could have a life together, until that is, his wife found out and that's when Granddad sacked him." John nodded, so that's how the sacking came about, he realised, Billy Dawson had paid the man off for using Nancy and deceiving his own wife.

"But, someone wrote and told my dad that Jim Murphy had been seen coming out of our house and he came home on 'compassionate leave' to sort things out." Billy's voice dropped to a near-whisper, "that's when he 'forced himself' on mum and threatened to kill her, before he stormed out and back to Gladys Kelly. Kevin was the result." John tried to force down his anger at Billy Donnelly and Jim Murphy's behaviour. If only Nancy had told him all this and Di Auchterlonie hadn't lied to him, perhaps they'd still be together, but too much water had flowed under the bridge for that to happen now.

John grimaced. "And why are you telling me this now?" he asked.

"Because you're a good man, John Brannan and it was thanks to me that mum turned you out. I was as bad as all the rest, despite knowing the truth, but I know now, that was the drink talking that day in our kitchen, and once you sobered me up and made me understand about missing my dad, I knew that I had been wrong about you."

John stood and shook Billy's hand, "it takes a big man to admit he's wrong and an even bigger man to forgive the past hurt," he said "and I'm glad you see me now as a friend and not the enemy."

John sat for a long time after wee Billy had gone, allowing the sadness of Nancy's life to settle into his soul. All she'd ever wanted was to be loved by a decent man who'd look after her and make her happy, but what she'd got was Billy Donnelly and Jim Murphy. No wonder she was wary of him and rightly so, when she'd needed him he'd let her down, like all the rest. And he couldn't blame Di Auchterlonie for that, John Brannan had only himself to blame.

Chapter 28

Billy drove to the Montrose Base ready to face whatever the day and Bo McGhee would bring. He'd already decided he was a 'wrong-un' but determined he would hear him out. After all, if all went as he planned, Bo would be his son-in-law.

Bo and Martin Kettlewell watched from the Comms Office window as Billy Dawson's car was waved through by the Guard and drew up at the front of the building.

Bo had never met Billy Dawson, but could see at a glance that he wasn't a man to be crossed. His whole demeanour was summed up in one word, strength. Tall and well built and with a purposeful walk, he came to the Office door and Bo knew his only hope was to be truthful and willing to do anything to appease Lexie's step-father except, of course, marry her.

A Secretary asked his name and picked up a telephone. "Mr Dawson is here to see you," she said, before nodding at the answer. "Wing Commander Kettlewell is expecting you," she said, "if you'll follow me?" After all the weeks of worry and distress that Annie and Lexie had had to endure, Billy was at last going to meet the elusive Mr McGhee.

Both men were standing when Billy entered the office, almost identically clad in their dress uniforms. "Mr Dawson," Martin said, "allow me to introduce Wing Commander McGhee from the Royal Canadian Air Force." Bo took a step forward and extended his hand but Billy remained unmoved. The man was very handsome, he gave him that and he could see what Lexie found attractive about him. However, 'never judge a book by its cover', he reminded himself, Bo McGhee may look honourable on the surface, but he couldn't hide behind his uniform and position for much longer, when the wrong he had done Lexie would be put to him. Bo felt himself tense as his offer of a handshake was rejected. "Maybe we should all sit down", Martin Kettlewell said "and try to get some understanding of what's been happening with your step-daughter and also my ex-Secretary, Lexie Melville. I would also add that Bo is a nephew of mine, but I can assure you, that will have no bearing on what is agreed here today to resolve the problem."

Billy's eyes narrowed and fixed onto Bo McGhee, "there's only one problem as I see it," he began, glaring at Bo McGhee, "this man took advantage of Lexie's feelings and trust, to talk her into going to bed with him, before returning to Canada with his son, never to contact Lexie again, despite her letters telling him that she was pregnant and he was the father."

Martin Kettlewell felt his heart sink, Billy Dawson couldn't have been clearer. Bo had taken advantage of Lexie to satisfy his own lust, then ditched her when he'd found out she was pregnant. "Answer the man, Bo," he said, refusing to look at his nephew.

Bo directed his full attention to Billy and began his answer. "During the war, Lexie and I met at Lossiemouth and fell in love, or so I thought. She agreed to marry me, but on the way over to Canada where we were to wed, she changed her mind and married the Captain of the ship called Robertson who had been her childhood sweetheart." Billy nodded, he knew all this, but a woman was allowed to change her mind and it was better she married the man she truly loved that live a lie. "Go on," he said, never taking his eyes of Bo's face. "I couldn't believe it, but had to accept her decision. To say my heart was broken is an understatement, I almost went out of my mind trying to accept what had happened and spent the next few weeks in Quebec, going from bar to bar........till one night, I met Angela Lafeyette. I didn't know it then, but Angela was what was called 'a good time gal,' and made it her business to show me that she could love me, far better than any other woman and before I knew it, we were married in Quebec."

Billy sighed audibly, "If you think I'm feeling sorry for you, then you're wrong," he said, "my problem isn't your 'good time gal' but what you've done to Lexie."

Bo nodded, before continuing. "It didn't take long before I realised that the marriage had been a mistake, but by that time, Angela announced that she was pregnant and 9 months later, Louie was born." Bo's words softened at the mention of his son's name. "I loved him from the minute I saw him, but I couldn't live with Angela any longer, so we made an agreement, that Louie could stay with me as often as my duties would allow and that I would pay money into Angela's bank account every month to cover the cost of everything Louie needed, but the marriage was over. Once this was in place, I returned to Moose Jaw and in1939 the war broke out and in 1943 I was sent overseas to Lossiemouth to fly the Lancasters in bombing raids over Norway and that's where Lexie came into the story."

"That's all very interesting Mr McGhee," Billy said, a degree of impatience creeping into his words, "but I'm more interested in what you're going to do about Lexie and YOUR bairn."

"I was coming to that Mr Dawson," Bo said, "but you need to understand that as far as I knew, Lexie had married someone else and that I'd never see her again, that is, until my Uncle, I mean, Wing Commander Kettlewell, got in touch and told me Lexie was now a widow and working at Montrose Base as his Secretary." Bo studied his boots for a while, remembering the elation he'd felt at the news. Lexie was alive and back in his life.

"I loved her when we first met," he told Billy "and realised that I loved her still and decided to do everything in my power to get to Montrose and let her know how I felt and hoped that there was still some glimmer of love in her heart for me. Well, Mr Dawson, there was, and that Christmas night before I flew back to Canada, we both realised that we were in love and...... well.......you know the rest."

"So you admit the bairn is yours?" Billy demanded to know.

"Of course, I admit the child is mine," Bo said, "but the story isn't finished. As soon as I got back to Canada I went straight to see Angela and demanded a divorce, but she refused." Bo shrugged in disbelief at the memory, "she said she'd never let me see Louie again and that she'd die before she let me go. She's Catholic, you see, and they believe in marriage 'till death do us part.'"

Billy could see where Bo's story was leading and it wasn't to a happy ending for Lexie. "She wrote to you several times, telling you about the pregnancy," Billy said, "but got no reply, answer me that one!" Bo held his head in his hands. "I never opened them," he said, "it was bad enough knowing that Lexie and I could never be together as husband and wife, but losing Louie if I went against Angela's wishes, was something I couldn't bear." Billy could see genuine tears in the man's eyes. "The first I knew about the pregnancy was when Uncle Martin told me that you'd been looking for me and that Lexie was pregnant. So, I'm here now and will do whatever it is that you wish in order to make things up to Lexie.......but I can't marry her."

There was no more to be said. Billy folded his arms and shook his head. His idea of forcing Bo to marry Lexie was a non-starter but, he decided, it was up to Bo to tell Lexie himself about his wife in Canada and then it would be up to her what she wanted done about the man.

"My wish," Billy said, "is that you come with me to Dundee NOW, and face Lexie like a man and tell her what you've told me, then it will be up to her what happens to you." Bo felt his blood rush through his heart, telling Lexie was going to be the hardest thing he'd ever have to do and then leaving her and his unborn child behind when he had to go back to Angela, was going to be even harder.

"Can I suggest something," Martin Kettlewell intervened, "perhaps it would be best if you spoke to Lexie first.....gauge from her what she wants to do regarding a meeting with Wing Commandeer McGhee, before we go any further?"

"And waste more time," Billy shot back, "time for......him.....to fly back to Canada again?"

Martin Kettlewell nodded in understanding. "Mr Dawson," he began, "you have my word as an officer and a gentleman that my nephew will be here until this situation is resolved, one way or another."

Billy pondered the words. Perhaps Martin Kettlewell was right. It might be too much of a shock to Lexie to have Bo McGhee just turn up, unannounced, especially with the news that there would be no marriage. "Very well," he said, "I will return to Dundee alone and once I've spoken to my step-daughter, I will telephone you with her wishes." And with a final look of scorn directed at Bo, Billy walked out of the office.

Chapter 29

Wee Billy came home from his visit to John Brannan, his shame at how he'd behaved towards him when he'd been grief-stricken and fuelled by drink, was gone. He'd made amends with John, now he needed to do the same with his mum. Confession, he had found, was good for the soul. He waited until Kevin was asleep in his cot and Mary Anne was out with her pal, now was as good a time as any, he felt, to broach the subject of John Brannan.

"I was speaking to Mr Brannan earlier on," he said, to no one in particular, "and I think he'd like to come over sometime...... .just for a wee visit, maybe?" Nancy turned away from putting more coal on the fire and eyed her son with a very suspicious eye. She knew she was grateful to John for his help with wee Billy, but his bedding of Di Auchterlonie was a step too far for her to tolerate allowing him back into her life.

"That's very nice, son," she said, "but I think Mr Brannan has other things on his mind that don't include us."

"Like what?"

Nancy lit a cigarette and sat down in her chair by the fireside. "If you must know," she said, blowing a stream of tobacco smoke into the air, "like Di Auchterlonie."

"Mmmmm!" Billy said, "would that be the same Di Auchterlonie that told John that Jim Murphy was Kevin's dad?"

Nancy almost dropped the cigarette onto her lap, as a surge of anger coursed through her. "SHE WHAT!"

Billy began to repeat the statement but Nancy stopped him. "No need to tell me again," she said, puffing at the cigarette until she was almost dizzy, "I knew she was up to something with

164

John Brannan, but thought she was just trying it on, but now...
..now I know different." Wee Billy waited as his mum's emotions
took over.

"And he believed her?" Nancy queried, angrily, hurt at John's
lack of trust in her. "And why didn't he ask me himself?" she
ranted on, "I've nothing to hide."

Wee Billy tried not to smile; his mum really did fancy John
Brannan to get herself in this state. "Maybe he tried," he said,
but thanks to me and my stupidity, you wouldn't let him near
you." Nancy's mind went back, to demanding John return the
key to her house and refusing to speak to him any further. Was
that where all this had begun with Di Auchterlonie?

But Nancy still rankled at the smug face of Di in the Canteen
when she'd poured milk over her to shut her up from boasting
about John Brannan and her being 'an item.'

She tossed the cigarette end into the fire, the fight ebbing out
of her. Too much water had passed under the bridge, she
fretted, to mend her troubled soul. Tomorrow was another day,
there would be work to do, Kevin to look after and plenty of
time to regret the past, but tonight, she just wanted to be alone
with her thoughts and feelings about her life since Billy
Donnelly's death, happy or sad, good or bad, but unable to be
altered. Life was what it was and, for Nancy, the fickle hand of
fate always seemed to win.

She looked at her son. "Be happy," she said, quietly, "live your
life as best you can and remember that your mum loves you."

"And I love you too mum," Billy responded, a tear glistening
in his eyes "and I'm sorry for giving you so much worry."

Nancy nodded, she had her son back and that was all that
mattered.

Billy started the drive back from Montrose to speak to Lexie,
but took a detour to Forfar to see Annie first. He'd hoped that
Bo McGhee would agree to marry Lexie once Billy had
threatened him enough, but now that he'd found out that the
man was already married, he realised that Lexie was going to
have to bring the bairn into the world without a husband,
whether she liked it or not and he could see life in Ireland with

their son, slipping away.

Isabella opened the door and welcomed him in. "Annie's in the kitchen," she said; smiling at the probability of her being anywhere else in the house, "and she's been fine," she whispered, "quiet, but fine."

Billy nodded his thanks, "I need to speak to her Isabella," he said, "alone."

"I understand," she said, stepping aside, "let me know if you need me."

Billy took a deep breath. "Annie," he called, gently, as he opened the kitchen door, the smell of baking wafting over him, "can I come in?"

At the sound of her husband's voice, Annie turned to face him and ran into his arms.

"Oh! Billy," she murmured, "I've missed you so much and I'm so glad you're here."

Billy hugged her tightly. "And, I've got news," he said, "about Bo McGhee."

Annie dropped her arms from his neck in astonishment. "You've found him?"

"I've found him," Billy repeated, "but let's get a cup of tea brewing, I'm parched and then I'll tell you all about it."

Annie bustled about the kitchen; now that Bo McGhee had been found, Lexie would be married and the bairn would have a father. But, once Billy told her the story of the wife in Canada and the impossibility of a divorce, she began to wilt. "So, there'll be no marriage?" she asked, wearily, already knowing the answer. Billy shook his head. "So," he said, "Lexie has some decisions to make and I think it best if we face this together."

Annie knew how hard it would be for Billy to remain in Dundee while their son lived in Ireland, but her love for Lexie and her need to be there for her, over-rode the option of going back there, together. "I'm ready," Annie said, "I'll just tell Isabella we're going."

Two hours later, Billy and Annie walked up the stairs to their house in Albert Street. Billy telephoned Lexie at Sarah's and asked her if they could come and speak with her as a matter of some urgency. Lexie agreed, more confused than ever, thinking her mother was in Irelend, only to find out she was in Dundee and that she and Billy wanted to speak to her urgently! Charlie and Sarah were both at work, so Lexie had the house to herself as usual; she'd been spending so much time alone with her thoughts, she'd begun to realise why 'waiting for the bairn to arrive' was called 'Confinement.' Truth be told, she was dreading the time when she'd be a mother with the bairn totally dependent on her for everything!

The knock at the door, though expected, made Lexie jump. Before she even saw her mother again, she could feel a lump forming in her throat at the impending encounter. She wrapped her hand protectively around the unborn bairn in her womb and took a deep breath. "C'mon," she whispered, "your grandma's come to visit us."

Whether it was Lexie or whether it was Annie who made the first move, it didn't matter, within seconds of seeing one another again, mother and daughter broke down, hugging one another for dear life. "Can we come in?" Billy finally asked, "we've just driven all the way from Forfar and could do with a nice cuppa tea."

Lexie wiped the tears from her face, "FORFAR," she exclaimed, I thought mum was in……." Billy smiled, "No Lexie," he said, "and if you'd have let me finish my telephone call to you, you'd have found that out."

"So, you've not gone to live in Ireland?" Lexie asked, gazing at her mother, wide-eyed with happiness.

"No," Billy answered before Annie could ask him any awkward questions, "but something has happened that you need to know about."

The trio hurried to the kitchen, Billy and Annie finding a seat at the large table, while Lexie made the tea.

Once settled Lexie looked expectantly at Billy, "well," she said, "what is it that I need to know?"

Billy glanced at Annie, who nodded her approval.

"Bo McGhee is at the Montrose Base," he said, "and he admits that the bairn is his."

Lexie almost dropped her cup, as her hand began to shake. "You've spoken to him?" she asked Billy, incredulously. Billy nodded, "I've spoken to him..... but the question is do YOU want to speak to him?"

Lexie tried to calm her thoughts. Bo was at Montrose! But so many questions began tumbling from her heart; why hadn't he replied to her letters, did he still love her, would they marry as he'd promised, when would he come for her......."YES," she said, "I want to speak to him, of course I do and I want to see him, he's the bairn's father." Her hand cradled her womb again as happiness filled her being, Bo had come for her, she knew he would, she'd prayed and prayed and God had answered at last. All thoughts of living alone with no man to support her and the bairn, flew out of the window. "Will he come here to see me?" Lexie asked, eagerly, "or maybe I should move back home with you and mum and meet Bo at Albert Street?"

"Now, now" Billy cautioned, "are you sure you want to see him?" Lexie frowned; what on earth was Billy talking about, with Bo back in her life, everything would be wonderful. Billy and her mum could go off to Ireland to live, as she would be married and going to Canada once the bairn was born and life would be just wonderful.

"Alright," Billy said, "I'll telephone Wing Commander Kettlewell and let him know Sarah's address, don't want you having to move again so soon, unsettling yourself and Sarah and, anyway, I'm sure she'd want to meet the bairn's dad, don't you?"

Lexie blinked back a tear of happiness. Sarah would be so pleased that everything was going to work out and she needn't worry about her or the bairn anymore.

Billy had considered telling Lexie the whole truth about Bo McGhee, but couldn't bring himself to be the bearer of such bad news. Anyway, he reasoned, it was Bo McGhee that had caused this mess, so it was up to him to face the music. And if Sarah's option of adopting Lexie's bairn came to pass, then she should meet the man who was the father.

The telephone call to the Wing Commander was brief. Lexie would see Bo McGhee the following day at 4 o'clock in the afternoon when Sarah would be home from school. He gave her address and replaced the receiver in its cradle.

"What's going to happen?" Annie asked, anxiously. Billy joined her on the sofa and held her hand, "whatever happens tomorrow," he said, "you AND me will be here when she needs us." Annie's eyes clouded over, "but that would mean...." Billy hushed her with a kiss, "I know," he said, "we won't be going to Ireland after all." Picking up the telephone again, he dialled Sarah's number and gave Lexie the news.

When Sarah came home from school, Lexie rushed to the door to meet her. She couldn't wait to tell her the good news. "Bo's at Montrose," she squealed, before Sarah had the chance to even remove her coat. At first, she didn't realise what Lexie was talking about. "Bow" she said, "as in ribbons and bows?"

"No, silly," Lexie grinned, "Bo McGhee, the bairn's father." Sarah felt her legs buckle and had to, quickly, sit down. Bo McGhee was in Scotland and all of her plans to be the bairn's mum, began disappearing like April snow.

"He's coming tomorrow at 4 o'clock, so you can meet him yourself and " Lexie added wistfully, "you're going to love him." Sarah nodded dumbly. There were no words to say, that would ease the emptiness that now filled her heart, as Lexie glowed before her. "I'm happy for you," she murmured, "but I think I need a lie down."

"Is everything alright?" she heard Lexie ask, her voice wondering why Sarah wasn't jumping for joy along with her. But there was no answer, just the closing of the door.

Chapter 30

Nancy's swirling thoughts had kept her awake most of the night and by the time the6 o'clock alarm clanged on Monday morning, she struggled to open her eyes, but Kevin's squeals forced her to react and she stumbled from bed.

"C'mon, King Kevin," she said, lifting him from his cot, "time and tide wait for no man, or woman for that matter, let's get you fed." A yawning Mary Anne trooped through from the back room, she'd stayed later than she should have at her pal Amy's house and was regretting it now.

"Start the porridge, will you?" Nancy asked, "while I get Kevin washed and dressed."

Gradually, energy began to build as Nancy's body wakened up and the start of another working week at Baxters began. Wee Billy, was the last to come into the kitchen, already dressed in his painters overalls and sober are a judge. Nancy smiled, she had all her family around her and had so much to be thankful for. From now on, she'd be happy with her life and stop searching for a man to come along and love her. She'd had enough heartache and as for John Brannan,

Di Auchterlonie was welcome to him!

For the next hour the kitchen was a hive of activity. Nancy's family rushing through the morning routine of washing, pulling on work-clothes and filling up on porridge, but by 7 o'clock, wee Billy had gone off to Ernie Griffiths house, Mary Anne was on her way to Baxters and Nancy was hurrying along the Cowgate to the nursery with Kevin.

"Here he is!" the Nurse said, taking Kevin by the hand, "the best wee laddie in Scotland." Nancy smiled, "I'll be back at the end of the shift," she said, "and be good," she added, patting Kevin on the head.

"Just a minute," the nurse called after her, I need to get in touch with Kevin's auntie but I've lost the telephone number she gave me. Nancy looked confused; surely Lexie wasn't trying to get her bairn into the nursery before it was even born? The nurse waited. "Sorry," Nancy said, "I didn't realise you could find a place for a bairn that hasn't been born yet?"

The nurse laughed. "Don't be daft," she said, "she was looking for work till her bairn arrived, but maybe she's changed her mind?"

"NO, no," Nancy told her hurriedly, "is there work for her here then?"

"There could be," the nurse said, "but if I can't get in touch with her, we'll look for someone else."

Nancy quickly scribbled her dad's telephone number on a scrap of paper and gave it to the nurse. "Her name's Melville, by the way, Lexie Melville."

Well, Nancy thought, as she hurried to the Weaving Flat, good for Lexie. It would have been easy to pass the bairn to Annie and her dad to bring up, but it looked like she was going to keep it and look after it herself.

The Weavers were spreading out across the flat, each one 'knocking on' to her pair of looms when Nancy hurried to her pair and set them going. This was what life was all about, she told herself, work and family and keeping away from gossips and men.

She'd visit Lexie at the weekend and hope that there was good news about the job at the nursery. The women hadn't been close over the years, but now that Lexie had come down from the lofty heights of being a WAAF and a Secretary to a Wing Commander at Montrose, she could see that, underneath, she was just like her, trying to survive in a world that had gone mad during six years of war and it was now 'survival of the fittest.'

Nancy was so lost in thought, she hadn't realised the dinner-time bummer had sounded and the Weaving Flat was quietening down as the looms were switched off. "Do you have a minute Nancy?" John Brannan's voice sounded in her ear, as she made her way to join the others heading for the Canteen.

"Not now, Mr Brannan," she said, hurrying on.

"Maybe later," John called to her disappearing back, but there was no answer.

John returned to the Overseer's desk in the Weaving Flat, took his flask of tea and sandwich from his haversack and began eating,if only Nancy would give him a chance to let her know he'd been wrong not to trust her and since the visit from wee Billy, when he'd felt renewed hope that there could be a future for them, he had to find a way to make her understand about everything, especially Di Auchterlonie and her lies.

Sarah had to brace herself to face Lexie at breakfast. The thought of teaching a class full of pupils, especially after Charlie's reaction to the arrival of Bo McGhee had left her bereft, with his delight that the father of Lexie's bairn had been found and was coming to see her that very day.

She turned up late at the breakfast table, and mumbled something about a headache before promising an excited Lexie that she'd be home in time to meet Bo McGhee.

"Don't forget!" Lexie called after her, oblivious to Sarah's bleakness.

Charlie left almost immediately after his wife, leaving Lexie alone with just the clock for company, that she couldn't take her eyes off, as it slowly ticked away the minutes to 4 o'clock.

At 3 o'clock Wing Commander Kettlewell's motor arrived at Albert Street. "Wait here," he told the driver, "we won't be long and we have a further meeting at 4 o'clock elsewhere."

The driver saluted as Martin Kettlewell, followed by Bo, stepped onto the pavement.

Both men looked around them at the grey tenements and rooftops of smoking chimneys. "This is where Lexie lives?" Bo asked, almost in disbelief. "It's Dundee, Bo, a working city fully of jute mills and hard-working people." Bo nodded towards the dark close leading to Lexie's home. "And is this where my child will live?"

Martin could see where Bo's mind was going. "It's not

Canada," he said, "but its Lexie's home and, yes, it's where your child will live."

The men climbed the dark stairwell to the front door and Martin Kettlewell knocked firmly. The door was opened by Billy, who nodded them through to the parlour where Annie was seated on the edge of the sofa.

"This is Lexie's mother, Mrs Annie Dawson," Billy said, "Wing Commander Martin Kettlewell and Bo McGhee," Billy told Annie, making the introduction. Annie felt overwhelmed by the two uniformed men who seemed to fill the room, but especially the figure of Bo McGhee. She didn't think she'd seen a man so handsome and quickly understood why Lexie had fallen for him. Don't judge the book by its cover, she told herself, this is the man who made Lexie pregnant, then deserted her and, if it hadn't been for Billy, he'd still be in Canada.

"Lexie isn't here at the moment," Billy said, "she's living with a very good friend of hers, who also happens to be my daughter. She is expecting you, Mr McGhee, to visit her at 16.00 hours," Billy stated, formally, making sure he used the military timescale, lest there be any doubt.

The Wing Commander turned to Annie. "I'm sorry, Mrs Dawson," he said, "that this circumstance has been brought to your door, but I am confident things will be resolved to everyone's satisfaction very soon." He turned to Bo, "the driver will take you to see Lexie and will wait for you, before returning here." His attention then turned to Billy, "if you'd be so kind to let Wing Commander McGhee have the address, he'll be on his way and I'd appreciate if you allow me to wait here till he returns."

"I'll make us some tea," Annie announced, finding her voice and, hastily, leaving the parlour to seek the refuge of her kitchen. She listened while Bo McGhee's footsteps faded before beginning to quietly sob. She knew the man's intention was to tell Lexie they couldn't marry and there was nothing she could do to protect her daughter from the hurt that would surely follow.

Lexie watched from behind the net curtains as Bo McGhee stepped from the Air Force motor car and her heart leapt, as a rush of love overwhelmed her. It didn't matter about anything else now, Bo was here and everything would be alright. Before he could even knock on the door, Lexie threw it open and flew into his arms. "Bo," she breathed, taking in the sight and scent of him, "you've come for me....I knew you would."

This wasn't how their romance was meant to work out, Bo's heart told him, folding his arms around Lexie. Angela was supposed to divorce him and Lexie would then become his wife and live with him and Louie in Canada, not exist in this awful grim world that was Lexie's lot.

"Come through," she said, "let me tell you about our child, I just hope he's as handsome as his dad." Bo followed her into the bright parlour over-looking the garden, "you know it's a boy?" he asked in disbelief. "No, of course not," Lexie replied, grinning, "I just hope it is." Her eyes were sparkling and not even in the plain dress that covered the bump could she hide the bloom of happiness that enveloped her. But Bo said nothing and Lexie felt her euphoria at seeing him deflate a little at his silence.

"Is everything alright?" she asked, a frisson of concern making its way into her heart. But there was still no response from the silent Bo.

"Everything is alright, isn't it?" Lexie asked again.

"Perhaps we should sit down," he said, grimly, there's something you need to know."

Slowly, Bo began to break Lexie's heart all over again. There would be no marriage, no life in Canada and no happy family. Bo was married to Angela and would remain so till the day she died, he told her, and she would make sure he'd never see Louie again if he tried to leave her.

All the dreams Lexie had allowed herself to believe could happen, crumbled to dust with his words. "You'd best go then," she said, her voice flat and emotionless, "we don't need you Bo," Lexie added, turning to face him, "I have people here who truly love me and who'll also love MY child when he's born, so fly away back to Angela and Canada and may God forgive you for what you've done, because I cannot."

"I'm sorry, Lexie," Bo said, "if there was any way I could make this right, you know I would......if it's a question of money, you just have to ask and I'll send you whatever you want....."

"SHUT UP AND GO," Lexie shouted, the tears of hurt just holding back, "there's nothing I want from you now or in the future." Her eyes held his until he couldn't look at her any longer. "Goodbye Lexie," he said, "be happy."

Lexie watched as he climbed into the back of the motor car, just as Sarah neared the gate. She hadn't had the courage to meet Bo McGhee in person, but could see by the look on his face that the meeting with Lexie hadn't gone well.

Sarah quickened her step into the house and opened the parlour door where Lexie sat, motionless and bleak.

"What happened?" she asked, taking Lexie's hand in hers. Lexie turned to face her. "There won't be a marriage," she whispered, "he's already married in Canada."

Sarah felt such a wave of sympathy for Lexie, for a minute she couldn't speak.

Even her own desire to adopt the bairn faded in shame that she'd tried to benefit from Lexie's disgrace. "We don't need him," Sarah said stoutly, "we'll manage one way or another and I won't let you down Lexie, nor will Charlie."

Silently, tears began to course down Lexie's cheeks. She'd been so sure that Bo would take her away to Canada and a wonderful life, but fate had decided otherwise, Lexie had been forced back to Dundee and despite all her efforts to break free from the jute mills and poverty, that's where she would have to stay.

The driver of Wing Commander Kettlewell's motor sounded the horn. "Look after Lexie," Martin said to Billy, preparing to leave and knowing what Bo would have told her, "she's a wonderful young woman and she's been through a lot, but with you and Mrs Dawson to support her, I'm sure everything will turn out for the best."

"No thanks to your nephew!" Billy retorted, leading Martin to the door, "you'll understand if I don't shake your hand," Billy added, before slamming the door behind the Wing Commander.

Annie stared at her hands, flexing the knuckles to try to get some circulation into their coldness. "C'mon," Billy said, "Lexie's needs you more than ever now, so get your coat and we'll take a walk up to Sarah's and let her know we're here for her as long as she needs us." Annie nodded, grasping Billy's hand. She knew what the words meant and thanked God for Billy's strength. He'd stay with her in Dundee and their son John would have to accept that there would be no future for them all in Ireland.

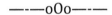

Chapter 31

Sarah opened the door to Annie and her dad. "Ssshhhh!" she hushed, "Lexie's exhausted and lying down in her room." Sarah ushered them into the kitchen and quietly closed the door. "How is she?" Annie asked, anxiously, "can you tell her we're here?"

Sarah nodded, "but let's have some tea first and give her a bit longer to settle, then I'll see if she's ready to speak about it all." Annie felt like one of Sarah's pupils, being told to sit and wait for the teacher, "I need to see her," she implored Billy, "she's my daughter and you can't keep me away!"

"Now, now, Annie," Billy said, stopping her from leaving the kitchen. "Sarah's right, Lexie needs to get some rest, for the bairn's sake," he emphasised, "let's drink our tea and wait a while." Annie sat down again, her face set in a defiant pose; who did Sarah think she was, telling her when she could or couldn't see her own daughter.

Sarah felt the beginnings of guilt settling into her soul. Her father knew her secret longing to adopt Lexie's bairn, but seeing Annie's determination to be with her daughter, made her realise that she would not be moving to Ireland with Billy, but remaining in Dundee with Lexie and her grandchild when it arrived. Sarah glanced at her dad, but Billy was just staring at his teacup. He was also suffering, she realised, his future with Annie and his son John in Ireland, had been shattered.

In the midst of the gloom, Charlie arrived home from work, hoping to hear the good news that the father of Lexie's bairn had turned up and would be whisking her away to Canada to marry her. But one look from Sarah told him, that hadn't happened.

"Mr Dawson," he said, awkwardly, "and Mrs Dawson, it's good to see you both."

"Lexie's had a bit of bad news," Sarah said, "and her mum and Billy are here to........take her home," the words almost sticking in her throat. Charlie tentatively sat down, "I'm sorry," he said, "not sure what he was sorry for, but knew it had to be about this man, Bo McGhee.

"It's alright Charlie," Lexie's voice sounded from the door, where she stood red-eyed but calm. "I'll be going home now," she said, "if my mother and Billy will have me that is......" Annie rushed over and wrapped her arm around her daughter's shoulder, tears of relief threatening to flow. "Of course you can come home," Annie assured her, "isn't that right, Billy?"

"Whenever you're ready," Billy said. The fates had won again, he had to concede, but even he could see that Lexie's needs and Annie's needs were greater than his own need to live in Ireland.

Before she could change her mind, Annie ushered Lexie into the hall and helped her on with her coat. "We can get your other things later on," she assured Lexie, "just let's get you home first." Lexie stood still as her mother fastened the buttons of her coat for her; so much for being independent, she pondered, she felt more like a bairn than the mum she was soon going to be.

Billy saw the despair in Sarah's eyes. All her plans had come to nothing and she was back where she began, barren. He took Charlie aside as they followed Annie and Lexie to the door, "she's going to need you more than ever, Charlie," he told him, "so be gentle with my daughter," he added, "she's not as strong as she looks."

Charlie nodded, grimly. No one knew better than him, the lengths Sarah had been prepared to go to in order to call Lexie's bairn her own.

Lexie was back home three days when the telephone rang. A bit of her still wanted it to be Bo, saying he'd changed his mind, that he'd forced Angela to divorce him and they'd be married at once, but it was a female asking to speak to her.

"Lexie Melville speaking," she said, uncertainly, "who is this?"

She heard the woman laugh, "well, you've got a short

memory," she said, "its Nurse Williams....from Baxters Nursery!"

Lexie's grip tightened on the telephone, "I'm sorry," she said, "is Kevin alright?"

"Kevin's fine," the nurse said, "it's you I want to speak to about a job that's come up at the nursery and I think you might fit the bill......if you're still interested that is?"

Lexie almost dropped the receiver. She'd forgotten all about her visit to the nursery to pick up King Kevin and the kindness of the nurse. "YES," she gasped, "very interested."

"Good," the nurse said, "then maybe you should come along and see me, tomorrow, if that's alright, and we'll see if it's what you're looking for." Lexie replaced the receiver in a daze. The plan that she'd tried to put into place of being independent and earning enough money to support herself and her bairn, seemed to be coming to pass without any effort on her part. She smiled, things were going to be alright, she told herself, earning her own money meant that she didn't need Bo McGhee nor anyone else to support her, she'd be like Nancy, a strong woman able to look after herself. She soothed the kicking bump, "everything's going to be alright," she told it, "the Fates are on our side, at last."

When Nancy turned up at Albert Street, the wave of happiness almost knocked her over. "Well, well," she said, plonking Kevin down onto the floor, "someone's in a good mood."

Annie smiling widely, before picking Kevin up and sitting him at the kitchen table before giving him a biscuit and cup of milk. "Tea?" she asked Nancy, filling the kettle, "Billy and Lexie have gone for a walk to the Swannie Ponds, while I get on with making the dinner."

"How is Lexie?" Nancy asked, wondering if Annie knew about her getting work at the nursery. "She's just fine," Annie said with satisfaction, deliberately omitting any reference to Sarah Mathieson "and so is the bairn, or should I say my grandchild," Annie added with obvious pride; although she was already grandma to Nancy's brood. But Nancy took no offence, she was just so pleased that everything seemed to be working out for Lexie and she'd gotten over the fear of what people would say about her being without a father for her bairn.

Annie poured out the tea and opened her usual baking tin. "Shortie," she said, "just baked yesterday. Nancy selected a triangle of the buttery treat and there was silence while they munched into the shortbread and sipped their tea.

"They shouldn't be long," Annie announced, brushing the crumbs from the table "and I'm sure Lexie will love seeing you and King Kevin again, especially since he's grown so tall," she noted, just as the door opened and Billy and Lexie came into the kitchen.

"KING KEVIN" Lexie gushed, on seeing the toddler, "how he's grown!"

Nancy beamed, he was a handsome little lad and would break a few hearts one day, she knew, just like his dad.

"And Nancy," Lexie crossed over to her and hugged her cousin, "I'm so pleased to see you and.........I've just told Billy my news."

"News" Annie queried, "what news?"

"Lexie's only got herself a job," Billy announced, "at Baxters Nursery."

"But.......she's going to have a bairn, how can she work as well?"

"Don't be so old fashioned Auntie Annie," Nancy interjected, grinning, "it's 1947, not 1847 and I'm sure Lexie's quite capable of working at the nursery till it's time."

"It's alright mum," Lexie assured Annie, "it's only three afternoons a week and I'll be sitting most of the time playing with the bairns and helping to feed them, that's all, then when my time comes, Nurse Williams says I can work more hours and the bairn will have a place at the nursery along with me."

Annie didn't know whether to be happy or not. She'd already decided that she would look after the new arrival at home and felt a bit cheated that Lexie had arranged everything herself and it didn't include her. Billy could see the disappointment in her face. "Why don't you and Nancy go through to the parlour," he suggested to Lexie "and you can tell her all about it. Annie and me will look after Kevin and we'll try not to eat all the Shortie."

"You have to give her a free rein, Annie," Billy said, when they were alone, "she's been beaten down by all that's happened, but this is a chance for her to 'plough her own furrow' and begin to see there's life after Bo McGhee."

"But, what about me?" Annie asked, crestfallen. Billy helped himself to the Shortie, "the bairn won't be at the nursery all the time," he said, dipping the sweet treat into his tea "and there'll be plenty of time to get to know your new grandchild, in fact," he said, with mock despair, "I just hope there'll still be a little place in your heart for me."

Annie snapped the lid back onto the cake tin. "If you eat any more Shortie, you'll be too big to fit into my heart," she chided her husband, but it was with a smile, Billy was right, Lexie had to learn to live in the real world if, she was going to cope with life when the bairn was born and it was her place to just be there for both of them.

Nancy sat enthralled as Lexie told her about Sarah's kindness and Bo's visit. "And he's gone back to Canada," Nancy said, stunned, "back to a woman he doesn't live with but who won't divorce him?" Lexie shrugged. "I think when I married Robbie instead of him, something in me knew that living in Canada and leaving everyone behind in Dundee wasn't right and now, it looks like the decision has been made for me."

"And the bairn?" Nancy asked, in a whisper, "are you keeping it?" Lexie nodded, firmly, "I'm keeping it," she said, "no matter what."

Nancy nodded, "that's good to hear," she said, "I know that men can come and go, but your family is the thing that's important.....blood is thicker than water," she assured Lexie, wisely, "and when the chips are down, it's your family that will be there for you, remember that."

"And what about you," Lexie said, "is the handsome John Brannan still in your life?"

"Well, he is and he isn't," Nancy replied, enigmatically, with a sigh. "Wee Billy didn't want him around, he said he wasn't his dad, but to cut a long story short, they're now thick as thieves, but I found out he's been bedding Di Auchterlonie, so that's that."

Lexie frowned. "He didn't strike me as a womaniser," she said, "are you sure?"

"Got it from the horse's mouth itself," she said, making a neighing noise and throwing Lexie into a fit of laughter. "So," Nancy concluded, "she's welcome to him and I've decided, a bit like you, to look after myself and the bairns and keep on working, but as for men, well, they'd better stay away from my door."

"What's all the laughter about then?" Billy asked, "carrying Kevin into the Parlour. "This wee laddie wants his mum," he winked at Nancy, as Kevin rushed to her side and clutched her skirt.

"C'mon," Nancy said, standing up, "time we got this one home for his sleep, he gets really grumpy if he doesn't have an hour in the afternoon. And good luck with the job at the nursery, Lexie," she added, grinning, "I know one wee man who'll love having his Auntie Lexie there."

After Nancy and Kevin had left, Billy and Annie settled down with Lexie in the peace of the parlour, each beginning to accept the way things had worked out. Nancy was right, Lexie conceded, looking at her mother, knitting yet another cardigan and Billy smoking a cigarette and doing the crossword in his newspaper, blood was thicker than water. The security she had lost on discovering she was pregnant and that Bo McGhee had no intention of marrying her, was now returning and settling into her soul. She would survive and so would her bairn.

——-—oOo——-—

Chapter 32

The letter with the Irish postmark landed with a soft whisper on the mat. Billy had written to John letting him know what was happening with Lexie and how they couldn't come over to Ireland to live with him and Mary, much as they wished to.

He'd tried to hold out hope that sometime, maybe, they'd be together again, but Bo McGhee's visit had made sure that any chance of that happening had been well and truly dashed.

He took the letter through to the kitchen where Annie was whisking up an omelette for him. "It's from John," he said, trying to keep his voice neutral, "probably just acknowledging our decision.   I'll read it after we've had breakfast." But Lexie wandered into the kitchen just then and Billy slipped the letter into his trouser pocket; no point in bringing the subject of Ireland up again, he decided, now that everyone was on a more even keel. He'd read it later.

Annie folded the omelette onto Billy's plate and set about making one for Lexie.

"Would you like to go into town today?" she asked over her shoulder, "can't start a Layette soon enough, Lexie," she smiled at the word, 'Layette' "and there's so much the new bairn will need." Billy glanced at Lexie, her mum was in her element and he was surprised that Lexie seemed glad to go along with whatever Annie suggested. But with only six weeks to go, Lexie had realised that the bairn would soon be here and she'd be a mum, but she'd never been less prepared for anything in her life.

With Lexie and Annie off to the shops, Billy eventually opened John's letter, his eyes misting as he read it.

Dear Dad and Mum

I hope Lexie is well and managing the pregnancy. Mary says it's a hard road she's on and understands that you can't come over to Ireland and be with us, as do I.

But I've missed out on so much, not knowing for years that you were my dad and Annie my mum and although Dr Adams and Mrs Adams were wonderful people who loved me very much, they weren't my real parents and I don't want to spend the rest of my life not having you and mum in it.

Maybe Mary and me could arrange to visit Dundee once Lexie's wee one is born. It'll be a good reason to come over, and who knows, once she's able to cope, maybe things could change?
I miss you both very much and pray all is well with you. Mary still lights that candle in the window to keep our hopes alive.

Your loving son, John.

Billy read the letter again and he could feel the tremble of his hands as he held on to it tightly; that his son missed him so much almost brought him to tears. He folded the letter and returned it to its envelope. The next few weeks, would be critical for Lexie, he knew, now that Bo McGhee had shattered her dream of marrying him, and Billy's only hope now was that Sarah would adopt the bairn once it arrived, leaving Annie and him free of all responsibility to live in Ireland for the rest of their days.

Annie and Lexie linked arms as they made their way to G L Wilson's Department Store. "We'll get everything 'White'", Annie announced, decisively, as they climbed the stairs to the counters displaying shelves and drawers full of baby clothes, "then it won't matter if it's a boy or a girl."

"May I be of any assistance?" the shop girl asked, looking from Annie to Lexie, "and perhaps madam would care to take a seat," she added, glancing at Lexie's swollen belly. Annie beamed, "my daughter is here to put together the Layette for her new baby, so perhaps you could show us some suitable items?"

Lexie sat bemused as the pile of baby clothing, woollen cot covers and fluffy nappies that Annie had selected on her behalf, grew. Not knowing what most of them were for and SO TINY that she couldn't believe how they would fit a kitten, never mind a bairn, but Lexie nodded in compliance every time Annie showed her another Mattinee Coat or pair of minute woollen booties.

Annie wrote down the address of where the store should deliver the goods and paid for all of it. "Once I'm working at the nursery," Lexie said, quickly, stunned at how much her mother had spent on the Layette, "I'll pay you back for all of it."

But Annie hushed her with a wave of her hand. "Allow me to spoil my new grandchild," she said, "and as for paying me back, there's no need to even think about it, I would pay this and more as long as you're happy." For a second Lexie thought of protesting further, the independence she had embraced of looking after the bairn and herself without any help, fading in the face of the reality of the cost of keeping the child and she could only nod in acceptance. The quicker next Monday came and she could begin her new job, the better.

"Let's take the Lift to the Tearoom," Annie suggested, happily, "a pot of tea and a slice of their fruit cake is just what we need... .. we don't want you tiring yourself out now, do we?" Annie fussed, as they waited for the Lift to arrive. Lexie felt herself diminish further back into childhood again, when her mum did everything for her and never allowed her to make any decisions on her own. But life in the WAAF had changed all that and Lexie found she could cope very well without her mother's attention, albeit, done with love.

Lexie felt a tremor of apprehension as she realised that over the weeks to come, her mother would be taking more and more control of their lives, making decisions for both herself and the bairn and she now knew, for certain, why she'd wanted to leave Dundee in the first place, she'd had to grow up and the only way to be independent and make her own decisions, was to leave home. But now, she was back and once again, dependent on her mother for everything.

"Lexie, Lexie, over here." Sarah Mathieson was at a window table, waving at Lexie to join her. Annie bristled, seeing Sarah as a competitor for Lexie's affection, she was in no mood to share her daughter with her; especially as they were having such a good time together. But Lexie was already on her way to Sarah's table, glad of the excuse to talk about anything other than the Layette and Annie had no option but to follow her.

"This is a surprise," Lexie said, pulling up a chair, "no school today?"

Sarah beamed. Lexie hadn't seen her as happy as this, since she'd moved in with her and Charlie. "No school," she echoed, "I've been to see the Doctor."

Lexie blinked, "you seem very happy to have been to the Doctor," she said, "I didn't even know you were ill?"

"I'm not ill," Sarah whispered, her tone conspiratorial, "I'm PREGNANT!"

Both Lexie and Annie were stunned into silence and it was Annie who found her voice first. "But I thought....?" "So did we!" Sarah interrupted, "but the Doctor has confirmed it, "I'm going to have a baby too!" She reached out and grasped Lexie's hands, "isn't it wonderful!" Lexie gazed at Sarah in her happiness and couldn't help compare it with her own situation. Sarah and Charlie were married, they'd bring their bairn into a world of warmth and security, it would have the best of everything and grow up in a loving home, whereas Lexie's bairn would have none of that, only the stigma of being a Bastard while she would remain dependent on her mother again. She could have wept.

"Yes," she finally managed to say, "wonderful and we're very happy for you, aren't we mum," Lexie added, bringing Annie into the conversation, "but we must get on," she said, standing up and taking Annie's arm, "mum's getting exhausted with all this shopping." Annie couldn't believe her ears, Lexie was making excuses to leave Sarah with her good news, but there was a part of her that was glad and at the same time, a bit confused. Tea and cake forgotten, Lexie steered her mum back to the Lift. "What was all that about?" Annie asked. "Nothing," Lexie clipped, "just a bit tired that's all." The Lift juddered to a halt and the Lift Attendant pulled back the metal door to let them enter. "Ground Floor," Lexie said. The doors clanged shut and mum and daughter stood in silence till they opened again.

Lexie was glad that Sarah was pregnant, but it meant that any hopes she had of her sharing responsibility for looking after her own bairn, as she'd promised, were now gone and, once again, she'd be totally dependent on her mother for the help that she now knew she was going to need. She could feel a depression setting into her system. There was no way out, Bo McGhee had failed her and now Sarah was no longer interested in her bairn, she was going to have one of her own!

As soon as they were home, Annie rushed to tell Billy the news. "Sarah's PREGNANT," she squealed, "we saw her today in G L Wilsons, didn't we Lexie, and she'd been to the Doctor's and........." "Hey," Billy said, trying to take in the news, "slow down." Lexie quietly slipped out of the room, she didn't need to hear the whole thing again. "Your daughter, Sarah," Annie began again, emphasising every word, "is going to have a BABY!" Billy could hardly believe his ears, Sarah had been so sure she'd never be a mother, that she'd even planned to adopt Lexie's bairn, but now, she was pregnant all that would change and Billy's heart sank, as his last hope of living with his son vanished with the news.

"Aren't you pleased?" Annie gushed as Billy tried to gather his wits together. "Of course I'm pleased," he said, "and I'll visit her this evening and tell her so."

He looked around for Lexie, but she was nowhere to be seen. "Where's Lexie" he asked? "Gone for a lie down, I think," Annie said, "she said she was a bit tired." Billy nodded, wondering how Lexie had taken the news; now that Sarah was also pregnant and no longer able to offer her support, "the best laid schemes of mice and men," Billy muttered to himself, quoting the Scottish Bard, "gang aft agley." The Fates had won again.

—-—oOo—-—

Chapter 33

Nancy returned from her visit to Albert Street, her thoughts so engrossed in what was happening to Lexie, with her determination to work for a living and keep the bairn, that she didn't see John Brannan watching her from the close across the road.

She was lifting the sleeping Kevin from his pram and struggling with the weight of him, when she heard a familiar voice. "Let me carry Kevin," John Brannan said, "he's too heavy for you to manage up these stairs alone."

"I can manage alright," Nancy responded, moving quickly forward, only to miss her footing on the first step and almost drop her sleeping bundle. "Here," John Brannan said, stepping forward and lifting Kevin into his arms, "let me help, Nancy... please?"

No one could miss the sincerity in his voice and the praise that her son had heaped on him came into her mind and for a moment, she hesitated. But then her heart felt the deceit of the man bedding Di Auchterlonie behind her back and it hardened again. "I said, I'll manage," she snapped, stretching her arms out to retrieve her son, who had started to whimper and blink open his eyes. "Now look what you've done," Nancy snapped, releasing the bairn from John's grip and setting his feet back on the ground. "Now if you don't mind, get on your way, I'm sure Di Auchterlonie is missing you." Lost for words, John could only watch as Nancy disappeared up the stairs.

She was hurting, that was for sure, John realised, but in a way it gave him hope that she, at least, felt something for him. Her indifference, he flinched at the thought, would have been harder to bear. Whatever it was that Di Auchterlonie had told Nancy needed to be uncovered and there was only one way he could see that it could be done, but that meant seeing Di Auchterlonie again, a prospect he didn't relish.

Nancy slammed the door behind her, threw her coat onto her bed, snatched up the kettle and banged it onto the stove, before kicking off her shoes into the corner of the kitchen, much to the amusement of the giggling Kevin, who began running after them. She could feel angry heat flushing her face as her mind raced. How dare John Brannan try to get her to forgive the unforgiveable!

With hands shaking, she lit a cigarette and forced herself to sit down, drawing heavily on the tobacco smoke, images of Di Auchterlonie's smug face as she taunted Nancy with her talk of 'how she'd have resisted John Brannan's advances had she known Nancy was interested in him.' "Huh!" Nancy said aloud; she was no more interested in John Brannan than she was in the lumps of coal she now tossed onto the fire. But Nancy could feel her throat tightening and tears of hurt blurring her eyes.

Kevin had pushed his feet into Nancy's shoes and was shuffling around the room, revelling in the noise they made as they clacked against the wooden floor and grinning from ear to ear. The innocence of her son enjoying himself with such a simple thing as wearing her old shoes was the last straw for Nancy and the tears that had been threatening since Di's first revelation that 'she and John had been for a drink in the Thrums before going back to her place where they couldn't keep their hands off one another......' still stung, badly.

The clock had ticked by an hour or so, when wee Billy came through the door.

He'd had a good day, walking along the Esplanade towards Invergowrie and had watched a group of youngsters trying to catch fish with their lengths of string and hooks dropped into the seaweed growing along the sea wall. For a while, he'd felt miles away from the grimness of the town with its smoke and the pervading smell of the jute and wondered what it must be like to live in the village of Invergowrie, away from it all. "Maybe one day," he said, turning back to Dundee and home, "maybe one day."

But his peace was shattered when he saw his mother's red-rimmed eyes and slumped shoulders. "Mum", he said, concern hurrying him across to where she sat, "what's wrong?" Nancy focussed on her eldest son, "your mum's a daft old woman," she said, "letting her heart rule her head."

Billy frowned, "what are you talking about?" he asked; surely, she wasn't still angry about his acceptance of John Brannan! Hadn't he told her he was a man to be trusted?

"Do you know what a friend is?" Nancy asked, huffily. Billy nodded, "someone you can trust," he said "and who you can turn too when there's bother, but you know that already." Nancy nodded, "you're right," she said, "but what if that FRIEND turns out to be a 'snake in the grass' who does things behind your back while smiling to your face?"

Billy pulled up a chair and sat beside her. "Who are you talking about?" he asked.

"DI AUCHTERLONIE!" came the reply.

Billy could feel his own temper bristle, as his mum told him the whole sorry story of what Di had been up to with John Brannan behind her back. He'd known the truth about Jim Murphy but this was something else. Had John Brannan fooled him as well as his mum?

"I need to go out for a while," he said, "Mary Anne will be in soon, so dry your eyes and I'll see you later."

"Where are you going?" Nancy queried, realising how much distress she was heaping on Billy's young shoulders, "you're not going to see the Kelly Brothers again?" she asked, anxiously.

"No mum," he said, "I'm going to find out the truth and I won't be back until I do."

All roads seemed to lead to Di Auchterlonie, Billy decided, making his way to her single-end. He well remembered her from the past; his dad had told him about Di and his mum going dancing and all about Jim Murphy's visits to Nancy's house. And he'd believed him at the time, until Kevin had been born and he could see for himself he was the image of their dad. If

Di Auchterlonie had spun a tale to John Brannan about Jim Murphy, then what else had she lied about? Billy knocked on her door, determined to find out.

"Wha is it?" Di's voice called out, anxiously, fearing a return visit from John Brannan.

"It's wee Billy Donnelly and I need to speak to you urgently, Di," he said, "I need you to get me some rum." He heard the bolt being slid back and saw a pair of bleary eyes trying to focus on him. "I've got plenty o' money," Billy said, waving a five pound note in his hand." Di's supply of rum was down to her last half bottle and the temptation of getting some more, even from Nancy's son, overrode any doubts about letting the lad in. After all, he was only a youngster and no threat to her.

She beckoned him in. "I ken whit it's like to be withoot the drink," she said, "so sit yoursel' doon and I'll see whut I can dae." She crossed to the sideboard and produced the half bottle of rum. "It's all I've got just now," she said, "but that fiver'll buy us baith enough to mak' merry."

Billy placed the note on the table in front of him. "Let's use up what we've got," he said, "there's plenty o' time before the Thrums shuts to buy some more."

"You're right," Di said, glad of an excuse to open the bottle and produced two small tumblers. "Doon the hatch," she murmured, swallowing the rum in one go. "That was quick," Billy said, taking hold of the bottle and pouring her another measure, while holding on to his own, untouched.

"I hear you've got a new man in your life?" Billy said, casually, "at least that's the talk on the street." He watched as a slow smile spread across Di's face; folk were talking about her. "Is that right?"

Billy topped up her glass again. "Aye," he said, "name of Brannan from the Mill?"

But the smile turned to a sneer at the mention of John's name. "HIM," she spat, "nuthin' but a chancer!"

"How's that then?" Billy asked, pretending concern, as he refilled Di's tumbler yet again.

"Kidded me on that he luv'd me," she whined, "but his heart

was somewhar else." Billy could see a tear begin to trickle down her face as she tried to focus on the words. "Yir mither disna' deserve'im," she slurred, "and eh've made shur she'll no' get'im either."

Billy knew a slack-mouthed drunk when he saw one and it wasn't long before Di had polished off the rum, including his own nip, but by then..... wee Billy knew the truth.

"Thanks for the rum," he said, loudly, but Di heard nothing, slumped as she was, over the table in a drunken sleep.

Mary Anne was spooning custard into Kevin's mouth and Nancy was peeling the tatties for their evening meal when Billy returned. With a sigh of relief, Nancy nodded to him that she was' alright now', so no more tears.

"Can Mary Anne mind Kevin for an hour," Billy said, "there's somebody you need to speak to."

Nancy drew her eyebrows together, regretting her tearful outburst in front of her son.

"Trust me," Billy said, "I told you I'd find out the truth and I have, so will you come with me?"

Nancy turned to Mary Anne, but before she could ask, her daughter was already nodding her consent. "It's no bother," she said, "and I'll finish the tattie peeling as well."

"Where are we going?" Nancy queried. "You'll see," Billy said, steering his mother into the close leading to John Brannan's house. He could feel her resisting and after what Di Auchterlonie had told him, he knew with good reason.

"It's alright," he said, "Di Auchterlonie isn't here, but John Brannan is and you both need to hear what I have to say, so just trust me."

Nancy had no option but to be dragged to John's front door and no one was more surprised than he, at the sight that met his eyes.

"Nancy!" he exclaimed, "and Billy! " His eyes going from one face to the other in confusion and his heartbeat rocketing.

"Can we come in John?" Billy asked, "I've been to see Di Auchterlonie and found out the truth."

Like two erring children caught plundering apples, they sat

and listened while Billy told them how Di had tricked both of them into believing that John was deceiving Nancy behind her back. It all made sense now and it was a draw as to who said 'sorry' first. Billy stood up, shook John's hand and kissed his mum on the cheek. "I'll just go and make sure Mary Anne's got the tatties peeled," he said, grinning at his mother, "someone's got to be the grown-up in the family."

Nancy sat staring at her hands in the silence that followed Billy's departure, unsure of herself about where things went from here, now that neither she nor John had been guilty of anything.......except that is, not trusting one another.

"I think I need to go home now," Nancy whispered, "her emotions fluctuating between relief that the truth was out, and fear of allowing herself to love John Brannan again.

"I'll understand if you want to go, Nancy," John said, "but I'll be here if you want me for.......anything."

After Nancy had gone, John sat in his chair till darkness fell. He loved Nancy, he knew that for certain, but could he trust her to be the wife that he'd dreamed of? Had too much water flown under the bridge? Only time would tell. He'd been badly burned by her rejection of him, without giving him a chance to explain, but believing, instead, Di Auchterlonie. Tomorrow was another day, he told himself and it being Sunday, he'd head for the hills and try to find some quiet for his soul and peace for his troubled heart.

—-—oOo—-—

Chapter 34

Lexie had worked her first three afternoons at the Nursery and Nurse Williams was very pleased with her efforts. She'd tried not to spend too much time with King Kevin, the toddler requiring more of her energy than she cared to admit, but focussed on feeding the babies instead.

"It'll get easier," Nurse Williams said, hoping she hadn't made a mistake in hiring someone who was so far on in her pregnancy; Lexie's flushed face and back rubbing were indicating she was struggling, but the nurse knew that things wouldn't get any easier for Lexie once her own child was born, in fact, she felt heart-sorry for what she would have to endure, without a husband to bring in the money she'd need to survive.

"See you next week, Lexie," Sadie Williams smiled. Sadly, she'd seen it all before, mill workers who had to carry on till they went into labour and get back to work when their bairns were barely a week old. She looked around the nursery, with its cots and nursing chairs, wooden boxes of simple toys and colouring books for the older ones and shuddered to think what would happen to the mums and their little'uns, if Baxters hadn't started the nursery for their workers.

Wearily, Lexie made her way onto King Street and boarded a tram home, unable to face the long walk uphill to Albert Street. She'd felt twinges of pain all day, but they'd come and gone without giving her too much worry, but as she stepped off the tram, there was a sharper pain and Lexie was glad to be near home.

Annie was waiting anxiously for her daughter's return. She'd never been happy with her working at the nursery, but Lexie had been determined to earn her own money and pay her mother back for the cost of the Layette.

"In here," Annie called, when she hear the front door opening, hurrying to reheat the kettle and get the biscuit barrel out. But instead of her daughter coming into the kitchen, Annie heard a cry of anguish and sound of something hitting the floor.

"LEXIE!" Annie shouted, hurrying to the kitchen door, "are you alright?"

But Lexie was on her knees, her arm wrapped around her womb and a wet patch beneath her. "The bairn's coming," she gasped, as the labour pains gripped her body.

"Your water's broken," Annie gasped, with the pain she had gone through, giving birth to her own children, flashing through her mind and galvanising her into action. "Hold on, Lexie," she said, hurrying to the telephone and dialling the doctor's number.

"Dr Andrews," she shouted, when he answered the telephone, "it's Lexie's bairn, it's coming NOW!"

"I'll be with you in ten minutes," the doctor said. He'd been looking after Lexie during the pregnancy and knew the child was at least four weeks early and that he would need to get Lexie to hospital. He picked up the telephone again, "Ambulance Depot," he asked, when his call was answered, "Dr Andrews here, we need your services," he said, "one of my patients has gone into early labour." He gave the ambulance driver Annie's address and hurried to his motor.

Dr Andrews had only just arrived and was reassuring Lexie that an ambulance was on its way, when the sound of heavy footsteps on the stair signalled the arrival of the men carrying a stretcher.

"Maryfield Hospital," Dr Andrews said, "quick as you can." The men loaded Lexie onto the stretcher and with the sound of her screams echoing in Annie's ears, they carried Lexie to the ambulance.

"Can you let the father know?" Dr Andrews asked, picking up his bag, "tell him to come to the Maternity Ward and I'll see him there." Annie could only nod as the doctor hurried away; but there is no father, she told herself, just a grandfather and a grandma, the weight of responsibility, not just for Lexie but for the new bairn, coming home to roost. "It shouldn't have been like this," Annie whispered. She picked up the telephone and gave Billy the news. "I'll be with you in five minutes," he said, "keep calm, everything will be fine."

Three hours later, Dr Andrews found Billy and Annie sitting in the Waiting Room. "It's a girl," he said, smiling "and Lexie and her new daughter are both fine."

Annie felt a surge of relief, surely, the worst was now over, but it had only just begun. "Dad not here yet" the doctor asked in surprise?

"He's......in Canada," Billy piped up, quickly adding, "on duty."

The doctor frowned momentarily, there had been no mention of the child's father during the pregnancy, but it was his patient that mattered and he just hoped that he'd turn up soon to register the birth of his daughter. "Well, we'll get the paperwork done later," Dr Andrews said, "in the meantime, congratulations all round and you can go in and see your new granddaughter for a few minutes, but not too long, the nurses have a lot to do to make her ready to 'meet her public.'"

Annie looked at her husband, "there'll be no dad's name on the birth certificate," she whispered, "just the word 'BASTARD.'" Billy held onto her, "now, now," he said, "we don't want to see our new granddaughter with a tear, do we?" Annie shook her head; she'd given birth to a Bastard when her son was born in Ireland and now, despite trying to shelter Lexie from the harsh realities of the life that she'd suffered, history had now repeated itself.

Lexie was sleeping in the hospital bed when Annie and Billy tiptoed into the Maternity Ward. "Mr and Mrs Dawson is it?" asked the Ward Sister, "Dr Andrews said you'd be looking in. Your granddaughter's in the Nursery.... this way."

Annie could hear the crying of bairns before they got to the Nursery door, where midwives and nurses were dealing with the newborns. She signalled to one of the midwives to bring over Lexie's bairn. The tiny bundle, red-faced with a shock of dark hair lay sleeping in the nurse's arms. "Is she like her mum or her dad," the nurse asked, pulling the shawl aside to show the bairn's face more clearly?

Annie frowned, the child had little or none of Lexie's features, in fact she was the spitting image of her father, Bo McGhee. Billy and Annie exchanged looks, "well, this little apple didn't fall far from the tree," Billy murmured. "She's like her dad," he said out loud to the nurse, his mind trying not to think of the fatherless future the bairn would have, "and she has all her fingers and toes I hope," he added, trying to bring some levity into the encounter for Annie's sake?

"Can we see mum?" Annie asked, "just for a wee while?"

"She's sleeping just now the Sister said, "better to come back at visiting time." Annie and Billy followed her to the Waiting Room. "But she's alright," Annie asked, anxiously? "She's perfectly fine," the Sister assured her, "but you'll see for yourself when you visit later."

Annie and Billy walked down Mains Loan into Albert Street and home, each lost in their thoughts for the future and how everything would now change for all of them, especially Lexie and Annie feared how she herself would cope with the heavy responsibility that now lay on her shoulders. She linked her arm through Billy's to calm her fears, as long as she had him by her side, she told herself, she'd manage.

Any thoughts of leaving Lexie and the bairn alone in Dundee and going to Ireland had now vanished completely and Billy was reluctant to let John know of the birth in case he came to Dundee and reawakened all the longing Billy had to be with his son. He was glad Annie knew nothing of the letter he'd received and now she never would. The door to Ireland had been well and truly slammed and had to be forgotten once and for all.

Annie and Billy waited till the Wall Clock showed 7 o'clock and the Sister opened the door to let everyone into the Ward. Lexie was sitting up in bed and smiled when she saw them, beckoning them over.

"It's a girl," she said, her eyes wide with wonder, "have you seen her?"

Annie nodded, "we saw her when we were here earlier, but

you were asleep."

Lexie sighed, "isn't she just the most beautiful child you've ever seen?"

"She is," Billy told her "and we're very proud of you both."

"Have you thought of a name for her," Annie asked, hoping her own name would be favoured?

Lexie nodded, "I've known what the bairn would be called, boy or girl, from the time I knew I was pregnant. Annie waited impatiently, "well" she said, getting confused? "I've named her Rainbow, after her father," Lexie announced, wistfully, "Rainbow Melville". Annie couldn't believe her ears, this was the man who'd caused all the trouble in the first place, who'd refused to marry Lexie and had gone back to Canada without a care in the world!

She was about to voice her anger, but Billy squeezed her arm to stop her. Lexie may have been rejected by the man, but it was obvious to Billy that she still had feelings for him. "I'll let Sarah know what's happened," Billy said, quickly changing the subject, "I'm sure she'll want to come to see you."

Why did Lexie want a constant reminder of Bo McGhee, Annie fumed, inwardly, by naming her daughter RAINBOW! As Billy steered the conversation onto who he needed to tell about Lexie's bairn, Annie remained tight-lipped for the remainder of the visit, watching the other mums being visited by their husbands, while her daughter only had, them, at her bedside.

The next day, Dr Andrews paid Lexie a visit. "Your husband will need this in order to register the birth," he said, handing Lexie an envelope. "I'll be registering the birth myself," Lexie told him, decisively, as soon as I'm discharged from Maryfield."

Dr Andrews was now more `sure than ever that Lexie wasn't married and that she was going to have to bring up her child without its father's help.

"Do you want to talk about it" he asked, assuring her that any conversation they had would go no further? Lexie fixed her eyes on her clasped hands. "My daughter's father lives in Canada and he already has a wife," she said, frankly, "but I'll not let him deny his daughter and when she's older, I'll tell her about her father and maybe, by then, things will have changed, but in the meantime, his name will be on my daughter's birth certificate and I will be writing to him to let him know that his beautiful little girl has been born."

Dr Andrews knew what it meant for a woman to admit she'd had an illegitimate child and of the stigma that society attached to it. "You're as brave, as I knew you to be, when you won the Empire Medal during the war, for helping with the rescue of the crew of the Wellington Bomber that had crashed into the sea at Lossiemouth."

"You knew about that?" cut in Lexie.

"Everyone in Dundee knew," the doctor smiled, "you were quite the little heroine."

How very different life had been then, she was living the dream she'd struggled to realise in the WAAF at Lossiemouth and was to sail to Halifax to marry Bo McGhee, but her change of mind on board Robbie Robertson's ship, meant that she married Robbie instead; how much had she hurt Bo then, she wondered, and knew her actions must have cut him deeply.

"My daughter's father is an honourable man," Lexie said "and I was in no doubt that he was married to someone else, when we met again last Christmas, but he expected she would agree to a divorce on his return...." Lexie's voice began to falter at the memory of the meeting with Bo, "so you see, he had no option but to leave me and go back to Canada."

Dr Andrews shook his head. "I wish you and your child every happiness in the world," he said, "and you must do whatever you feel is right for your daughter, no one can judge you and nor should they," he counselled, "but I'm sure there will be those who will try."

Over the next two weeks at Maryfield Hospital, Lexie learned how to look after the tiny scrap that was Rainbow Melville. The nurses took the time to show Lexie how to bath her baby, change her nappies and feed her, keep her warm in Scotland's cold climate, but most of all, let her know how much she was loved. The bond that Annie had formed with Lexie when she was born, was now repeating itself with Lexie and Rainbow and she knew that nothing or no one would separate them from one another, no matter what.

But for all her good intentions, the first day back at Albert Street, saw Lexie conflicting with her mother when she produced a large tin of dried milk and two little glass bottles. Annie had been aghast; surely, a bairn needed its mother's milk and not some strange looking powder? But Lexie had been adamant, as she was intending returning to work at the Nursery, she wouldn't be able to breastfeed Rainbow, so she'd be bottle-fed just like all the other babies there.

"Why is Lexie being so difficult," she'd asked Billy, time and again?"

"Mothers and daughters," Billy muttered to himself, remembering John's wife Mary, wondering if Annie had been upset about sharing the kitchen with her.

"Maybe we need another visit to Forfar," Billy suggested one day to Annie, when the bickering had gotten particularly loud. Annie had burst into tears at feeling she was the worst grandmother in the world, but took Billy's advice anyway and, later that day he'd driven Annie to Isabella's at Forfar, for a few days rest.

It had been agreed with Nurse Williams that Lexie would remain working three afternoons a week until Rainbow was 12 weeks old, then her shifts would increase to 5 afternoons a week. Fortunately, Rainbow wasn't one of the 'crying babies' that Lexie dealt with at the Nursery and would sleep throughout the night, giving her the rest needed for her recovery.

Lexie had registered Rainbow's birth as she had planned, naming Bo McGhee as the father and on a sunny Saturday, she dressed herself in her finest and set off into the town, pushing Rainbow in her pram, complete with warm bonnet and the cosy pink coat, that Isabella had made for her. She stopped outside a shop selling cameras. "Time to show your daddy what a beautiful little girl you are," she cooed, pushing open the shop door.

"Well, well," the shop assistant said, leaning over the counter and looking at Rainbow, "what have we here?"

"I'd like some photographs taken please," Lexie said, "one with myself and my daughter together, one with just my daughter and one just with me."

The assistant beamed. "Of course," she said, "I'll get Mr Jessop."

Lexie and Rainbow were ushered into a back room where a huge camera sat on a tripod and seats and tables were arranged in front of a 'swagged and tailed' curtain.

Lexie posed for her own photograph and then lifted Rainbow out of her pram and into her arms. Finally, cushions were arranged around Rainbow to support her and the photograph of her with her toothless smile, was taken.

"They'll be ready next Saturday," Mr Jessop told her and you can pay for them when you collect them."

Lexie thanked him. "Her daddy will love these photographs," she said, "he really misses us."

Chapter 35

The news of Lexie's bairn spread like wildfire amongst the workers at Baxters. They knew she was the Mill Manager's step-daughter and of her heroism when she'd received the Empire Medal for her bravery during the war, but they also knew that something was wrong. There was no sign of the man who fathered her bairn, nor of any wedding having taken place and the gossiping began.

Nancy could see them whispering and sniggering in the canteen, but they always shut up when she came within hearing distance. For weeks, she had been the topic of conversation amongst the Weavers and she knew how 'arms and legs' could be added to their story to paint the blackest of pictures and now, it looked like it was Lexie's turn. Nancy decided she'd defend her cousin to the hilt against the gossips and, as soon as Lexie was home from hospital, she'd go and see her and her new niece and make sure Lexie knew she could depend on her support.

A week later, with a fine crocheted shawl for the bairn and a box of embroidered hankies for Lexie, Nancy knocked on Annie's door, fully expecting Annie to answer, but it was Lexie who came to the door, carefully carrying her daughter in her arms.

"Well done, Lexie," she said, following her into the kitchen, where a bottle of dried milk had been prepared for the bairn.

"She's just about to be fed," Lexie said, "but then she'll be going for her sleep and we can have a catch-up."

Nancy watched as Lexie, tenderly, fed the bottle of warm milk into her babe's mouth. "Not the breast then," she asked?

Lexie smiled. "I start work back at the Nursery next week, so it's the bottle for Rainbow."

Nancy's eyes widened, "RAINBOW! Isn't that HIS name?"

Lexie nodded. "He's her father," she said, evenly, "so if she can't have his last name, she'll have his first."

If Nancy had thought that Lexie needed protection from the gossips, she was being proven wrong. Now that her daughter had been born, Lexie seemed to have taken on a determination to face the world alone and be answerable to no one!

She felt a wave of admiration for Lexie, she'd taken the worst that life could throw at her and she seemed stronger than ever, not weaker. She wouldn't have to defend her against the gossips, she realised, Lexie would face them all.

Lexie carried the sleeping Rainbow to her crib and returned to find Nancy had begun to make a pot of tea. "Has your mum left any of her baking in the cake-tin," Nancy asked, smiling at the memory of how Annie always made sure there was a treat there for her brood when they visited?

"She's not here," Lexie told her, simply, taking some biscuits from the Biscuit Barrel and putting them on a plate, "things were getting a bit fractious, you know, two women in the kitchen doesn't work and if you add in a bairn, then.......so, Billy suggested mum went for a few days at Isabella's in Forfar....let things settle." Once again, Nancy was amazed at how Lexie had taken control of not only her own life, but that of her mother as well!

Nancy dipped her biscuit into her tea and savoured the soft sweetness. "I can't believe you've got over that man, Bo McGhee, so quickly," Nancy wondered aloud, pouring herself another cup of tea.

"Who says I'm over him," Lexie replied, "just because he's in Canada, doesn't mean 'out of sight, out of mind.'"

Nancy couldn't believe her ears, "but surely, after what happened, you don't still want him in your life?"

Lexie sighed, "he's Rainbow's father, so he'll always be in my life and I'm going to make sure, he's also in his daughter's life."

"But he's in Canada," Nancy reminded Lexie, "aren't you just fooling yourself..... he'll never come back to Scotland?"

"Never say never," Lexie replied, enigmatically, "it may look like he's given up on me, but I know he loved me and now that our daughter has been born, he needs to know that she needs his love too."

All the way home, Nancy marvelled at the change in Lexie since the birth of Rainbow. From being a self-centred young girl who always got her way, with Annie and Billy meeting her every need, she had morphed into a confident and determined woman, fighting to get Bo McGhee into her and Rainbow's lives.

Back home, Nancy looked in the mirror above the fireplace. She was 35 years old now and had the beginnings of fine lines around her eyes and mouth. She fluffed her hair, her dark curls had always been her pride and joy, but now, her hair felt dry and lifeless. Her enthusiasm for an independent life began wilting like her hair, as she considered Lexie's need to still want Bo McGhee in her and Rainbow's lives and her own, denied need, for John Brannan, in her own.

In another five years, wee Billy and Mary Anne would be in their twenties and probably left home and King Kevin would be almost 10 and at school. But worse than that, Nancy felt her stomach tighten, she would be 40 and well and truly an 'auld maid,' living alone in this house in the Cowgate and working her fingers to the bone weaving the jute into cloth at Baxters.

She lit a cigarette and began to worry about her future. Even the independent Lexie wasn't what she seemed, she mused, but was, actually, doing everything she could to get Bo McGhee back into her life and using Rainbow as the reason. She was lost in her anxious thoughts when Mary Anne and King Kevin returned from their walk in Baxters Park. "We've had a great time, haven't we Kevin," she tickled her wee brother in the ribs. "We went on the Slide and the Swings and played 'Chasies' around the flower beds."

Mary Anne prattled on for a while till she realised that her mum wasn't saying anything, just sitting by the fire, smoking her cigarette and with a distant look in her eyes.

"Is everything alright, mum," she said, taking a closer look at Nancy, who knew everything was far from alright. Her visit to Lexie had forced her to examine her own way of life and realise, like Lexie, that if anything was going to change, it was up to her to make it happen. Lexie was going to fight to get Bo McGhee back in her life, but what was Nancy going to do about John Brannan, now the truth was out about Di Auchterlonie and her lies?

"Everything's fine," Nancy said, pulling herself together, "now, how about you go over to the Chipper in King Street and get us both a Fish Supper and extra chips for Kevin. We'll give ourselves a Saturday treat and worry about tomorrow when tomorrow comes." And tomorrow, Nancy told herself, as she buttered some bread and made a pot of tea, she would find a way to make him believe that she was really sorry and that she'd never mistrust him again.

Annie had been at Isabella's for over a week now and had managed to calm her thoughts about the rift that had developed between herself and Lexie. She hadn't realised how much Lexie had changed with the arrival of Rainbow. She'd tried getting used to the name, but still couldn't understand why Lexie had chosen to call her granddaughter Rainbow, instead of Alexandra Ann, as Annie had hoped.

But Isabella, as usual, had been able to show her another way of thinking, getting her to understand that Lexie was no longer a child and couldn't keep doing what Annie told her. She had to live life her own way and that was what the problem was. Two women in one kitchen, as Isabella had put it, was always a recipe for disaster, but especially when the daughter becomes a mother and the mother becomes a grandmother!

Isabella and John Anderson had never had any children of their own, but as Salvationists, they'd witnessed many arguments about the best way to rear the young and Isabella had even ran a crèche for Baxters workers, till the company had opened their own Nursery.

"Is Billy coming to take you back to Dundee tomorrow," Isabella asked, bringing a tray of tea and cake into the parlour and interrupting Annie's thoughts?

"He is," Annie said, "but I'm not sure if I'm ready for another clash with Lexie. Isabella could see that Annie was still hurt at Lexie shutting her out of helping with her daughter and understood why Billy had brought her to Forfar.

"How would it be if I came back with you," Isabella suggested, "after all, I haven't seen Rainbow yet and John can manage quite well without me for a couple of days."

"Could you" Annie asked, immediately? "Maybe you can make Lexie see sense and let me help her." But Isabella just nodded. She'd been here before, when Lexie had wanted to join the WAAF and Annie had tried to stop her and she hoped, as before, that she could 'pour oil over troubled waters' and bring some harmony back into both women's lives. "Good," said Annie, "I'll telephone Billy later and let him know we're both coming back to Dundee with him."

Chapter 36

Sunday dawned quiet and clear as Nancy nursed her first cup of tea of the day.

She'd thought about her life, long and hard, since her encounter with Lexie and decided that 'fences needed to be mended' with John Brannan, just couldn't think of a way to do it. She had said so many harsh words to the man and accused him of cheating and lying every time he'd tried to talk to her and she'd been WRONG!

All along, she'd listened to the twisted story spun by Di Auchterlonie and never gave John a chance to speak and she could feel her insides recoil at her jealous behaviour. She wouldn't blame him if he never spoke to her again, she conceded, but the thought of losing him, forever, filled her with dread. Somehow, she had to win him back.

Nancy was still lost in her thoughts when wee Billy came into the kitchen, fully dressed and hungry. "Where are you off to so early," Nancy asked, surprised, knowing that her son usually spent his Sundays asleep?

"Hill walking with John," he said, simply, beginning to slice into a loaf of bread. Nancy watched as her son made himself a jam sandwich and filled an empty lemonade bottle with water from the tap. "This'll do," he said, packing the food into his rucksack, "we're heading for Glen Clova, so we'll be away all day." And with that, he was gone.

Her son's obvious trust in John made Nancy question her own distrust of him even more! Was she so blinded by her past hurts that she couldn't see a good man when he stood in front of her?

Mary Anne, with Kevin holding onto her nightgown ambled, sleepily, into the kitchen.

"Where's Billy gone," she asked the silent Nancy, "he wakened Kevin up with all the noise he was making."

"Gone hill walking, with John Brannan."

"Mmmmm," Mary Anne murmured, yawning and cutting slices of bread for their breakfast toast. "Aren't you surprised," Nancy asked, "after all the trouble he's caused?" Mary Anne blinked awake, "trouble," she repeated, "you mean about Di Auchterlonie?" Nancy nodded. "But Billy said that was all sorted and everything was fine now," she said, before asking, "isn't it?"

Nancy sighed, taking the bread and laying it on the metal-rack for grilling; it seemed that Mary Anne saw no harm in John either!

"Not yet," Nancy replied, in answer to her question, "but it will be."

But Mary Anne just shrugged at her mother's reply; she'd gotten used to her mum's erratic behaviour over the years, especially where men were concerned and knew not to react to her moods. At seventeen years of age, she just wanted to have some fun in her life and as soon as she could, fall in love, get married and live happily ever after......unlike her mum!

Nancy fretted for the entire day and couldn't settle to any of her Sunday chores. All her thoughts kept coming back to how she'd misjudged John and how much the idea of him not being in her life was affecting her. Was being independent, like Lexie, what she really wanted, or was it life with John Brannan she yearned for?

Wee Billy returned home just as daylight was beginning to fade and Nancy couldn't wait to question him on how the day went, but more importantly, had John Brannan asked after her. She watched as he dumped his haversack by the door and pulled off his jacket with a contented sigh. "Something smells good," he said, sniffing the air. "Just mince and tatties, as usual," Nancy shrugged.

Billy joined the rest of the family at the table. "Is there

enough for another plateful," he asked, pulling up a chair. "I've invited John to join us......if that's alright with you," he added, slowly?"   Nancy felt her heart skip a beat, but she didn't say 'NO'.

"He's just changing out of his boots, then he'll be over," Billy added, holding his mother's gaze.

Before any more could be said, there was a knock at the door and Nancy hurried to open it. John Brannan had been weathered on the hills over the years and the sun that day had added its colour to his face, but it couldn't match the rosy flush that had suddenly appeared on Nancy's. "Billy said....." he began, but Nancy just stepped aside and pointed to the table. "It's Mince and tatties," Billy grinned, "and there's plenty to go round."

Nancy had thought of a thousand things to say during the day, but now John was sitting across from her, she couldn't think of a thing. Man and boy chatted about the trip to Glen Clova, Mary Anne asked if she could go next time and even Kevin, who was on Mary Anne's knee, kept dipping his bread into John's gravy and giggling when John pretended to look shocked.

"Well," John said, rising from the table as soon as the meal was finished and Nancy's Apple Tart had been eaten, "time I was on my way, work tomorrow for us all, but thanks Nancy," he said, extending his hand towards her, "for letting me join you and your family, it's not much fun eating alone." His grip was warm and strong, while Nancy's was weak and tentative. Was he really going to go already, without as much as a 'longing look' in her direction? She followed him to the door. "Thanks again," he said, turning towards her, "it's good to know I have a friend."

It took a minute or so for Nancy to react as a full-blown wave of rejection swept over her. "FRIEND!" she said aloud, "We'll see about that." She took off her apron and pushed her feet into her shoes. "Mind Kevin," she instructed Mary Anne, "this won't take long."

"Here we go again," her daughter said shaking her head, "another mad mood."

Wee Billy said nothing, but smiled as he began clearing the

dishes from the table.

John was just turning his key in the lock when he heard footsteps running up the stairs and Nancy's voice muttering incoherently. She slapped him on the shoulder and he turned to face her, he'd never seen her so inflamed, nor so beautiful.

"Do you want to come in," he asked, amiably, "or do you want to give my neighbours something to gossip about?" How dare he look so calm, Nancy winced, didn't he even care a little bit about her? "Open the door," she said, her hands on her hips and her eyes blazing, there would be no 'half-measures' she'd decided and his 'friendship' wasn't an option. She knew now, that she wanted this man more than she wanted anything else in the world and she wanted all of him.

"What's wrong?" John asked, with a sigh of resignation as he sat down in his chair, indicating to Nancy to also sit down "and before you tell me, ask yourself this, is there anything I can do about it?"

The simple question stopped Nancy in her tracks; what did he mean, of course he could do something about it, he could tell her he loved her!

"Well," John said, "I'm listening?"

Nancy clasped her hands together and focussed her gaze on them. "I don't want to be your friend!"

"I'm sorry to hear that, but I wouldn't worry about it, John said, "I don't want to be your friend either."

Nancy felt the second wave of rejection hit her and, try as she might, she couldn't stop her eyes beginning to sting with tears. "Then there's no more to be said," Nancy murmured, all her bravado and confidence that she could just flash her eyes at John Brannan and he'd come running, drained from her heart.

Whether she liked it or not, by her own selfish actions, she'd consigned herself to a life alone and without the love of this good man.

With head bent and her eyes blurred with tears, Nancy made her way to the door. "Don't go," John said, hoarsely, "I don't want to be your friend, Nancy, I want to be your husband."

Nancy couldn't believe her ears. "Husband" she whispered?

"I love you," he said, "always have, I just don't know if you love me enough to trust me not to hurt you like all the others?"

"Of course I love you," Nancy told him, "with all my heart," knowing for certain that she did and realising that her distrust of him must have hurt him more than she had known.

"I'll never doubt you again," she said, running into his arms "and if you'll forgive me, I'll show you how much I love you, but not as your friend," she added, glowing with happiness, "as your wife."

All the pent up passion that had been denied for so long was released in that first kiss and it was dark before their love for one another was sated.

"Shall I go and tell Mary Anne and Billy we're to be married," Nancy whispered as she snuggled her naked body into John's. John pulled her tightly against him and kissed her hair, "let tonight be the start of our life together," he said "and let's tell them together....although I think my friend Billy may have already guessed; and John was right, wee Billy already had.

—-—oOo—-—

Chapter 37

Billy drove Annie and Isabella back home to Albert Street.

"Lexie will be at work at the Nursery," he told both women, "so it'll give you time to get settled in before she comes home." He carried the two suitcases from the car into the house. "I've work to do too," he said, briskly, "but I'll be home around six." He kissed Annie on the cheek and was glad he wouldn't have to be there when Lexie came home and also glad that Isabella would be there when mother and daughter were reunited.

"You can have Ian's old room," Annie told Isabella, "it hasn't been used for a while, but some clean bedding and a bit of a dust should make it comfortable enough." But when Annie and Isabella entered the room, they found it spotlessly clean and the bed already made up. "Looks like Lexie's become quite the housewife as well as a mum," Isabella said, appreciatively. Annie frowned, "let's see Lexie's room, it's always a bit of a mess." But Lexie's room had been turned into a Nursery. Alongside her single bed, there was a crib, a nursing chair, and a chest of drawers, painted white! Annie was speechless as she opened the door to her own bedroom. Once again, everything was spotlessly clean and in its place. Lexie had been busy even there!

"But, this is wonderful," Isabella said, applauding Lexie's efforts, I can't wait to see the rest of the house." Annie nodded, bleakly and led the way. The parlour furniture had been moved around, and the fireplace now had a Fireguard in front of it and a new coal-box with a lock on it! When they were, finally, in the kitchen Annie broke down, "it feels as though I've never lived here," she wailed; it was Lexie's house now and Annie had no place in it.

"Don't be silly, Annie," Isabella said, "of course it's still your home, Lexie's just made it safe for little Rainbow that's all." She put a comforting arm around Annie, "and when Lexie and Rainbow come home, I'm sure she'll be delighted to have you back where you belong." But the joy of being home was gone and Annie felt she no longer belonged there.

Isabella knew how Annie had felt when Lexie left home to join the WAAF, but this was different. Not only was she losing Lexie again, she was also losing the grandchild she'd longed for. Isabella knew that Lexie had grown up years ago, but Annie was still seeing her as her bairn, who needed to be looked after. But the reality was that Lexie was more than capable of looking after both herself and Rainbow and earn money to support them into the bargain. Annie had to understand this and let her daughter go!

The sound of the door opening signalled Lexie's return. "It's only me," she called out, coming into the kitchen with Rainbow on one arm and a bagful of shopping on the other. Smiling widely, she immediately handed Rainbow over the Annie, "Billy said you and Isabella were coming today," she beamed, "can you hold her for a minute, mum, while I get our Bridies out of this bag."

Isabella had to suppress a smile at Lexie ordering Annie about. Now she knew why Billy had brought her to Forfar, but the break seemed to have allowed Lexie to establish herself in the house and she could see how happy she was with her new-found independence. But, Isabella had to admit, Annie was right, Lexie didn't need her mother anymore.

She watched as Lexie prepared Rainbow's bottle and offered it to Annie. "Could you feed her," she asked, "she needs to get to know her Grannie?" Annie's eyes lit up, she wasn't totally unwanted after all and began to feed the hungry Rainbow her milk while Lexie got on with preparing their meal.

Isabella was given the task of peeling the vegetables, while Lexie told her all about the rush to Maryfield Hospital and Dr Andrews kindness and understanding when she told him she would be bringing up Rainbow alone. "So, I refuse to hide from the gossips," Lexie stated boldly, "or from anyone else for that matter and I'll make sure Rainbow knows of her dad and he knows she's his daughter."

Isabella listened in awe as Lexie told her story, without any sign of the shame that had blighted her mother's early life; in fact, since the war ended, life as Isabella and Annie knew it, was fast disappearing and this new generation of women were making themselves seen and heard and Lexie was one of them.

Billy crept into the house at 6 o'clock, expecting to hear mum and daughter at loggerheads, but instead he found them in the warm kitchen, with Isabella rocking Rainbow to sleep and Annie and Lexie sharing the washing up. Billy sighed with relief, he'd seen how Lexie had managed the house and looked after Rainbow and knew that she didn't need Annie anymore and it looked like Annie had realised it too!

By 8 o'clock, Rainbow was asleep in her crib and Isabella had gone to her room tired-out but happy, leaving Lexie with Annie and Billy in the parlour.

"I've something to tell you both," Lexie said, producing a brown envelope. Annie felt a jolt of the unknown hit her; she'd just begun to feel at home and now Lexie was awakening her insecurity again. Billy turned off the Wireless and lit his cigarette.

"We're listening," he said, taking Annie's hand in his to reassure her that whatever Lexie had to say, he was beside her.

Lexie opened the envelope and produced the three photographs taken by Mr Jessop a week ago. Annie and Billy gazed at the face of Rainbow surrounded by cushions, then Lexie holding her in her arms and finally, Lexie standing alone. "They're beautiful," Annie breathed, "I'll get frames for them tomorrow."

But Lexie shook her head, "they're not for you," she said, "I'm sending them to Rainbow's father, Bo McGhee." Billy faced her in confusion, "do you really think he deserves to see them" he demanded, "after all he's done?" Lexie knew there would be objections but she was ready for them.

"I've registered Rainbow's birth and Bo is named as her

214

father. Although he's thousands of miles away, I will make sure that he knows his daughter and, more importantly, that she knows him."

"But, what good will that do" Billy asked, exasperated that Bo McGhee's name was even being mentioned? "He's already made it quite clear he's married to some woman in Canada and as far as he's concerned, that's the end of it."

"I'm not telling you this to ask your permission," Lexie said, plainly, taking back the photographs and returning them to the envelope, "I will be writing to Bo tonight, letting him know that his daughter has been born and showing him what she looks like. What he does about it, is up to him," she added, decisively, "I just wanted you to know, that no matter what the future holds, Bo will know everything about Rainbow as she grows up, just as if he was here."

In the silence that followed, Lexie bade them goodnight. "I love you both, very much," she said, making her way to the door, "and I hope you understand that I have to do what's right for me now and for Rainbow."

Once again, Lexie had proven that she was the master of her own destiny and not Annie nor Billy, nor anyone else could tell her what to do; and Annie, finally, knew that her daughter may still love her, but she certainly didn't need her.

"C'mon," Billy said, "let's get some sleep. Things will be different in the morning."

But although Annie agreed with a nod, she knew that her old life had changed forever and not for the better.

Back in the make-shift Nursery, Lexie kissed her daughter's sleeping head, before picking up her pen. This was the most important letter of her life and she had to get it right. Bo not only had to know about his daughter, but also that Lexie still loved him.

The flight back to Moose Jaw was long and turbulent and much as Bo tried to sleep and blot out the misery he'd caused Lexie and the turmoil he felt on leaving her and his unborn child, he was awake all night and arrived back to the base, emotionally and physically exhausted.

'If only,' he kept repeating to himself till he at last, fell asleep, but his dreams were fraught with anxiety and the following day saw no relief from his guilt, as he travelled to the Cape to pick up Louie.

"Papa!" shouted his son as soon as he saw Bo walking up the path to the front door of his Grandmama's house, "I've missed you." Louis threw himself into his father's arms, "and I've missed you too Louie," Bo said, swinging him onto his shoulders and carrying him into the house.

"Papa has to hurry today," he told Louie, "so get your things together and we'll be back in Moose Jaw by evening." But Angela was watching from the doorway. "Going so soon," she said, slipping off her shoes and allowing the strap from her dress to slip down over her shoulder, "what's all the hurry?"

Bo stood still. "I'm needed back at the base," he said, "that's all."

"Don't you think I need you too Bo," Angela whispered in his ear as she trailed her fingers over his arm? "It's not just Louie who's missed you."

Bo felt every muscle tense. Angela was well schooled in the art of love and Bo closed his eyes. He knew his wife of old, every time Bo had tried to break away from her, she knew just how to pull him back in. But, not this time, Lexie was going to have his baby and that changed things, especially staying married to Angela.

He untangled her arms from around his neck and held them at her sides. "Lexie is PREGNANT," he said "and she needs me."

Angela shook her arms free and stepped back, her hands on her hips. "NEEDS YOU!" she shouted, "your son needs you, the Air Force needs you and now your Scottish girlfriend needs you, but WHAT ABOUT ME," she cried tearfully, "I NEED YOU."

"STOP IT!" Angela's mama had heard everything from the shadows. "I think you should take Louie and go," she said, "My daughter has been hurt enough by you and it is I who will have to pick up the pieces."

"I'm sorry, Madam Lafyette," Bo said, "for disturbing you, especially after the loss of Monsieur Lafyette....." But Angela's mother brushed away his apology. "Leave, please," she said, "I have nothing more to say to you."

"Tell Louie to be quick," she instructed her daughter, "my patience has run out."

Louie was so pleased to be going home with Bo, that he didn't notice the grim face of his Grandmama or the tearstained face of his Mama, as Bo hurried him out to the waiting Jeep.

He'd made a mess of everything, he scolded himself, harshly and now there was no way out. In fact, he'd probably made things worse by telling Angela about Lexie's pregnancy. She'd never divorce him now and he'd never see Lexie ever again.

The days turned into weeks and Bo wrote to his Uncle Martin at Montrose.

Dear Uncle Martin

I hope you are well and I'm sorry for all the trouble I've brought to everyone's door.

Angela is still refusing a divorce, even though she now knows that Lexie is pregnant, in fact, it seems to have made her more determined than ever to live this sham existence. But Louie is well and growing taller every day, as for me, well the world keeps on turning and I can't wait till my 18 years service is up and I can find some peace of mind, maybe fur trapping in Alaska. After all, it's what my dad did and he never seemed to worry about anything.

Forgive me for everything,
Bo

The next day, Bo handed his letter to his Secretary, to be airmailed to Montrose and received in return, a letter from Scotland. He slipped it inside his coat, he'd read it later, pleased that his Uncle had written to him and hadn't disowned him.

It was late in the evening when Bo remembered the letter

and sat down with a glass of Whisky to read it. He broke the seal and was surprised to find three photographs inside, along with the letter. He went to the last page, unsure now of who had sent it, only to see Lexie's signature.

One by one he turned over the photographs. There was one of Lexie, looking more beautiful than ever, then another holding a baby in her arms and the third photograph was of a tiny child, propped up by cushions, with dark hair and a toothless smile peeping out from the folds of a shawl. With trembling hands and heart, Bo read the letter.

Dear Bo

By now you will have looked at the photographs of our daughter, yes I gave birth to a wee girl four weeks early and I've named her Rainbow, after you, her father. Things have changed for me since you last saw me, not only am I a mum, or 'mama' as you'd say, but I've found work and am living back at my old home in Albert Street.

I know that you and I will never marry, but that doesn't mean that you can't know your daughter and I hope that you will let her come to know you too.

Whatever happened in the past and whatever the future holds, I want you to know that I loved you that Christmas and I know you will always be in my heart, but I need to make a new life for myself and Rainbow, without you in it.

I ask for nothing from you, but that you allow me to keep in touch to let you know how our daughter is growing and who knows, maybe one day you'll be able to meet her in person, but not now, maybe when she's old enough to understand about everything.

Our love to Louie and to you,
Lexie and Rainbow

Long into the night, Bo gazed at the photographs of Lexie and Rainbow. "Rainbow," he whispered, smiling through a blur of tears, "we'll meet some day, I promise."

—-—oOo—-—

Chapter 38

Nancy couldn't wait to tell everyone her news. John had posted their Bans at the Registry Office and in three weeks time, they'd be married and she'd be Mrs Nancy Brannan. Mary Anne hadn't been surprised that her mother had left the house determined to hate John Brannan, but returned with the news of their marriage. She was used to her mother's erratic moods and wondered how long it would be before they would cause trouble again, after John moved in as her husband.

But Mary Anne had said nothing and asked, instead, if she could be the Bridesmaid.

Wee Billy had given a knowing smile to John and shook his hand like the man he was turning out to be. "Can I be your Best Man," he'd asked John and had beamed when he'd said "yes!"

With Kevin skipping alongside her, Nancy made her way to Annie's to tell her the news, but she and Isabella had taken Rainbow out in her pram to Baxters Park and it was Lexie who answered her knocking. "I've got some wonderful news!" Nancy announced, breathless from her rapid climb up the stairs to the house, "you'll never believe what's happened!" "Well," I won't know about that till you tell me," Lexie replied, grinning, taking Kevin's hand and leading her nephew into the kitchen.

"Well" Lexie said when the tea had been poured and the biscuits passed around, "what's this exciting news?" Nancy clasped her hands and held them under her chin, "I'm getting married," she breathed, "in three weeks time."

"To John Brannan, I assume," Lexie asked, ready to be contradicted given Nancy's history with men?"

Nancy's eyes widened, "of course, John Brannan," she said, "who else?"

"Well, that is wonderful news," Lexie said, a slight hesitation in her voice, "no more doubts?" It didn't seem that long ago to Lexie, that Nancy had sworn that John Brannan wouldn't 'darken her doorstep' ever again! Nancy lowered her eyes and her hands, "well," she said, "I was wrong about John," she admitted, sheepishly, "and......" she met Lexie's eyes with her own, "I don't want to 'die an auld maid.'"

Lexie couldn't believe her ears! This was the phrase that Nancy had tossed at her all those years ago and one of the reasons that had made her join the WAAF in the first place! How things had changed, the beautiful and bold Nancy now admitting that she needed a man in her life and, despite her previous misgivings about him, that man was John Brannan.

Lexie refilled her teacup and gave Kevin another biscuit and some milk. "Mum and your dad will be delighted to hear your news," she said, "I know he was worried about you and the bairns living on your own when they went over to Ireland to live with John."

Nancy clasped her hand over her lips, "I quite forgot about him," she said, "he's a doctor now, isn't he, our half-brother?" Lexie agreed, "I'm sure Billy will write and let him know in good time to come to the wedding," Lexie smiled, "and let him know about Rainbow being born earlier than expected."

A distant look came over Nancy's face as she nodded in agreement. "Sometimes, I can't believe all that's happened to us over the years and how so much has changed since the war." She lifted Kevin onto her lap and hugged him close, "what's going to happen to our bairns, Lexie," she asked, "will Kevin and Rainbow have a happy life, now the fighting is over and they can grow up in a safe place?"

Lexie took Nancy's hand, "I hope so," she said, "and if I have anything to do with it, Rainbow will be the happiest girl on earth."

Annie and Isabella returned with Rainbow and Annie glowed with happiness on hearing Nancy's news. "But that's wonderful

Nancy," Annie said "and your dad will be so pleased that you'll be settled at last, after all the heartache you've had in the past."

"And how is King Kevin," Isabella asked, beaming at the toddler? "I remember when you were a wee bairn," she said, "and your mum used to bring you to my little nursery to be minded." Nancy acknowledged the memory "and you and Mr Anderson must come to the wedding," she said, "you haven't met John yet, but I'm sure you'll love him."

Amidst all the talk of weddings and congratulations, Lexie lifted Rainbow out of her pram and took her through to her room. "Have a wee sleep Rainbow," she whispered to her child, tucking the woollen blanket around her babe and gently stroking her hair. "You will have a wonderful life," she promised her sleepy child, "and be the happiest girl on earth." She kissed the top of Rainbow's head, wistfully, "if the fates allow," she added, "and your dad falls in love with you."

When Billy came home from his Masonic meeting, he was met with a gaggle of voices. "Hold on," he said, picking up the odd word and the mention of Nancy's name. "Annie," he asked directly, "what's happened?"

"It's Nancy and John Brannan," Annie said excitedly, "they're to be married!"

"When did all this happen," Billy asked, barely managing to hang his coat up on the Hallstand, before being pulled by the arm into the kitchen? "I don't know," Annie said, honestly, "but we're all invited to the wedding..... even John and Mary!"

"And you've to write and tell them to come over to Scotland," Isabella added, quietly, giving Billy a questioning look; she knew how much he'd wanted to remain in Ireland with their son, but with Lexie and her troubles, Annie had insisted that they return to Dundee, but now.......had the fates changed their minds, she wondered?

When everyone had settled down much later that night, Billy and Annie sat in the welcome silence of the parlour. "Well, old girl," he said, "what's to do now?

Do you want our son and Mary to come here for the wedding and meet Rainbow, who they don't even know has been born?"

Annie frowned, realising that John needed to know that Lexie had given birth, but if they came over, they would then see for themselves, that she didn't need her mother to support her anymore and John would be asking Billy when they were coming back to Ireland.

"What's wrong?" Billy asked, seeing the look of concern on Annie's face.

"Lexie may not need her mother anymore," Annie murmured, defensively, turning bleak eyes to face Billy, "but Rainbow will still need her Grannie's love!"

The possibility of returning to Ireland, now that Lexie and Nancy were both living their lives, quite nicely, without either her or Billy's help, had not gone unrealised by Annie, but in her heart of hearts, she couldn't bring herself to break the bonds of love she had forged with Lexie over the years......and no one could make her, she told herself.......not even her son.

Billy tried not to feel disappointed with Annie's answer, but would never force her to do anything she didn't want to do. She'd had enough pain in her past caused, not only by Lexie's father, Alex Melville, but by Billy himself, when he'd married Annie's pregnant sister, Mary, and unbeknown to him ,left Annie in Ireland also pregnant in the Poor House in Belfast.

"Hush now, Annie," he said, "we'll stay here as long as you want to, as long as we're together, it doesn't matter where we live, now let's get some sleep and I'll write to John tomorrow and invite him and Mary to Nancy's wedding and tell them about Rainbow." Annie felt the tension ease from her system, Billy was right, as long as they were together that was what really mattered.

Isabella was returning to Forfar the next day and once Billy had written his letter, he'd drive her back to her home and post it on the way.

"Have you got everything," Annie fussed, as Billy helped Isabella into her coat?

"Yes, Annie," she said, patiently, "now say goodbye to Lexie and Rainbow when they come home from the Nursery and I'll see you at the wedding."

The women hugged and Annie returned to her kitchen to tackle the pile of breakfast dishes. She lifted the net curtain aside and watched as Isabella and Billy drove off, before beginning the washing up with a sigh: Everyone seemed to have their lives under control except her. Lexie knew where her life was going, but she'd made it clear that Annie had no place in it any longer and despite assurances from Billy, she felt lost. Everything that she'd known and lived through had gone and she found herself in a world where she felt no longer at home.

"Will you write to John," Isabella asked as they drove to Forfar?"

"I already have," Billy said, "I'll post it when we get near your home."

"Lexie seems very happy being a mum?" Isabella continued, "and Rainbow is a beautiful child."

"Mmmmmm!" Billy grunted; "it's pretty plain that Lexie doesn't need Annie around anymore, but she's now saying that Rainbow needs her, so she has to stay in Dundee, but it's really Lexie she can't let go off."

Isabella squeezed Billy's arm. "Maybe she'll change her mind when John and Mary get here." Billy nodded, signalling that he was stopping at the Pillar Box. "I'll just post this and hope you're right, but if not, we'll be staying in Dundee."

—-—oOo—-—

Chapter 39

As soon as John came home from his shift at the hospital, Mary ran to meet him waving an envelope in her hand. "It's from Scotland," she said, excitedly, "maybe it's news about Lexie and the pregnancy and that your mum and dad are coming back!"

"Let's not count our chickens," John said, "let me get my jacket off and we'll read it together." It had been a while since his father had written to him and he had to assume that things hadn't changed much, but he was wrong, everything had changed.

Dear John and Mary

I have news about Lexie and also about your other half-sister, Nancy.

Firstly, Lexie gave birth to a wee girl on the 6th of September, (4 weeks early).

Both of them are well and thriving and Lexie has taken to being a mum far better than we'd been expecting, given that the father won't marry her and has gone back to Canada and to his legal wife. John looked at Mary in astonishment. "Read on," Mary said, "poor Lexie, she must be so hurt."

Then there's the news about Nancy. She's to be married on the 7th of November to an Overseer at Baxters, name of John Brannan and you're both invited, so please make arrangements to travel to Scotland as soon as you can, both to attend the wedding and to see Lexie's new bairn.

However, I have to tell you that although Lexie and her daughter are fine, your mum still feels she has to remain in Dundee for the sake of Rainbow, that's the bairn's name, so when you come across for the wedding, don't think anything has changed on our wish that we come to live with you both in Ireland, I'm so sorry to say.

We are looking forward to seeing you both, so stay as long as you can, your absence from the hospital permitting, John.
I await your reply with anticipation,

Your loving dad and mum,

"First the good news, then the bad," John said, dejectedly, "this means we'll have to sell this lovely old house where I'd hoped we all could live, now that mum won't leave Lexie and Dundee."

Mary linked her arm into her husband's as they tried to accept the news and what it meant for the future. John folded the letter and replaced it in the envelope. "Do you want to go to Scotland," he asked, bleakly, not sure if he could handle seeing Annie and Billy again and then returning to Ireland without them.

Mary understood what was troubling him, but could do nothing to change things. He'd built so much around having Billy and Annie in his life and making up for all the years they'd missed, that seeing the dream, finally disappearing, was almost unbearable. "Maybe if we go, we'll understand your mum's decision," Mary mooted, "she must have her reasons for staying and we have to respect that....?" John sighed, "you're right, of course," he said, "I just hoped that there would be room enough in her heart for me as well."

Mary knew there was no point in saying anymore about it, John was hurting too much. "Let's sleep on it, she said, softly, "then maybe tomorrow things will be clearer."

John wrapped his arms around his wife. "You'll never leave me, Mary, will you?"

"NEVER!" Mary assured him, "I'll never stop loving you, as long as I live;"

His mother had said that to him, when they'd met for the first time, at the old Church in the Nethergate, but now, he couldn't be sure if the words were still true. It was only words, after all, and don't actions speak louder than words and Annie's actions were speaking volumes.

Bo McGhee read Lexie's letter again and again, before folding it around the photographs and putting it in his desk drawer. There was no point in torturing himself about not being able to marry Lexie and be Rainbow's father, the fact was that he was married to Angela and would remain so 'till death do us part.'

Although Lexie wanted nothing from him, he decided that he would send money every month towards Rainbow's upkeep, then, if some day he should see her, she'd know that he'd cared in the only way he could. But apart from that, he could do nothing to be with the woman he truly loved and the daughter he'd fathered.

Lexie hurried home from the Nursery with Rainbow fretting all the way. Some of the toddlers had gone down with Measles and Lexie was worried that Rainbow may have picked up the infection. There was no rash, but she was hot and bothered and barely managed her last bottle.

"I need to phone Dr Andrews," she said, immediately on arriving home. "I think Rainbow may have Measles," she told Annie urgently and she's so young....."

Annie lifted Rainbow from her pram and took her into the light of the kitchen.

The bairn was certainly hot and grumpy as Annie removed her woollen coat and mittens, but with no rash, she decided it may just be a cold. "Dr Andrews will come after the surgery closes at six," Lexie said, rapidly, returning to the kitchen after making the telephone call to the Surgery,"but in the meantime, we've to keep her cool and quiet and try to get her to take some warm water with a little sugar."

"I think it may just be a cold," Annie said, trying to reassure Lexie, but Lexie was having none of it. "You're suddenly a doctor then, are you," she said, angrily, "and what if it is the Measles and Rainbow's really ill......what then?" And with that, Lexie took her daughter from Annie's arms and whisked her through to her crib in the Nursery.

Annie sat down on one of the kitchen chairs, her soul reverberating at Lexie's onslaught. If she ever thought that she would be trusted to look after Rainbow, she knew now, she wouldn't. Dr Andrews arrived as promised and Annie pointed him in the direction of the Nursery. With a quick nod, the Doctor knocked and entered Lexie's room, closing the door behind him, leaving Annie to wait alone for his diagnosis.

Skillfully, Dr Andrews examined Rainbow and checked her temperature. "She's certainly got a bit of a fever," he said to Lexie, "but it's not Measles." Lexie breathed a sigh of relief. "There's Measles at the Nursery where I work," she explained "and I was so worried for Rainbow, being so young....."

"And you did exactly the right thing in calling me in," Dr Andrews assured her, "it's always better to be safe than sorry where babies are concerned," he added, putting away the stethoscope in his Gladstone Bag. "Now, add a few drops of this into her feed," he said, handing Lexie a small brown bottle "and by morning I'm sure she'll be fine, but if you're worried about her, telephone me again."

Lexie flopped down in the Nursing Chair. "Thank you Dr Andrews," she said, "for coming so quickly, we're so lucky to have you to take care of us."

Dr Andrews watched as Lexie wrapped Rainbow in her shawl and returned her to her crrib. He remembered again, reading about her heroism during the war and now, that same heroic woman was embarking into the unknown as the mother of an illegitimate child and he was full of admiration for her courage.

"I hope I'm not talking out of place," he said, as he reached the door, "as I am your Doctor, but if you ever need a friend, Lexie, then let me know and I'll do what I can to help you or Rainbow."

"Thank you for your offer Dr Andrews," Lexie smiled, "I'll bear it in mind."

Dr Andrews nodded. "And it's Christopher by the way, but my friends call me Chris."

Lexie's mind flashed back to her first meeting with Bo McGhee. 'My name is Rainbow McGhee,' he'd said, 'but my friends call me Bo.'

"Rainbow's got a bit of a temperature," the doctor told the waiting Annie, "but it's not Measles." Annie felt exonerated. "I told her it wasn't Measles," she said, but she wouldn't believe her old mother. "No harm done," Dr Andrews said, "I'm sure Rainbow will be fine by morning."

Lexie came through to the kitchen to prepare Rainbow's bottle adding three drops of the medicine into the mix. "I'm sorry I shouted earlier," she said, "but you need to understand that it's me who makes the decisions about Rainbow's health, not you."

"But I was right," Annie stammered, "it wasn't Measles!" But Lexie wasn't listening, she knew she now had another one to call on if she was worried and he was a Doctor. "Chris Andrews" he said to Rainbow, "is going to look after us both."

When Billy came home from the Lodge Meeting, he found Annie alone in the parlour, her mouth set and her eyes fixed on her knitting.

Surely, not already, he asked himself, had the mother and daughter truce broken down again and so soon?

"Is everything alright" he asked, fearful of the answer? "No," Annie replied, the needles clicking faster. Billy sat down beside her on the sofa. "Do you want to speak about it," he said, hoping Annie would say' no' again, but instead she began to tell him the whole story from start to finish until her chin began to wobble and she couldn't say any more.

Billy sighed; he'd been doing that a lot lately, he thought. "C'mon," he said, taking the knitting from her hands and laying it aside, "time for bed. Everything will look better in the morning." But, for Annie after a restless night, everything was still the same and she could feel the atmosphere chill whenever mum and daughter were in the same room.

With her usual briskness, Lexie got herself and Rainbow dressed and fed. "I'm just going to the Nursery to tell Nurse

Williams I won't be staying today," she said without making eye contact with Annie, "I can't risk Rainbow's health with the Measles going around, so I'll be back in an hour or so." And with that, they were gone, leaving Annie and Billy, but especially Billy, weary of it all.

"I know Nancy's wedding is just two weeks away," Annie said, clattering the dishes into the sink, determination in every word, "but I want to go back to Forfar..... till nearer the time."

Billy nodded. "If that's what you want," he said.

"It's not what I want," Annie responded, "it's what.....my daughter wants!

She HATES me."

Before the situation got any worse, Billy held up both his hands in resignation. "I'll telephone Isabella now and let her know we're on our way."

The drive to Forfar was taken in silence, no one wishing to broach the subject of Annie's perceived rejection by Lexie and it was with relief that Billy handed the problem over to Isabella to bring calm to the' troubled waters' yet again.

On his return he found Lexie and her best friend, Sarah, enjoying tea and a Victoria Sponge that Sarah had brought amidst much talk about pregnancy and babies.

"Sarah!" Billy exclaimed, pleased to see his pregnant daughter and Lexie close again, "how's Charlie," he asked, unwittingly, "looking forward to being a dad?"

Sarah glanced at Lexie, who would be bringing Rainbow up alone, but she needn't have worried, "wait till he has to try changing a nappy," Lexie laughed, "men never seem to get the hang of that!"

"Your mum's paying another visit to Isabella," Billy said, "just till the wedding," he added, "seems Isabella's not feeling too well and wanted your mum for company."

Lexie blinked; she knew this was a lie, but it saved any more arguments, so let it pass.

"Speaking of weddings," Lexie suddenly remembered, "this came for you."

She handed the envelope with the Irish postmark on it.

"Hope John and Mary will be able to come over," she said "and to see Rainbow, of course," she added as she lifted her daughter from her pram and into her arms.

Sarah's eyes sparkled, "isn't she just beautiful," she said, gently stroking the dark hair off Rainbow's forehead. "And she looks just like her dad," Lexie cooed, "don't you Rainbow. Would you like to hold her?" Lexie asked Sarah and with a nod, she held the babe in her arms.

Sarah gazed at the child, remembering all the distress that Lexie had been in when she'd been pregnant and Bo McGhee had gone back to his wife in Canada and couldn't believe the change that the birth of Rainbow had brought to Lexie

If she had ever believed that Lexie would give up her bairn, she didn't now and couldn't wait until her own baby was born and the two women could watch them grow up together. If Sarah had any thoughts about Lexie ever leaving Dundee, they had now been dismissed. Lexie and Rainbow were here to stay.

Billy left the women happily chatting and took himself into the parlour with his letter from John, hoping it would be good news and that his son would, at least, be visiting him in Scotland and they could spend a little time together, before they'd have to part again. Billy unfolded the single sheet of notepaper and felt his heart sink as he read.

Dear dad and mum

Thank you for the welcome news that Lexie has safely given birth to a little girl and that all is well. We've been worried about how things were going with you both, but it seems that everything is fine and mum is happier being a Grandma to Rainbow, than living in Belfast, so you will both be remaining in Dundee after all.

We were also pleased to hear about Nancy and John Brannan and their wedding and thank them for the invite but, unfortunately, work commitments mean that we won't be able to attend, nor see the new baby.

Love to you both and glad that you and mum are happy.
John and Mary.

Billy lit a cigarette and inhaled the tobacco smoke deeply into his lungs. His dream of spending the rest of his life with his son was, finally, over. The last time Billy had prayed, was when he'd sat at the hospital bedside of Nancy's tiny son, Kevin, as he fought for his life. Then a miracle had happened and the bairn recovered and Billy knew God had heard his prayer. He closed his eyes and bowed his head and for the second time in his life, he prayed to God again, asking for another miracle, so he could be with his son in Ireland.

Chapter 40

"Today's the day," Nancy smiled to Mary Anne. Over the past three weeks, she had planned every step of the day and all she had to do now was turn up at the Registrar's Office in King Street. Her dad had arranged her wedding breakfast at the Masonic Hall and one of Baxters drivers would be taking her and Mary Anne to the ceremony.

Nancy stroked the cream-coloured linen suit with its black buttons and trimmed pockets and gave a final polish to her matching shoes. Although it was November, she'd also chosen a cream straw hat, its wide brim to be held in place with a ribbon and one of Annie's hatpins. Mary Anne had chosen a simple belted shift dress, also in cream, but with a brown belt and shoes. Whatever she had chosen would have looked good on Nancy's daughter; she was nearly 18 now and was turning many a young man's head as she walked past them. Thanks again to Annie, she also had a little fur cape for her shoulders and long cream gloves to keep her warm.

"Let's have a bit of breakfast," Nancy said "then it will be time to get ready!"

"I'll waken Billy," Mary Anne said, "if he's to be John's Best Man, he'd better get over there and make sure the Groom turns up!" It was meant as a joke, but Nancy felt a flutter of anxiety at the words. "You don't think...?." She looked at Mary Anne. "Of course not," her daughter assured her, "if anyone was going to run away," she added with a knowing wink, "it would be YOU!"

Annie had returned from Forfar two days before the wedding and it looked like Isabella had worked her magic again. She seemed relaxed as she made herself and Billy their breakfast, leaving Lexie to make her own when she woke up. She'd finally learned that the best way to deal with her daughter was to do as she was told and not interfere, but it was a hard price she was paying, when every inch of her still wanted to be Lexie's mum as well as Rainbow's Grannie.

She turned the bread under the grill, wondering why they hadn't heard anything from John and Mary. "No word from Belfast then" she asked Billy as she watched the bread turn brown? "No," Billy lied, "I think they would have came over if it had been possible, but you know John works very hard at the hospital."

"Do you miss Ireland," Annie asked, buttering the toast? Billy lifted his head from the newspaper, "that's a strange thing to ask," he said, "you know I miss being there."

She handed Billy his toast, "I miss Ireland too," she said, almost to herself.

Billy hesitated to ask further, but before he could say anything, Lexie and Rainbow came into the kitchen.

"Today's the big day then," she said aloud but to no one in particular, "let's hope Nancy has better luck this time with her soon-to-be husband!" Billy couldn't help but notice a tinge of regret in her voice, that it wasn't her and Bo McGhee who were to be married, but said nothing. What was past was past and there was no going back and it wasn't only Lexie who had regrets about the hand fate had dealt her, Billy did too.

"We'll leave at half past ten" he told the women, bristly, taking a last gulp of his tea, "so get all your finery on in good time, we don't want to be later than the bride."

"I thought Billy had written to John and Mary inviting them to the wedding," Lexie asked casually, as she prepared Rainbow's bottle?

Annie bristled; she only wished John had come, to show Lexie how much HE loved his mother. "He's very busy at the hospital," Annie said, "but maybe we'll go and visit HIM instead." If she thought that this would bring a reaction of protest from her daughter, she was disappointed. "That'll be nice," was the response and Annie felt the stab of rejection again.

234

"I'll better get ready then," she said instead, turning her head to hide the hurt. "Billy doesn't like to be kept waiting." Lexie watched her mother leave the kitchen: "When is she going to understand that it's not that I don't love her," she told Rainbow, "it's just that I need to be strong enough to look after me and you and stop depending on her."

Annie splashed some water on her face and dabbed her eyes. Somehow, she'd be happy for Nancy and John Brannan and try to enjoy their wedding, but once it was over, she determined to speak to Billy about Lexie and Rainbow and how unhappy she was feeling.

Wee Billy had scrubbed up pretty well and Nancy glowed with pride as she pinned a flower on the lapel of his suit jacket. "Now take this one with you for John and make sure he remembers to wear it or else..........! "I will," Biiy said, stopping her in mid-flow, "I'm the Best Man, remember AND I've got the ring right here in my pocket." He patted his jacket, "now just be ready when the motor comes and we'll see you and Mary Anne at the Registrar's."

John Brannan couldn't believe how nervous he felt. All his doubts about trusting Nancy were resurfacing: "What if I'm making a terrible mistake," he asked himself as he gazed at his reflection in the mirror? "What if Nancy doubts me in the future and storms out without listening again?" His hands shook as he tried to knot his tie, "and what if......what if she doesn't turn up for the wedding.....what then?"

The knock at the door made him almost jump out of his skin: He'd never been married before and, even though he'd been through the war in the Scots Guards, this felt worse than anything he'd had to face in the conflict.

The knocking became louder. "John," he heard his name called, "it's Billy, can I come in?"

With no response, Billy knocked again, but this time, turned the door handle and the door opened. He looked through the gap and into the dimness of the tiny room.

John Brannan stood at the mirror, with his back to Billy. "I can't get this tie right," he said, "my hands are shaking."

Billy laughed until he saw John's face in the mirror as he got nearer. He was as white as a sheet and Billy stopped laughing.

"What's wrong," he asked, concern for his friend and mentor forming in his stomach.

John turned to face him. "I'm not sure I'm doing the right thing!"

With John's help, Billy may have grown up, but he wasn't able to comprehend what was being said.

"I don't understand," Billy said, "I thought that this was what you wanted?"

"I did too," John replied, "but now.....now I don't know if.....if, I'm man enough for someone like your mum?"

Billy frowned, "mum's getting ready to marry you, John," he said, "but if it's not what you want, then maybe you should tell her now, before it's too late."

John's eyes had never looked so bleak, nor his heart so heavy. "You don't understand," he said, "I love her very much, but what if she leaves me like she did before, when she believed Di Auchterlonie and wouldn't even listen to me. WHAT THEN?"

Billy didn't know how to answer him, nor give him any assurances that his mum would never leave him. He knew her too well and how her moods could change on the turn of a sixpence. "I'll be at the Registrar's at 11 o'clock," Billy said, solemnly, "and so will mum and everyone else. Whether you will be there to marry her is up to you." John stood still in the silence Billy left behind: He was right, the decision was his and his alone. He poured himself a measure of rum and downed it in one swig. His decision was made.

Baxters motor car and driver arrived at eleven minutes to eleven. A crowd of neighbours had formed at the end of their closes to wave Nancy and Mary Anne on their way. "Isn't she a bonny wumman," one said, looking admiringly at Nancy in her cream outfit, "and would you jist look at Mary Anne in ah her finery," another added as John Brannan watched from his window.

Billy and Annie, with Lexie and Rainbow in the back seat, set out from Albert Street. "Well," Billy said, "let's have a lovely day and a lovely wedding for my daughter," as he pulled away from the kerb and towards King Street. Isabella and John Anderson were already there when they arrived and took their seats. He could see wee Billy seated at the front of the room. "Where's the groom?" he whispered to Annie, "shouldn't he be here with wee Billy?" Annie looked around her, "Nancy's not here either," she whispered back, looking at her watch.

"I'll just have a word with the 'Best Man'," Billy said, walking to the front of the room where wee Billy sat, alone.

"Where's John Brannan," he asked, "shouldn't he be here by now?"

Wee Billy raised his eyes to meet those of his Grandfather. "He's having doubts or something," he said, hoarsely, "and I didn't know what to do, so I left him and came here." Billy felt anger rising at the man. "Don't move from here till I get back," he said, "I'll see to John Brannan."

He'd been here before, when Billy Donnelly had tried to get out of marrying Nancy when she was pregnant with his bairn. It didn't take Euan McPherson and Billy long to show him the 'error of his ways' and the marriage went ahead. And now, it looked like he was going to have to do it all again, but this time with John Brannan.

He waved to Annie that he was leaving and as he stepped out into the street, Baxters motor car pulled up with Nancy and Mary Anne in the back.

"Come back in 20 minutes," he told the driver, urgently, "the Registrar's not ready," and with that, he waved the driver on his way, before getting into his own motor and heading for the Cowgate and John Brannan's house.

His door was open and Billy walked in to find John where wee Billy had left him, but now he was nursing another measure of rum. Billy took it from his hand and slapped him hard across the face. "My daughter's waiting to marry you," he said, "so unless you've got a fatal disease, I'm here to make sure you do!"

The slap seemed to bring John out of his malaise and he burst into tears.

"I'M SCARED" he cried, his head in his hands "I'm not man enough for her!"

Billy pulled him to his feet, Billy Donnelly had said the same thing and it turned out that he was right, but John Brannan was different, he'd have trusted this man with his life. He was man enough alright, Billy knew, he just had to make John believe it too.

"What are you talking about, John," he said, "you're an ex-Scots Guard and the one who I trusted to look after Nancy and her bairns when Billy Donnelly threatened them. It's thanks to you that they're all safe now and if you think Nancy doesn't know that you're a man she can turn to, then you're mistaken." John Brannan listened, intently as Billy talked. "I've never seen her so happy than when she told us you and she were to be married, so put any doubts out of your head, John, and come with me to the Registrar's and marry your Nancy."

John felt his shoulders straighten. "I love her, Mr Dawson," he told Billy, wiping his eyes, "and I'll never hurt her like the rest did."

"That's all I need to hear," Billy said, "now let's get you out of here and take Nancy as your wife, like the man I know you are."

"Where are we going?" Nancy asked the driver, as he pulled away from the kerb without depositing her and Mary Anne at the Registrar's. "Some problem," he said, "but Mr Dawson's fixing it."

Mary Anne shrugged, "I don't know either," she said to her mum's questioning look, as the driver steered the motorcar up King Street.

"You don't think John's ill or anything, do you," she fretted, her daughter's words about John not turning up, now beginning to feel prophetic."

Mary Anne took her mother's hand. "Everything will be fine," she said, assuredly, "and if Granddad's sorting things out, you know that too."

At quarter past eleven, wee Billy breathed a sigh of relief as his Granddad and John Brannan came hurrying into the room. "The Registrar says, if we don't start soon, he'll have to postpone the ceremony," he whispered to Billy."

"Just keep your eyes on John Brannan," Billy told him, "the Registrar's a Mason and he'll not be cancelling anything."

With two minutes to spare, Nancy and Mary Anne walked into the room as Billy joined Annie and Lexie in their seats. "What was all that about," Annie asked?

"Something and nothing," Billy told her, "now let's enjoy this wedding."

Nancy and John were showered with confetti as they emerged from the Registrar's to a crowd of well-wishers from Baxters and the Cowgate. "Happy," asked John, his doubts all gone and kissing Nancy as the motor car drove them to the Masonic Hall, "happy ever after," Nancy replied, "with you by my side."

Billy scattered a shower of pennies from the motor car window, to the bunch of bairns shouting 'SCRAMBLE' as they left the Registrar's. "The cook will have the Beef and vegetables ready," Billy said, "and a nice wee Wedding Cake should have been delivered for afters." Annie leaned over and pressed her hand on Billy's arm. "What would I do without you," she whispered, "I'm so glad you married me, even when I was unsure." Billy smiled, "so am I," he said, "so am I."

The tables were set out and everyone was seated when Billy, Annie, Lexie and Rainbow arrived at the Masonic Hall. When everyone's glasses had been charged for a toast to the Bride and Groom, Billy took to his feet. "Before we enjoy the delicious feast the cook has prepared for us, would you all stand and raise your glasses to the Bride and Groom, Mr and Mrs John Brannan." A cheer went up and glasses were clinked as the whisky and sherry was drunk.

"And I have another toast," John Brannan said, standing up and raising his glass again, "to absent friends," he said, "especially those from Belfast."

"I'll drink to that," Billy heard John's voice say from somewhere behind him.

He swung around. "John," he cried out "and Mary, YOU'RE HERE!"

Father and son hugged one another while Mary and Annie

watched, tears filling their eyes. "I didn't think you were coming!" Billy exclaimed, "when you wrote....?"

"I know," his son stopped him saying anything more, "but Mary made me understand that love knows no boundaries, so here we are!"

"Is there room for your old mum too," Annie asked, joining in the welcome.

Lexie watched the four of them, revelling in being together. "I think your Grannie and Granddad may be leaving us soon," she whispered to Rainbow: The past was well and truly behind Lexie now and she knew that the future would be whatever she made it, with or without Bo McGhee in her life.

The celebrations went on till all the food had been eaten and the wedding cake shared amongst the guests, with an extra piece for Lexie to keep, for when Rainbow was christened. It had been a wonderful day, made more so with the arrival of John and Mary and when all were bedded down for the night, Annie turned to Billy. "Do you remember when we were with John and Mary in Belfast last Christmas, when I asked you to take me home?" Billy turned towards her, "and I did," he whispered. "Well," Annie said, "can I ask you to take me home again?" Billy switched on the bedside light, to make sure he wasn't dreaming. "But you are home," he said, "aren't you?"

"Not anymore," Annie whispered back, "I think it's time to go home to Ireland where he once belonged and be with John and Mary, if you'll take me?"

Billy kissed Annie, "I'll take you home to Ireland Annie Pepper," he whispered, "if you're sure?" Annie had never been more certain of anything in her life. "I'm sure," she said, as they fell asleep in one another's arms; just like they had done the first time they'd made love down by the river during the flax harvesting all those years ago. The Wheel of Fate had turned its full circle and Annie Pepper was truly going home at last.

THE END

Lightning Source UK Ltd.
Milton Keynes UK
UKHW010720200220
359001UK00005B/410